Nerea

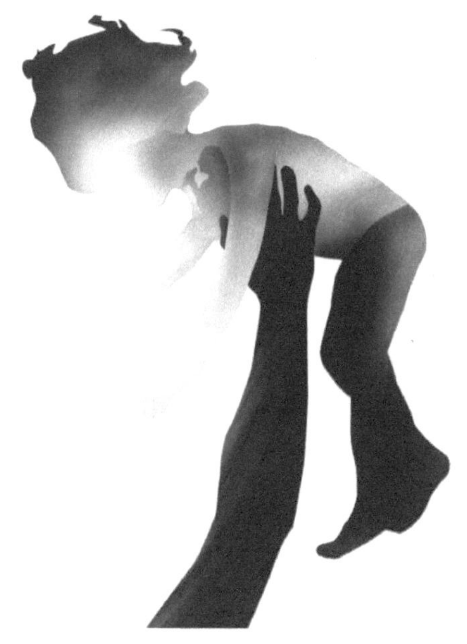

James Snow

Act II

Act III

Dedication

14/06/2020 – The Awe Experience

Dear Reader: Thank you for spending your valuable time with me.

Océane and Violette: You are the two most amazing people I have ever met. Being your father fills me with endless pride, admiration and wonder. I wrote this story so that one day, I can share it with you and discuss the wandering ideas within. You are my audience. I love you both so much.

Barbara: You inspired every page of this novel and cared for me while unrelentingly nourishing your deepest dreams. Your sparkle has brought joy and incredible life experiences into our family. I love you deep, my heart.

Prologue

Journal entry from Sven (2015)

Bellis perennis or 'eternal beauty' is considered by many to be an invasive weed; but to a child, the common daisy inspires exploration and must be shared with those they love.

21/10/2224 – The Anticipation Experience

Nerea sat inside the sun-warmed windowsill and counted the daisy's petals. 48.

Small chocolates remained untouched on the hotel's plush pillows, and her shoes were tucked neatly in the closet. She rested her temple against the cold glass and hugged her knees tight. Seventeen floors was a long way down.

'Control yourself.'

'Be still.'

Criss-crossing strangers wandered far below. Why was life so cruel? Their interactions, for all their urgency, were meaningless. Repetition and routine imprisoned infinite potential.

She brushed the daisy across her cheek.

How could she enjoy this moment while billions of others stumbled through an unrelenting monotony? There must be someone more deserving.

For twenty-one and a half years, Nerea hid loneliness and shame behind an expressionless exterior. She was a champion at asking questions people most wanted to answer, and a master at avoiding them herself. The real Nerea hid in silence behind a wall.

And now, she waited nervously for the door to open.

'Your Decision is power—seize it! Join us. Come with me!'

In a flash of spontaneity, Nerea had accepted Sloan's proposal and now awaited his arrival. He promised the unexpected and dared her to leave her comfort zone.

'Maybe…'

Nerea took a deep breath, pinched one of the flower's long, white petals and pulled it gently from its core. She brought it to her lips and practiced a small kiss.

'…he loves me.'

Who knows where the afternoon would lead? Could she open up? A shiver of electric joy flowed from her knees to her knuckles and her face had to fight against a smile.

She released the petal and watched it float gently to the floor.

Sloan was late.

Nerea pulled a second petal from the daisy and paused. Like everyone she encountered, it was beginning to die. Hope dripped from her body and made room for deep-rooted boundaries and fears. She should not have agreed to this. Trust was a mistake. Nerea looked to the closed door. Had he abandoned her?

BANG! BANG! BANG!

Sloan's fist pounded loudly against the outside window, mere centimeters from her face. Nerea tossed the flower, flash-rolled and fell to the floor.

He hung perilously, seventy meters above the ground; one hand on the windowsill and the other in a narrow space between building panels. He grinned with inexplicable confidence and looked straight into Nerea's eye. Her heart pounded in admiration as she stood. He had definitely delivered the unexpected.

Sloan pointed to the window's handle. Nerea approached and cautiously swung it open. "You're insane! Come inside."

The invitation was dangerous.

His smile widened as he shook his head. "No." He placed his hand on top of the window. "Follow me!" Sloan stepped onto the window ledge, gripped a piece of structure above and continued his ascent.

Nerea watched his feet rise and disappear upwards. Cool air blew calm intensity into the space, and Nerea was left with an empty room and a call to adventure. Should she dare? So much of her life had already drifted by without meaning or consequence; maybe it was time for change.

She hopped onto the open windowsill and peered to the oblivious people wandering far below. It was a long fall to the pavement. Her body teetered, and for a moment, she imagined the freedom of plummeting to an early end.

A gust of wind brought a shiver of fear, and Nerea pulled back into the room.

She spotted the daisy dying safely on the floor. Was that a better way to go? Nerea closed her eyes and embraced the breeze.

'Breathe.'

'Relax.'

A sliver of smirk betrayed her indecision. Nerea opened her eyes and whispered to the wind, "It's time to dance." She stuck her head outside and scanned the towering wall. Sloan was now two floors up and moving quickly. She grabbed the frame above the window, twisted to a foothold and pulled herself onto the building's face.

Her right hand found a solid side grip, and she extended her leg to leverage against the sill. Up she went. After quick hand adjustments on shaky holds, Nerea gripped an inner-joint that gave confidence. There were modest cracks for toes and occasional big cracks to rest fingertips. Nerea found a rhythm and began to flow up the naked structure.

Technique came from years of scaling the sheer and overhanging boulders on Clara's private island. Climbing without a rope brought freedom and exhilarating danger into her over-controlled life. Trained focus blocked out the growing void under her feet.

Nerea danced up the wall with a gecko's grace. Each smooth movement deepened her confidence and strength; she was taking control.

Ten floors up, there was a new challenge: the building changed from vertical to horizontal panels, and Sloan had stopped. He was contemplating his next move. Nerea caught up and understood the next hold was out of reach by an arm's length.

"Too much for you?" she poked. He did not answer. His breathing had changed. They both pinched delicate holds, but while Nerea's confidence remained, Sloan's left leg was beginning to shake.

He was stuck.

Nerea needed to act, and down was not an option. "Stay with

me!" She looked up, pulled her toes into the next crack, curled into a spring and leapt to the distant hold. Nerea flew free in the air with both hands stretched far above her head. After an eternal split second, she stuck three fingertips from each hand into a tiny crack. 'Shit!' It was only three millimeters deep, and the friction was already failing. Her legs dangled in the wind.

She pulled with all her strength and shot her left hand to a higher joint-hold. It stuck! She brought her feet to the finger crack and found a rest point. Safety!

Nerea exhaled and looked down. The soul below her was panicking. His legs wobbled as he looked to the ground.

Her pulse raced. "Jump! You can do it. The first hold's thin, but the second's a jug!"

Sweat dripped from his forehead. He was not listening. His fingers were ghost white and losing grip.

"Focus on my voice. You can do it! It's not far. Come-on!"

His jittering slowed to a stop and his shoulders drooped in resignation. Sloan would not make it.

He was giving up.

Sloan looked up into Nerea's eye and smirked with a defeated grin. He shook his head, let go of the wall and dropped backward with eyes locked into hers. Nerea watched the fall in slow motion as Sloan descended to the ground. His empty stare remained fixed on hers until the instant he exploded on the pavement. Her stomach tightened with the splat, and Nerea was amazed at the instant lifelessness of the body that remained.

The wind kept blowing, and the sun kept shining. The panicked screams of the crowd below were the only signs that anything had changed.

In that instant, Nerea buried her soul even deeper inside. She looked upwards to focus on the task at hand and continue the impossible flow up the wall. Nobody was between her and the sky above.

And nobody was there to help.

~

Nerea opened her eyes and looked over to the empty simulator beside her. Sloan had left. All flash and no depth. He would not get a second chance.

Nerea was empty and alone.

Act I

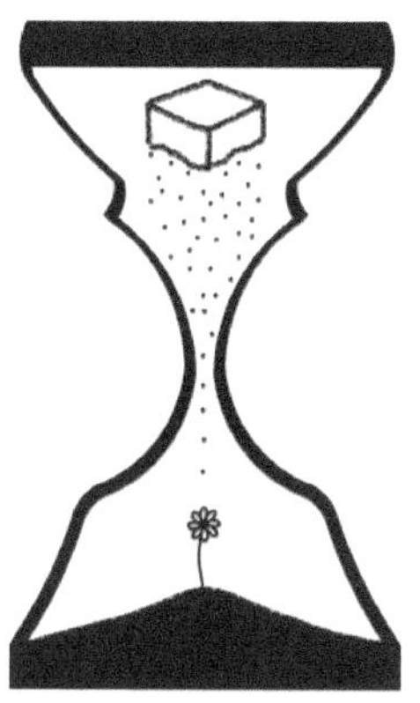

Journal entry from Sven (2023)

The pinus longaeve is a bristlecone pine tree that is biologically immortal; some are older than the Egyptian pyramids.

Chapter 1

07/04/2226 – The Guilt Experience

Wealth was a curse. It separated her from the suffering and made her less human.

Nerea looked around the office and knew she didn't deserve its luxury. No one did.

She turned her locket one last time and peeked at the discreet timer. There were only 48 hours and four minutes remaining before the most important Decision of her life.

The unspoken reality of Waldon's Life Contract was simple: sell your body to a corporation and rent it back one day at a time. Unfortunately, the strain of the next payment was unbearable for so many, and those who chose aging's cure marched forward in two distinct camps: the rich and the miserable.

Waldon was pure evil; rejecting their offer should be easy, but the allure of eternal youth was undeniable.

Nerea laid back in the egg-shaped simulator and pulled the near-invisible lace over her body and head. Sensors in the neural webbing and bed lining would monitor every cell in her body and transmit new data into countless nerve endings.

She turned to the woman sitting in a second simulator. "Did Clara share the files?"

"Everything is prepared. Are you ready to begin?"

She closed her eyes in resignation. "Yes."

~

Nerea inhaled with a shiver as cold, beach fog hit her nose. She hunched forward and opened her eyes to an overwhelming grey that hid all color, muffled all sound and dampened all smell. A seaward path disappeared into freezing, moist clouds and left her wondering if the ocean was even there. The wet bench dampened her dress and tiny splinters clawed at her bum—the beach-house garden offered no comfort this morning. Then: the woman's soothing voice broke the silence. "We will start with a few baseline questions. What is today's date?"

"April 7, 2226." Nerea grabbed a blanket as the unwelcoming air needled her skin.

"What do you know about the Decision?"

"In two days, I turn twenty-three and can choose to stop the aging process of my body. While not immortal, a twenty-three-year-old body has a death rate under 0.01% per year and with medicine and risk avoidance, can survive tens of thousands of years."

"Why do you have the Decision?"

She braced herself. Everyone knew the happy propaganda hammered into their trusting minds as children. Nerea reluctantly recited the answer: "Waldon's Decision is available to all through governments around the world. Waldon believed death was a preventable sickness and developed medicine that stops aging. Waldon defined the rules for who has access to it and when they can use it. At the age of twenty-three, every person is granted the Decision and can enter into a Life Contract with Waldon. If we do, we agree to pay a Life Tax. If we don't, we will grow old and die as it has always been."

Nerea took a deep breath and quietly swallowed her anger. The Life Tax imprisoned so much potential, and the Penalty applied to those who didn't pay was vicious and cruel. Despite happy brochures that promised the opposite, Waldon's cure drained hope from its customers.

"Why are you working with me?" For the first time since they met, Nerea looked into the eyes of her Decision Coach. They were golden and held a glimmer of honesty that invited Nerea to open up. Her name was Seren.

"I'm here because you have an excellent reputation and I can afford your fee. You will accompany my journey and help me reflect on the options."

"The Decision is a big moment in a young life. You don't sound excited."

Nerea stared into the grey and filled her lungs with its cool air. "I believe Waldon was wrong to release their 'cure' to the world."

Seren raised her eyebrows. "That was almost two hundred years ago. The government praises Waldon as humanity's greatest achievement; the savior who gave us eternal life."

Nerea instinctively yearned to conceal her true thoughts, but today was not a day for secrets. "Governments are part of the problem. Waldon has given them the power to control their people, and enabled tyrants to dominate for far too long. Countries are blinded by their tax revenue and created a system that ensures their people stay silent." She was shocked by the quaver in her own voice. "In many countries, the Penalty for those who cannot pay is death, and we accept it! We accept the world as it is and no longer seek to make it better. We're so paralyzed by the fear of dying, that we ignore the lunacy of a corporation controlling life. We need to find the courage to reject their power; we need to stop Waldon."

Seren tilted her head. "It sounds like you plan to reject their offer. Have you already made up your mind?"

Nerea rubbed her arms and lowered her gaze shamefully to a white pebble on the ground. "No." The whisper was barely audible.

"So, despite your disdain, you remain open to a contract with Waldon?"

Nerea nodded silently, embarrassed by her weakness.

"What are you scared of?"

Her throat welled. "I'm terrified of finding joy in Waldon's wickedness."

"Everyone deserves to know joy."

Nerea did not agree. "If you're dancing with the Devil, you're blind to her evil. Death used to be a great equalizer—it made things right. But now, the rich can enjoy eternal sin, while the poor suffer endlessly. I just want to do my part to make things a little bit better."

The coffeemaker beeped.

Seren smiled with a mix of admiration and kindness. "By the time we finish, I hope you will embrace your Decision with certainty. Clara has prepared ten simulations for you to experience and asked that you follow them in order. In 48 hours, you will make your Decision: continue aging as it has always been or enter into a Life Contract with Waldon and live for a very long time."

Nerea had no desire to die; but like a story with no end, the absence of death seemed to negate life itself—it made no sense.

Seren brought the coffee pot to Nerea. As she poured a cup, she explained what would happen next: "I like to use drinks to start experiences. You will enter each simulation by taking a sip." Seren motioned down to the coffee, and Nerea understood it was her pathway into another life.

Nerea loved coffee—a lot. And the smell of the dark, earthy roast whisked her back to her favorite mountaintops. She held the warm mug and breathed it in. "What type of coffee is this?"

"I call it Phil."

Nerea took a sip. Darkness was followed by a flash of light.

~~

14/02/2000 – The Love Experience

Rejection loomed. Phil wanted to chicken out, but my God, those eyes—ocean storms swirling around an undiscovered pole. Then: the buzz of a text in his pocket. It was from Louis: 'good luck!'

He typed a response: 'thx!'

The clean, white bathroom was near the museum entrance. It was late, and there were only a couple of staff left in the building. He looked in the mirror and saw happiness staring back. His heart raced, and his dark skin flushed with nervous joy. He cupped water in his hands and splashed it over his face.

Thank God for Louis. When he arrived to university, he was a lonely mess. His high-school crushes had been knowingly unattainable, and he found cruel ways to reject any girls that got past his shyness. The day he told Louis: 'I think I might be gay' changed everything. As he let go of shame and bared his true feelings, an invisible bag of rocks fell from his shoulders. He didn't even realize its weight until it was gone. Louis listened and asked questions that allowed him to gain confidence. He was finally free to embrace and accept his own soul. Phil liked the smell of other men and would catch himself admiring the way they moved. When he was alone in his bed at night, his thoughts would wander inevitably to the shape, movements and strength of men. Yup, he was gay.

But he had never touched another man.

It had been impossible to concentrate on his internship today; the anticipation of tonight had become an uncontrollable distraction.

Phil took one final look in the mirror and had one last pee to relax. He opened the door, breathed deep and affirmed to himself: "This will make me happy."

He turned the corner and froze. There he was: fifty steps away, floating like a dream at the desk, strong shoulders and long blonde hair pulled back in a bun—a soft Viking. The strongest magnet in the world was simultaneously pulling him forward and repelling him back, but lust was winning. Sven sat unaware and magnificent, eating a sandwich and reading one of Phil's favorite books, by B.F. Skinner.

Sven worked security and the two had been meeting eyes heavily every night for weeks, but Phil only managed quiet 'Goodnight's as he blushed his way out the door.

'What if he isn't gay?'

'What if he's offended?'

'What if he gets violent?'

The imagined strength of Sven's hands shot a dose of fear through Phil's mind before he recalled their erotic potential. He took a step forward and began the long walk down the hall and into the echoing entrance.

Sven looked up and smiled. His alluring gaze locked into Phil's. He stood from his desk and the two walked towards each other without glancing away. They met in the middle of the museum hall. Sven broke the silence. "Hello." His voice was timid; maybe he was nervous as well.

Sven tucked a few loose strands of hair neatly behind his ear and glanced down. Phil almost drowned in the blueness of those ocean-eyes. He summoned the air and courage to finally answer. "Hi." Suddenly: something was wrong! There was a piece of bread on the upper part of Sven's chin! 'Wow, that's big! Look away! Look away!' But it was too late. Phil was now 100% fixated on the bit of sandwich that had stuck itself below the corner of Sven's mouth.

"Workin' late again?"

Phil responded in a confused, distracted stutter: "Yes." He forgot what he was there to say. His mind raced. 'Should I tell him about the bread? We're almost alone in the building. Holy crap, that's big! How is it even staying on?'

The two fidgeted in awkward silence. Sven continued to glance down nervously, and Phil's eyes widened at the sight and confusion of the crumb. It was a full-on crisis! 'If I can't tell him about a piece of bread, how am I going to tell him he's beautiful, and I want to eat him up? Is it rude to say something? Would it embarrass him? Am I being crazy? That is a massive crumb!'

Sven looked like he wanted to speak.

Phil was paralyzed. 'What should I say?'

The phone rang at the desk. Both looked to it with relief.

It rang a second time. Phil was not sure if it was saving or ruining his night.

It rang a third time.

"I should get that," Sven announced reluctantly.

"Okay. Goodnight," answered Phil instinctively and to his immediate regret. 'Oh, NO! Why did I say goodnight? Noooooooo!!! That's not what I wanted to say. No! No! No! No! No!'

Sven took steps towards the phone, and Phil followed through with his mistake and unwillingly moved to the exit.

He walked quickly to and through the front door. Before he knew it, Phil was outside the building in a sickening shame. The door locked shut behind him, and he stumbled straight over to his favorite bench in the museum's garden.

Crushing embarrassment flushed through his body. His thoughts raced: 'How old am I? Five? Why could I not tell him about a simple piece of bread? Idiot! Idiot! Idiot!'

Phil sat on the bench, put his head down into his hands and whispered: "I'm such an idiot!"

He opened his eyes. "Holy crap." Phil was staring directly at his own crotch: his zipper was wide open! It could not be any more open; like a giant 'O' wide open.

It must have been like that since the toilet.

And Sven did not tell him.

Sven was having the same experience he was: the zipper and the crumb.

"Bastard." Phil's shame washed into a soft giggle of relief. He sheepishly did his zipper and laughed alone on the bench.

The universe had spoken: this was destiny. Unhinged inspiration flowed through his body. He turned swiftly and hustled back to the museum.

Sven stood watching him through the glass door and they locked eyes once again. Phil ran until only the thin, glass door separated him from his crush. Sven looked happy. Their stare held each other tight. Sven gently brushed his own chin, letting Phil know that he knew about the bread. Phil mimed the action of doing up his zipper.

Sven smirked. Phil smiled. They both began to laugh.

Sven bit his bottom lip and reached for the handle. He opened the door slowly.

Phil took a giant breath. "Do you want to get a coffee with me?"

Sven glowed. "I do."

~~

Nerea inhaled desperately and woke in a panicked flash.

Primal adrenaline sought to protect her naked vulnerability. 'Where am I? Who am I?' Her eyes darted, and her mind searched for clarity. 'What's happening?' Nerea grasped for the limits of her body. She was Nerea, and the woman beside her was Seren. Sunshine now pierced through the fog. A million questions tumbled though her mind; the first jumped out instinctively: "What the hell?!?!"

Seren smiled. "Was that the first time you experienced an empathetic simulation?"

Nerea nodded. She often entered level-one simulations in her own body, or level-two as an audience to someone else's life. But she had never before became a level-three passenger to empathy—genuine thoughts and emotions.

"Simulations of other people used to be observational; like watching a movie. Then Waldon created this level-three technique that masks the conscious of passengers and allows you to fully become another person. You start with their memories and live their experiences—in their bodies. It is extremely intense, but you will get used to coming back. How did it feel?"

Intense was an understatement. "Like I traveled to a new planet with different gravity. But beautiful. Who were they?" Phil was incredibly familiar; like she had known him forever.

"They became parents to Yves, one of the founders of Waldon. The morals of Phil and Sven shaped Yves and ultimately, the Decision you are about to make."

For protection, Waldon's founders remained anonymous, and Nerea found it difficult to rebel against a faceless tyrant. Now she finally had a small detail about one of them. "Why did Clara want me to meet them? Are they alive?"

"No. Phil, Sven and Yves died many years ago, long before you were born."

Nerea was puzzled. "A founder of Waldon died? How?"

"Patience. Clara has selected simulations that follow the history of Waldon chronologically. She wants you to understand its creation and the motivation of the founders."

Waldon had turned life into a commodity and destroyed the joy of living. Nerea imagined a corporate money-dragon smoking a cigar and defining rules that would extract the most profit from the world. How could Phil and Sven have raised a dragon?

She was anxious for answers and curious about the accuracy of what she had lived. "Did Phil's experience really happen?"

"These simulations are as real as possible based on available data. Waldon's Artificial Intelligence program, named Aurora, built them."

"How could they possibly be accurate?" Nerea faded off in reflection.

"Waldon has an exceptional license for an A.I. technology that has long been illegal around the world. Aurora is not like any A.I. you know. She has access to the largest farms of quantum computers, and most importantly, Aurora has the Waldon Record. The Record contains endless information from the turn of the millennium, a period when people ignored the value of their data. She has communication logs, security videos, photos, medical records, brain scans, DNA samples, location trackers and infinitely more sources. Aurora builds simulations starting from a single, known data point, such as a video, or a photograph. She then tests every sequence of events, thoughts and movements that could possibly lead to the next known data point. It is trial and error connecting data in the most probable path forward. The more data points you have, the more sequences you can eliminate. Until there is only one sequence remaining: the truth."

Seren took Nerea's hands. "You have now experienced the earliest simulation that Aurora has ever created."

She was not convinced. "But thoughts? I knew what Phil was thinking! He didn't walk around with a thought recorder; that data can't possibly exist."

"While we are each unique, our thoughts follow patterns. Some are easy to guess, like when we are reading or reacting to a video. Others require an understanding of health, exercise, events and our long-term emotional patterns. With hundreds of gigabytes of data per person per day, Aurora can calculate the personality and unique sequence of thoughts that connect it all together."

"Who else has experienced Phil? Have you?"

"No. Clara has access to Aurora and asked her to create this unique experience for you. The only other human to have lived this moment is Phil. Clara gave me an overview, but I do not know the details. I must confess that I have never attempted level-two or level-three simulations. While I coach many people, I doubt I have the strength to come back and remain whole. But you grew up on Clara's island with a simulator and seem to have a keen sense of reality."

Living someone else's feelings was an invasion of privacy. It was fantastic but felt so wrong. Even if he was dead, she had explored the most private parts of Phil's mind. Where did this fit in her morals? How would Phil feel, knowing that others could explore the hidden corners of his soul? Would it enrich the experience of life or kill freedom of thought?

As she wandered through Phil's memories, a flash hit her: if she could experience Phil, could someone else experience her? What if her life was a simulation, and others were experiencing it right now? Some day in the future when she was dead… what if they experienced her most private moments? Her showers? Her dirty fantasies? Imagining murder and death? Exploring uncertainty and fear? The thoughts were mortifying, and embarrassed blood pumped swiftly through her cheeks.

But Phil may not have cared. He had found a new confidence in life and may have been happy to share. Nerea contemplated the familiarity of his body and embraced its differences to her own. His movements were unnoticeable and liquid compared to her decisive rigidity. His face was itchy, and his pants were tight. Having a penis was not as vulnerable as she had imagined. Openness and freed desire sharply contrasted her own closed heart. While they shared the pained history of disguise, Phil had broken free of his, and Nerea loved the liberty that remained. She longed to return to the smell of Sven as he opened the door of the museum. It was the most intense and pure moment of her life.

Except it was not her life.

Chapter 2

07/04/2226 – The Amazement Experience

Nerea closed her eyes and appreciated the rolling crash of the waves; the sea was part of her. A chickadee beckoned playfully in the distance, and the garden offered fresh wafts of basil and mint.

Seren spoke softly. "You have chosen a perfect home-base. This is paradise."

"Thank you." Nerea had never visited this place in the real world but knew it well from simulations; she escaped to it often as a private space of dreams and security. It was home in a way that her childhood island could never be: the home of her grandparents. A narrow path led directly onto the beach and invited them to go for a swim. They admired the ocean from a long dining table in the shaded oasis.

"Do you miss waking near the ocean?"

Nerea had buried her childhood long ago, but it was time to dig. She sifted lightly through mornings of her youth and recalled a lonely little girl, ignorant of the suffering across the water. "I miss the sunrises, but the island was a prison where Clara isolated me from the world. I was allowed only rose-tinted simulations to see off the island, and they filtered out so much pain."

"Honesty is important, but as you grow, you will understand that too much transparency can crush a childhood. Sometimes, it is the role of adults to protect the young until they are strong enough to survive the truth."

"Hiding the sadness of others does not magically bring happiness. In fact, it left me empty. Clara is a terrible liar, and even as a child, I knew she was hiding something. One day during math class, I started crying for no reason. My video-teacher said that when life gifts you challenge, it is your time to dance. I decided surviving Clara was my challenge and distanced myself from her. I built a wall to protect myself, and those childhood tears were the last ones I ever shed."

Nerea's stomach knotted and she rubbed her hands to hide their tremble. "Through the years, small glimpses outside allowed me to understand that life off the island was not the paradise that Clara wished it to be. When I wondered aloud about inequality or poverty, she reacted with fury. I swallowed my questions and allowed anger to gnaw at my core. At sixteen, I left the island, and we have barely spoken since."

"You escaped?"

"There's a bridge, and Clara let me go. I left, but there was no escape. Life off the island was even more lonely than the solitude on it. I was embarrassingly unprepared, an alien—awkward and naked everywhere I went. I hid my wealth from the judgment of others and suffocated as I learned the true extent of suffering and imbalance."

"You left almost seven years ago yet link every experience back to Clara. Today began with anger towards Waldon, but it sounds like your most profound anger is towards your mother. You do not even refer to her as your mother, yet she is present in every sentence of your story. Why?"

Nerea stared blankly into the garden. "Clara is both the hero and the victim of every story she tells. She controls the narrative and leaves no space for others. Silence and untold stories left me empty and confused. I know nothing of my father and little of my grandparents. Clara is void of uncertainty, humility and self-doubt, and her lack of empathy for humankind is unforgivable. I'm ashamed to share her wealth. I reject her completely, yet her shadow is cast on everything I do. While I cannot recall ever feeling her physical touch, her invisible control chokes me every evening when I lie in bed, every night when I dream and every morning when I wake. I needed a mother, but she never acted like one. The title of 'mother' is earned through acts of love, not by squeezing out a baby. Clara never earned that title, so I stripped it from her. I try not to judge the people I meet, but from the bottom of my heart, I hate Clara."

And there it was: hate. It had a name. She looked to Seren for validation. "You met her; did you not see her arrogance?"

A saddened smile crossed Seren's face. "Each of us inherits burdens at birth. Some are obvious, but the most dangerous are often unspoken. I met Clara briefly, and she is one of the most fascinating people I have ever encountered. Her burdens are unimaginable, and she wanted you to make your Decision innocently: free from the weights of your ancestors. She is relieved to finally share these stories with you.

"Clara constructed a childhood that does not exist anymore: a childhood from a different era, like the one she was given. She raised you on that island to protect your innocence and assumed you would love it as she did, but your curiosity far exceeded her ability to protect you."

Nerea looked to the sky. Clara could tell a good story and had seduced Seren. What had her mother tried to protect her from?

"Are you ready for the next simulation?"

Nerea was not ready. "Let's go."

Seren reached into a cooler and pulled out a glass bottle of water branded 'Eva.' Nerea froze in excitement.

"Is that…?" Her voice vanished in anticipation.

Seren poured a glass and handed it to Nerea.

"It is."

Nerea was going to meet her grandmother.

~~

12/07/2008 – The Rage Experience

Eva's heart raced as her body clenched in anger. Rapid-fire air seethed through her teeth. There was no will left to contain the fury. Injustice, frustration, and revenge stomped through her mind. Jagged movements betrayed her normal dexterity as she laced her shoes with the grace of a horse.

Escape!

Louis yelled from the kitchen: "YOU CRITICIZE EVERYTHING I DO!"

It bounced back instinctively: "JUST TAKE CARE OF THE THINGS YOU SAID YOU WOULD!!!!"

"GET OUT!"

The front door flew open. Eva tore outside and used every ounce of strength to slam it shut.

She stomped into the shaded garden and emptied her lungs at the beach: "AAAAAHHHH!!!"

Breathe. Headphones. Play. Eva sprinted away from the water, up her favorite forest pathway.

'Why's he being like that?!?'

She had worked so hard—three shows in the last two weeks. Her career was finally moving, and she should be on top of the world, but Louis kept letting her down. When she wasn't busy, she took care of everything. Now she asked for one simple thing: get the dry cleaning done. Easy. But no. Now she did not have the right dress for dinner.

Eva accelerated into the tree-cooled trail, stirred forward by an aggressive mix of metal and rap. She loved the thumping contrast to the serene beauty around her.

It wasn't just the dry-cleaning; the dirty laundry was still in the basket. He said he was waiting for a full load, but that was just lazy. Anytime Eva saw washing to do, she did it. 'It takes ten seconds. Why the hell wait? And why does he refuse to spray clean the toilet?' She did it every day, and it only took a second. She couldn't even remember the last time he had done it.

A raven landed on the path in front of her and paused before flying away.

'It was right there! He was at the market, and the dry cleaner was right beside him! There was time for the tax guy, but not for my dress!'

Eva's jogging slowed as she crossed her favorite little bridge. An angler cast her line into the water.

Her husband had let her sleep in this morning after last night's show. And he was doing all the work preparing the meal for their friends, even though she had organized it.

Why were they fighting so much?

A woman with a push-buggy walked towards her, singing to her baby. With music blaring, Eva focused straight ahead.

Her dream had taken so much work: years of jingles, bullshit cover bands and failed projects. And now, she finally had an album out! And a concert tour! Regular gigs and good money.

But it was incomplete.

As she jogged past the mother and child, the baby looked straight into Eva's eye and smiled: a punch in the belly.

Eva wanted a baby.

It might be too late.

Crap.

Louis would be a wonderful father but wouldn't dare push her to start a family. They occasionally spoke of kids, but always in an abstract 'someday.' Louis supported her dreams while letting go of his own.

She fantasized about holding a baby to her chest and breastfeeding—pure connection.

Thirty-eight. Friends her age had been trying to have a baby for years. Could she even get pregnant? She'd been on birth control for over twenty years. Could they adopt? Louis was young enough, but not her. No agency would grant a child to a mother so old.

Maybe if they went overseas?

… after she had established herself…

… in two, or four years…

… maybe it would still work…

The lump in her throat pushed a pair of tears to roll down her cheek and Eva slowed to a walk. Half of her dreams were slipping away. She turned off the path and wandered through the woods to a secluded part of the river—her personal secret.

Abandon her music?

No. Eva shook herself and was back on stage with the same vision she always had: leather pants, pyrotechnics and a stadium filled with adoring fans. The audience chanted along to her powerful anthem; spirits bathing in its joy. Their hearts beat to the rhythm she had brought into the world.

She loved her dream.

Eva got naked and enjoyed the forest air steaming sweat from her skin. She stepped onto her favorite rock, closed her eyes and stretched her arms like an apple tree. 'Observe the wind's touch. Listen to the water's babble.' Were the birds admiring her confidence? She was proud of her body; Louis had helped with that. Eva raised her arms above her head and dove into the cool river.

She surfaced on her back, stretched into a star and looked up to the bristling leaves. Thousands of fans sung along to her chorus. She held the last note in ways that only years of relentless training could allow and triumphantly walked offstage and into her dressing room.

There was that baby again; in her chair. So cute. The crowd chanted for an encore. She picked up her smiling angel, lifted her shirt and began to breastfeed. The room vibrated under the arena's stomping as they called her name in unison.

Eva touched her breast and floated in the water.

The audience did not fade but waited patiently for her to finish. Her guitarist began the chords to her Celtic Lullaby, and the crowd immediately started singing without her. When the baby fell asleep, Louis took the child, and Eva ran back onto the stage to finish the song. Her fans would leave as they did every night: inspired and changed forever.

Eva swam underwater back to the shore.

Maybe she could have it all.

She climbed onto her favorite rock, closed her eyes and embraced the hot sun drying her body. Eva dressed and strolled home, enjoying the newness of her dream. She paused to smell the garden's basil and mint, then snuck upstairs to take a long, hot shower. Her mind was calm for the first time in forever, and she knew exactly what she wanted.

Eva slipped a cute silk dress over her naked skin and loved the sexy woman that looked back in the mirror.

She walked down the stairs through the modest home. Their big investment was the kitchen: a dream workshop made for cooks and feasts.

Louis was chopping vegetables and looked up shyly as Eva entered. She allowed a moment of feigned anger before letting go and smiling at her deepest love. The scene was familiar to both, and Louis was relieved to know peace had returned.

Eva had brought the morning anger into their home, and they

both knew that her dress and smile were the beginning of a long dance of forgiveness that would end when she managed to seduce him.

She looked across the counter full of fresh produce, oils and spices. "What can I do?" She loved cooking with her man. They shared a passion for incredible cuisine and knew how to build a meal together.

Louis acknowledged the peace offering. "You can make dessert: peach cobbler."

Eva picked up a peach from the fruit bowl, squeezed and smelled it. Bright, golden and sinful; these peaches were gloriously sweet and syrupy. Louis always knew where to find the right ingredients. "Cobbler is perfect."

Together, they prepared an elaborate, multi-course meal. Small portions were vital in maintaining desire and joy throughout the feast. Moon-apple and spinach salad. Salmon sashimi with ginger, seared with olive and sesame oil. Steamed asparagus covered in butter. White-truffle parmesan ravioli. Oven-roasted blackened halibut. And of course, the peach cobbler.

Cooking was an aphrodisiac for Eva. She glanced to Louis every moment she could and fought to steal his gaze with her posture. He focused straight ahead and chopped apple with the hands of a head chef. When he asked her to pass the oil, she bent more than necessary, looked away and brushed his skin with her fingertips. Louis noticed, and a smile let her know to behave. Eva's favorite game was interrupting dinner preparations with lovemaking in the kitchen. She opened a bottle of chilled Saint-Nicolas-de-Bourgueil and handed him a glass when he put the last pan in the oven. Louis wiped his hands, tossed the towel over his shoulder, and his look let Eva know that she could come close. Her body swelled with excitement. Eva swayed back and forth in a seductive dance while her fingertips started to hike up the bottom of her long silk dress.

She had never needed to make love this much in her entire life. Louis took a sip of wine and put his glass down on the counter.

The doorbell rang.

Eva looked to the clock. "Oh, no."

Louis closed his eyes and reluctantly turned towards the door.

"Noooooooo!!!" whispered Eva half-jokingly. "Make them go away!!!"

Louis turned, grabbed Eva and pulled her tight. "I love you."

Eva smiled. "I love you."

They held each other until there was a second ring at the door.

The evening began.

During the next three hours, Eva, Louis and the four guests enjoyed an incredible meal that left each in a state of bliss.

Santy played classical guitar as Eva brought the desserts to the table. The precision and passion of every strophe brought chills down her spine. His ferocious talent was mesmerizing. Eva slid her fingers up the back of Louis' neck.

As the last chord echoed in the room, the friends erupted into applause. Janet gave Santy a big kiss.

Louis was stunned. "You are unbelievable!"

He shrugged with humble confidence. "It is nothing that six hours a day for twenty-five years cannot teach."

The steaming peach cobbler beckoned each of them. Eva

gestured to everyone to eat and turned to Janet as she picked up her spoon. "Where did you two meet?"

"It's embarrassing." Eva loved Janet's colorful stories. "I saw him perform a while back and became a little obsessed. I found out he gave private lessons, so I booked a two-hour beginner's session. Instead of a guitar, I arrived with two bottles of wine and my best bra."

Santy blushed and the table laughed at the ridiculousness of their friend. Janet put her hand under Santy's chin and continued with a smile. "I still have not learned to play a single chord."

The table all knew that Janet was telling the truth, and they loved her for it. One by one, their laughter turned into delicious grunts as they savored the dessert.

Phil directed attention back to the hosts. "Eva, Louis, you have outdone yourselves once again. You have to give us the recipe for this cobbler!! It is AMAZING!!!"

Sven added, "OH MY GOD YES! We need it! It is THE MOST amazing deliciousness I have ever experienced!" Eva loved Sven's penchant for exaggeration. Everything they had ever prepared was 'the-best-thing-ever.'

Phil contemplated his next bite and turned to the newest addition to the table. "Santy, I've known Louis for seventeen years. When I visited his parent's house, his mom would always make us a new dessert, and every dessert had a story. Every dessert that Sven and I have shared with Louis has a story." He turned to Louis. "So, what's the story?"

Eva loved her partner for this family tradition; he always managed to surprise her. Louis feigned confusion, then relented. "I was in China last month and had dinner with a friend. He explained to me that in Taoist mythology, the Jade Emperor and his wife, the Queen Mother of the West, ensured the everlasting existence of the deities by inviting them to an extravagant banquet called the Feast of the Peaches. Somewhere on a Tian Shan mountainside in the west, there's a peach tree of immortality, and it blooms only once every three-thousand years. The Queen Mother guards this tree, and legend has it that it will soon bloom again.

"So, this morning, I went to the market, and in the corner was a rickety booth that I had never seen before. An old, mysterious Chinese lady was there selling peaches. I'm not 100% certain, but I strongly suspect she's the Queen Mother, and we've eaten some of her immortal peaches. Now, we're destined to live forever."

Janet picked up her empty plate and held it out to Eva. "Could I please have some more?" The whole table laughed. She then grabbed Santy's plate and asked him to join her. "Come, honey; I wanna make mad love to you FOR-EV-ER!!!!"

Santy turned red, and the whole table enjoyed his continued embarrassment. Janet insisted. "Can you imagine having time to realize all of your dreams?!? Learn all musical instruments? Travel everywhere? Meet everyone? It would be AMAZING!!!"

Phil contemplated his bowl and responded in a more serious tone: "I love the story but living forever would be terrible. I mean, it's the newness of experience that makes life great: the preciousness of time. We live our choices. But if we lived forever, no choice would have consequence or relevance; just change your mind a thousand years later. Can you imagine having already done everything? Having nothing new to taste?"

Sven interrupted and asked in his best sweetie-voice: "What about me? Do you want to choose me forever?"

Phil snuck into baby-talk and caressed Sven's cheek. "I'll choose you every time and always." The table rejoiced. "But living forever would be awful." Phil reached for the sugar bowl and took a cube between his fingers. He held it purposefully above an empty plate. "Did you know that one large cube of sugar has thirty-six thousand grains? If you imagine for a second that each grain represents one day, this cube contains a hundred years." He then shaved off a tiny piece and let the sugar fall to his plate. "Most of us will not live to 100, so the amount of sugar that is left represents the days of an average life. This is the only wealth that matters: the days of our lives and how we choose to spend them."

The cube was so small.

Phil twisted it in his fingers. "Today, half of my days are behind me." He broke the cube in two and crushed one side, letting the grains fall. "I'm proud of those days, but they are only memories." He looked to the dwindling remains. "The last bit of my life will probably be of limited health and capacity." He scraped off a corner from the ever-shrinking shape. Eva stared depressingly at it.

Phil looked into the eyes of each of his dearest friends. "With this modest cube, I can imagine how valuable each and every grain is. I need to savor each moment to its fullest." Phil put a single grain on his finger. "I'm happy with how I chose to spend this day: with you, with people I love. I do not wish for endless mountains of sugar, because then this grain, this day, this choice, would be infinitely less important.

"I love you all too much to wish for that."

Eva considered the overflowing sugar bowl. She did not want to live forever.

Phil held the cube and asked Santy one of his famously provocative questions: "So what do you want most with your remaining days?"

Santy paused. "To play my music for people who appreciate it."

Phil turned to Janet. "And you?"

Janet grew serious. "I want to give more of myself to others."

Phil looked at Eva. "And you, Rock Star?"

Eva closed her eyes and hunched forward. Even amongst people she cared for deeply, she had never shared her baby thoughts. Her rock-star dreams were legendary, and she knew the answer everyone was expecting; the answer Louis was expecting. Eva looked at the meager cube in Phil's fingers. Her voice cracked as she whispered: "I want a baby."

Eyes widened, but no one made a sound. A tidal wave of pressure flowed out, freed from her body. It was replaced by warmth as Louis put his hand on her back. His love was clear and limitless.

Phil turned to Louis with a smile. "And what do you want?"

Louis looked Eva in the eye. He was ready to cry, and she felt a little bad for sharing in front of everyone. "A baby sounds good."

After letting the couple enjoy the moment, Phil moved on and looked to Sven. "You're my heart, and I don't want to waste any more of these precious grains working in jobs we hate." He explained to the table: "The earth is losing too much of its botanical diversity. We need to find ways to preserve nature's wonders, and Sven had the idea to build a giant atrium and fill it with endangered plants from around the planet. It's time for us to quit our jobs and follow this dream." Phil turned back to his partner. "Is that what you want, my love?"

Sven grew a big mischievous smile. "Yes. And can I ask for a baby too?"

The table laughed as Sven had intended. But Louis didn't laugh. He looked at Phil. "Do you want a baby, Phil?"

"Well, yes. If we could adopt or find someone to have our baby, I would love to raise a child. We have so much to give."

"That would be one lucky baby." Louis moved to the stereo and started looking through CDs. He found what he was looking for and put it in the player. "When we were twenty, I walked into Phil's apartment and found him alone, making ridiculous dance moves to this song."

Louis hit play and began to imitate his friend's flailing arms and silly legs. Eva knew this was Louis' way to get the party started. He was the only engineer she had ever met who loved to dance. One by one, they got up from their chairs and joined the bopping.

The next hours were a mix of wine, laughter and dancing. Louis and Eva could not stop touching and flirting with each other. He pulled her close whenever a new song came on, and she put her hair up, knowing the nape of her neck drove him wild.

As they waved to the last guests driving away, Eva turned to the ocean and let her dress fall to the ground. Fresh air and goosebumps tightened her naked body. Behind her, the clumsy sounds of Louis frantically taking his pants off made her smile. She sauntered across the beach with swiveling hips, stepped into the cool water and waded until it rose to her waist. Stars poked holes through the night's black canvas and connected her to all purpose and wonder in the universe. She closed her eyes and listened to slow water movements as Louis approached. He paused centimeters away and warmth filled her heart. His head touched the back of hers. His hands stroked down her shoulders and wrapped deliberately to her front. She felt his nakedness as he kissed the back of her neck and caressed her stomach.

Desire and excitement pulsated through her body.

~~

Basil and mint and awe. An endless tingle warmed her body as Nerea opened her eyes in the candle-lit garden.

Eva was incredible.

Waking from her body was natural. Nerea now sat on the same bench, at the same beach where Eva had lived. She breathed the ocean air and embraced its inspiration. There was comfort in her grandmother; they shared a soul. It was beyond her deepest fantasies: a family, separated only by time. Eva was everything that Nerea wished she could be: passionate and open and free.

The simulation was perfect. Eva was perfect. Nerea allowed a moment of sadness as the details of the memory began to fade.

It was late. The hours had passed as they had in the simulation.

She stretched her fingers and toes and turned to Seren. "My grandparents were deeply in love."

Seren smiled. "Yes. Eva and Louis had your mother nine months later, and after Santy and Janet broke up, Janet became a surrogate mother for Phil and Sven. They had Yves eighteen months later. This beautiful dinner played an important role in the birth of Waldon."

It hit hard. Her mind darted left and right. "Holy crap! Did Clara know the founder of Waldon?" She began to shake her head. "Was my blood part of the destructive undertaking? Is that where our money came from?"

Seren invited Nerea to take deep breaths and embrace the calm evening. "Slow down; answers are coming. Our lineage shapes us. We cannot escape our patterns and write our own stories until we acknowledge our pasts. Your story and the story of

Waldon are intertwined. Your questions are important, and you will learn more tomorrow morning. Now, you need sleep."

Nerea's mind exploded in every direction but grogginess clouded the clarity of each thought. She breathed deeply as sudden exhaustion became unbearable. Seren offered a quilt and suggested lying down on the patio couch.

For the first night in ten years, shame and loneliness would not keep her awake. Nerea stretched into a big yawn, lay back and allowed the inner chaos put her to sleep.

Chapter 3

08/04/2226 – The Pensiveness Experience

Nerea woke to the warm, pink light of a sunrise over the ocean. The sea begged her to bathe. She took a towel onto the beach and undressed. Sunrise swims were her favorite thing in the world. In some ways, it had been a privilege to grow up in Clara's beautiful prison.

'Pick a wave. Dive. Glide. Float.' The underwater silence made her feel safe. While it was strange knowing her body was asleep back in Seren's office, she appreciated the quiet of this simulated reality. How would the next hours affect her Decision? Where would today take her? Would she be seduced or repulsed by Yves and the monsters of Waldon?

The soft sand slowed her walk to the beach house, and she found Seren smelling flowers in the garden. The golden sun sparkled off her skin and radiated an aura of pure kindness. There was something pure in Seren—she was sublime: a stunning beauty with a giant heart. Nerea spoke softly. "Good morning."

Seren turned with an alluring smile, walked closer and put a hand on Nerea's shoulder. "How are you?" Touch. Nerea twitched to pull away, but the comforting grip opened something inside—something lost. Seren wore a light, seductive scent of lilac and lemon. Why had she not noticed yesterday? Lived wisdom and reflective guidance waited patiently behind that glow. She was honest and pure.

"I'm nervous." Seren nodded and allowed the honesty of the answer to float freely in the air. Nerea wondered if, under different circumstances, they could have become friends. She thought so. At least, she hoped so. Seren let go of her shoulder, and Nerea's body somehow felt heavier. "How old are you?"

"Fifty-five."

"Was your Decision easy?"

"No. I had a wonderful childhood and loved my parents. I imagined growing old with them and having a family; but when my older brother chose to stop aging, I knew I had to follow in his footsteps. He was my hero, and I didn't want him to be alone. Unfortunately, he couldn't handle his new reality; he grew hopeless, vanished and death caught up to him. We were heartbroken, and my parents never recovered. They died soon after."

Nerea's belly plummeted; Seren's pain flowed directly from her grandparent's innocent dinner. Waldon's Decision tore families apart and crushed countless souls with its gift of eternal emptiness. She felt queasy. The air thinned as she attempted to speak. "Waldon has done awful things to families. My blood is tied to inhumanity and has done nothing to fix it. Our wealth lays dormant while billions of people suffer. When our work together is complete, I will be free to cut Clara from my life and slice the final strings of our dying bond. I want to dedicate my life and money to helping families like yours. I want to repair some small part of the damage Waldon has caused. No one should suffer as you have." Nerea's hands trembled, and her eyes welled; it was unbearable.

But there was a lifeboat in Seren's eye, free of judgment. "There is so much tension in you. You are young, with so much life in front of you. Let go. Your wealth is not your fault. Your family was part of Waldon, not you. Waldon's actions are not your actions. Waldon is not your responsibility. The sadness I knew was not your fault."

Nerea slouched forward and gasped. A single tear forged an unchartered path down her cheek. Seren passed a tissue and spoke soothingly. "Life is shaped in how we deal with the inherited burden of our ancestors. Today, you must begin to shed weights that you have unknowingly held for too long. You need to release the guilt that is crushing you. You need to be clear about your own opinions and beliefs. You need to separate yourself from your mother, create your own space and make your own Decision. So, tell me: what do you believe in?"

Nerea looked to the sea and slumped back in her chair. A breeze brought basil and mint from the garden. Her guarded beliefs had formed through observation and reflection. They had taken shape in coffee shops, on cliff-tops and through books, and had forged a relentless need to understand the spark that drove others. Her voice cracked. "I believe life is meant to be a brief moment of exploration and connection, not an eternity of repetition. I believe that death is a necessity to life and not a disease in need of a cure. I believe pain is necessary to joy and challenge is necessary to success, but I refuse to accept the misery that Waldon has brought to the world."

Seren smiled, went to the bar and made an espresso. "Yesterday's experiences were the ancestors of Waldon. Today begins at its birth. This is the first investor and is based on a brain scan from many years ago. This person is still alive and does not know this simulation exists. Are you comfortable with that?"

It was illegal to live the life of someone alive without explicit permission, but Nerea trusted Seren. "I'm okay with that."

Seren brought the double ristretto to the table. Nerea held the warm cup, inhaled and fantasized about her first sip. "Where am I going now?"

"This is Mathieu."

~~

20/03/2031 – The Hope Experience

Mathieu drove through the town in the back of his electric limo. Every muscle in his body was tense and tired, but an unrelenting desperation kept his bones moving at full speed. The answer that once seemed so close, was slipping away.

Failure was not an option. He had made a promise to Grampa.

Raindrops hit the car and isolated him further from the wet people on the sidewalk. As the years would roll by, each of them was scheduled to die. Death was inevitable.

Why?

Mathieu did not want to die a predetermined death.

He did not want to die at all.

His fortune had been dedicated to unlocking the cure to aging. Most promising studies focused on improving cell survival and neuron replacement, but each had hit limitations. So much had been wasted following the lies of con men.

But this was different.

The ridiculed thesis that brought him here sat on the seat beside him. The draft had arrived two days ago from the professor of two young graduate students: Clara Woodruff and Mohammed Korman. The title was 'Reprogrammed Telomerase Boosts Protecting Chromosome Caps,' and Mathieu had already spent many hours reading it backward and forwards. The first page was highlighted: '…encouraging results with significant costs that must be addressed."

A VIP barrier opened, and his car passed through the university's main gate. Mathieu appreciated the energy and potential that flourished only on campuses—invisible to most students but crystal clear once they looked back. He had left school during his first year and promised Grampa he would one day return and get his degree. 'When time is no longer limited,' he would tell himself.

They stopped in front of the Health and Sciences building. Tom got out and opened Mathieu's door holding an umbrella and a badge. "The lab is twenty-five meters straight ahead, fourth door on the left. Mr. Korman and Ms. Woodruff are in there now."

"Thank you." He appreciated Tom. Mathieu paid him well, and he had become the closest thing to a 'friend' he could allow: a reflective confidant with a beard and a gun.

Tom warned him one last time. "Be cautious. The leaps they made don't make any sense, and our experts have already discredited their work."

"I don't think they made leaps; I think they made edits. There's something in the writing that intrigues me. It could be the path I'm looking for."

Tom nodded and moved aside. "I'm not convinced, but good luck."

Mathieu walked up the stairs and into the building. The interior was faceless and bland—the worst type of beige. He walked towards the fourth door, terrified that the same lifeless atmosphere would extend into the lab he financed. The badge opened the lock, and he stepped inside.

Relief! The room basked in natural light and breathed with fresh air. A powerful, optimistic energy flowed through the space. His soreness was swept away with adrenaline of anticipation.

This was it.

Two students stared at him with guilty eyes and open mouths. His unexpected entrance had startled them. They were doing things they should not be doing.

Mathieu surveyed the lab. It was different than other labs he knew. There were no mice nor animals. Whiteboards were full of furious writing and brainstorming sessions. A couple of mattresses lay under tables, and there was a pizza box on the counter. Recycled servers were stacked and running in the corner, while odd bits and hard drives were tethered to several of his million-dollar robots. Every one of the machines hummed with active calculations. Half of the space was sealed behind a glass wall, with a clean-room changing area at its entrance.

Mathieu's shoulders straightened.

The stunning young lady with olive skin and black hair was Clara. Despite scholarship offers to every elite school in North America, she chose to study here: at Grampa's alma-mater. In her scholarship acceptance letter, Clara stated that she selected the university because of the lab. She did her undergraduate degree in half the usual time and was now working on her master's thesis.

Mohammed Rahimi Korman came to study in the States after growing up in Canada. He had arrived with a wave of Afghan refugees in 2010 after his family died in the war. His adoptive parents were an older, light-spirited couple with big hearts and a farm. They could not have children and gave everything they could to Mohammed: stability, love, humor and space. They even converted to Islam to support the spiritual path of his birth parents. His best friends were the farm animals and the veterinarians that would visit. Mohammed was obsessed with cell behavior and microbiology.

Clara broke the long silence: "Sir. Can I help you? You're not allowed in here."

"Hello, Clara."

Mohammed gave an awkward glance towards his friend. "Do you know him?"

"No. Who are you?"

"Mathieu Baird. Hello, Mohammed."

Their stares rose over his head and froze. He followed their eyes to the plaque that hung in many labs around the world: 'Baird Advanced Medical Studies Laboratory.' Mathieu enjoyed these moments and the focus they brought to discussions. "They give you a plaque if you donate a bit of money."

Clara appeared nervous as her benefactor explored the room. "What can we do for you?"

"I read your paper."

Clara focused on the floor. "I guess we wasted a bit of your money."

"According to your professor, you need another six months before you can resubmit and graduate."

"I guess we got a bit sloppy."

Clara kept avoiding his eyes. The lab was not a defeated space—
it was one of breakthroughs and victories. The woman before
him was not ashamed—she was confident, knowledgeable and
in complete control.

"Do you trust your professor?"

Clara looked up. "Yes. She gives us a lot of freedom. Why?"

"It's bizarre that you got so far without submitting a draft."

"She's very busy. It's my fault we didn't give her one till it was
too late."

Mathieu knew their professor was not too busy; she was too
drunk. The school should have fired her years ago. "In the last
few days, I've read every paper you have submitted. Your writing
is flawless. It's why you had access to such advanced equipment
before your masters even started. You're thorough. The work
you have done in your young career is extremely impressive."

Clara sounded worried. "Thank you."

Mathieu turned to Mohammed. "You're one of the most gifted
microbiology students to come to this school in twenty
years. And your previous writing and submissions were perfect."

He spoke with a soft yet proud tone. "That's a bit much but
thank you."

"I think the two of you know more than you published. I think
your work on maintaining the protective caps of chromosomes
is significant."

Clara and Mohammed looked again to the ground; they were
definitely hiding something. Mathieu's heart accelerated.

"Why not publish your actual results?"

Mohammed tried to make eye contact but glanced away as he spoke. "We did." He shuffled his weight.

Clara's stare rose to Mathieu and locked. There was growing confidence in her gaze, like she was getting caught for a good deed. Mathieu's voice trembled as he whispered. "I've been taken advantage of by some of the world's most skilled liars, but you two are terrible. What have you found?"

Clara looked at her friend and nodded. She began: "At first, we were scared because we assumed we were wrong. Every day, we tried to find our mistake. And then, I was talking to a friend and became terrified of another possibility: what if we're right?"

"If you're right, you have figured out how to cure aging."

Mohammed interjected, "Not cure; slow it down."

Mathieu's core was beginning to float. "That's just one step from a cure."

The three looked at each other in silence. Mathieu could no longer hide his excitement, and a grin belied his controlling tone. He pulled up a chair and motioned for the others to do the same. Like a teenager seeking weekend tales from his best-friends, Mathieu opened the floor, "What you have found? Tell me."

Clara's confidence grew with each sentence. "As you read, there are many different theories on how to maintain the protective caps on chromosomes. When this is accomplished, human cells could almost endlessly duplicate—essentially stopping aging. While experiments have shown promise in mice, the leap to humans was thought to be fifty years away. Our bodies are full of complex interactions and Moe and I did not like the over-simplified approaches in today's single-factor studies; we began multi-targeting approaches on human stem-cells with complex protein and gene treatment combinations. Through a precise modification of a few strands of DNA, combined with a complex cocktail of enzymes, cells establish a new balance, and are able to produce micro-boosts of telomerase that prevent degradation of telomeres. The cells rapidly infect surrounding cells with the same, superior mutation. Our tests show that the Hayflick limit does not constrain the resulting cells, and their epigenetic clocks remain constant."

"How many divisions have you achieved? Did you get beyond sixty?"

Nerea nodded towards a live microscopic camera-feed from the clean-room. "We are at four hundred and eighty-three, and there are new divisions every seven hours. The cells remain in perfect health."

His eyes welled with happiness, and his voice cracked as he whispered: "So, you've done it? You've found a way to prevent age-related cell degradation?"

Moe and Clara nodded in unison, and Mathieu's body tingled. He asked question after question around the methods, assumptions and experiments they had run. With each answer, he was more and more confident that this was the real deal. There was a strong possibility that the two young people in front of him had unlocked the fountain of youth.

His dream had begun.

As the conversation wound down, Clara asked, "And now what?"

He would not lose this opportunity. "I want to know what you need. I want to get you out of this cramped lab and into a place where you can spread your wings. I want to build on what you have started. I want to help you change the world."

Clara took a deep breath. "When?"

"Tonight. Put together a list of things you need to form a new company, and we can discuss it later. I like to move quickly. Life's too short…" he smiled wide and continued, "…for now."

Clara allowed herself a chuckle. She ripped down a small, pink flier pinned awkwardly on the wall between science papers. It was for a poetry reading at a café. "Can we meet here at 8:30?"

Mathieu liked the idea of starting a company at a coffee shop. "I'll be there."

He spent the rest of the day in a euphoric state of giddiness. The plan was simple: his lawyer drew up paperwork, and he calculated how much money he had left. After so many wasted investments, this could be his last shot.

Mathieu arrived at the 'The Flagrant Fowl' cafe with Tom. The place was half full, with couches and chairs that had been collected from garbage bins and garage sales. There was a quiet mix of students, young artists and old hippies, and they were split between tea and wine. Clara and Moe sat in a round booth at the back. Mathieu and Tom walked back and joined them.

A tipsy announcer in a Hawaiian shirt and sandals introduced the following performance. "…And next up is one of my favorites here at the Fowl. Please give your undivided attention to the observations of Yves!!!!!" There was scattered applause.

Yves was a beautiful man: dark skin, short hair and a genuine smile. He took the microphone.

"Hi. Tonight, I want to share an untitled work written by a Jewish poet. He was born to a generation that could be governed alternately by Pharaohs, Babylonians, Persians and Greeks without ever leaving home. It was a confusing time for truth seekers. Pharaohs proclaimed to be literal gods, while

Babylonian gods controlled everything from fires to the wind. The single Persian God, Ahura, guaranteed the ultimate destruction of all evil, while Alexander the Great's beliefs were shaped with the father of Western Philosophy, Aristotle.

"It was a dangerous period to be a Jew, yet this poet is now recognized as a Prophet in both Islam and Christianity, and his words are more relevant today than they have ever been.

"For tonight only, I want to give this poem a name. I call it 'The Garden of Yves.'

> On the day you were created,
> you were the seal of perfection,
> full of wisdom
> and perfect in beauty.
> You were in Eden,
> the garden of God.
> Every precious stone adorned you,
> settings made of gold.
>
> On the day you were created,
> they were prepared.
> An angel there to guard you,
> on the holy mountain of God.
> You walked among the fiery stones.
>
> On the day you were created,
> you were blameless in your ways,
>
> until wickedness was found in you.
>
> By the vastness of your trade,
> you were filled with violence,
> and you sinned.
> You became more cruel
> and evil.

Now, you must exit in disgrace
from the mountain of God.
The creature, your protector
will chase you from the jewels.
Banished.
All nations appalled.
You have come to a horrible end,
and will never exist again.

On the day you were created,
you were the seal of perfection.

Ezekiel 28:12-19"

Yves put the microphone down as the audience clapped in sparse approval. He made his way to the table and sat beside Clara. Mathieu took a moment to observe each of the three friends as they pushed together in the booth. They were close.

Mathieu nodded to the poet. "So, you're Yves."

"Hello, Mr. Baird."

"Call me Mathieu. This is Tom."

Tom offered a half-nod. "Who's the poem for?"

"I don't know yet. Prophets words can only be understood when we look back from the end."

Tom ordered a glass of Minervois for Mathieu and a tea for himself. The others asked for water. Empty glasses scattered around the table let Mathieu know that the three had been there a while.

Tom began: "Mathieu tells me that the two of you 'might' have found a cure for death? Very exciting." There was a huge dose of doubt in his voice.

Moe corrected: "Not death—aging."

Clara expanded, "We have solid preliminary results, but don't have the computing power to understand the long-term impact."

"Why would you publish partial, edited findings?"

Yves looked leery of Tom: "The world is not ready."

Tom rolled his eyes. "And what's your role on the team?"

Yves looked at Clara. "There are significant moral challenges in front of us. Clara and I have known each other since we were babies, and she appreciates the way I see the world. She asked for my help."

"Based on my research, you have spent your life avoiding responsibilities. You finished high-school with excellent grades but have done little more than travel the globe and work in your fathers' atrium for the past few years."

"I go where I'm needed, but if I'm not needed, I go. Right now, I'm here to protect Clara from people like you. And how do you know where I've been?"

Mathieu calmed everyone down. "Tom does homework before I invest in people. As you protect Clara, Tom protects me."

Clara spoke softly. "Yves is more than my protector—he sees the bigger picture and reminds us of the stakes. When we first got results, Yves convinced me not to publish the details. We need more certainty before sharing with the world. Because if we're right, a lot will change."

Yves turned to Mathieu. "Why is aging's cure important for you?"

"Humanity needs it."

"I didn't ask about humanity; I asked about your personal motivation. Why is this important for <u>you</u>?"

Few people ever dared to question him; most were only interested in his money. But these three kids looked intent on digging deeper. After a pause, Mathieu decided to share. "I never met my father, and my mother was not strong enough to raise a child. My grandfather was poor but gave me everything he had: time, love, food and a roof. He was the kindest person I ever met. I loved him so much and worked tirelessly to repay him and make him proud. By twenty-six, I sold my first company. I was very wealthy, and he was very sick. I was powerless to help during Grampa's long, painful crawl towards death. I had limitless resources but could not help the one person who had loved me unconditionally. On his deathbed, I promised him I would help others avoid the suffering that he knew. He smiled, nodded, and fell asleep for the last time. His body was no longer strong enough to heal itself. His cells were programed to fail— a planned obsolescence. Why? Aging is unnecessary, a disease. Humanity is better than death."

He stared at the empty stage and remembered Grampa, holding his bent fingers as he wheezed towards his last breath; then silence. Despite many years that had passed, the wound was still raw. Mathieu took a deep breath and turned to Clara decisively. "What do you need?"

Clara looked to Yves and Moe. They nodded, and she began. "The same tools we have in the lab, plus another fifty million dollars for more powerful computing and equipment. Yves' fathers have the perfect spot to build our lab – in an atrium. I need complete control over the release of our cure. Today, I trust you, but as money comes into the picture, I need to make sure we continue to do the right thing."

Tom shook his head. "Fifty million! This is a joke. You're wasting Mathieu's time! You're just beginning, and the chances of success are tiny." Tom started to stand. He could intimidate when he chose.

Mathieu interrupted softly and looked straight into Clara's eye. "No games tonight, Tom. Sit down." The stare between Mathieu and Clara remained unbroken. "You don't care about money; that's clear. According to security data, you have been using the equipment I bought almost twenty-four hours a day for the last eighteen months, but nothing was saved to the network as designed. You have been stealing from the school and stealing from me. You have been left almost entirely alone to play in my very expensive lab.

"Despite that, I'm beginning to trust you. I believe your results are accurate, and I like your approach a lot. To be clear: will this work?"

Clara smirked and straightened her shoulders. "It works."

He turned to Moe. "So, you have found the cure for aging."

Moe could no longer hide his pride. "Yes."

He turned to Yves with a grin: "And what do you think, Mr. Conscience?"

Yves looked away from Clara and stared down to his glass of water. He hesitated. "I think we're playing with fire. Transhumanist ideas have been around since humanity learned to reason. Our earliest religions dreamed of eternal life: ancient Egyptians and the Caribbean Taíno discovered and lost death's cure in the waters of Kollam and Bimini, while Japanese Shinto has always yearned for life to live, not to die. Our search has never stopped, and every scientific breakthrough we have made has been in chaotic pursuit of this goal. Our DNA is driving us relentlessly towards an ultimate survival; we can't possibly stop it. Sooner or later, someone will solve the problem of death; it's inevitable. And given the choice of how a cure should be released, I trust the morals of these two infinitely more than I would anyone else. But this scares me: it changes everything, and I'm not sure it's for the better."

Tom rolled his eyes, and Mathieu smiled wide. He liked the philosopher and knew this team was the right one to change the world. He looked each of them in the eye. "What does fifty million dollars buy me?"

Clara stared at the flickering candle on their table. "Thirty-one percent of the company. I take thirty-two percent, fifteen for Moe, eight for Yves, seven for a key new technical role, two for early employees, and five for future investors."

Clara had just assessed the value of the company at 167 million dollars. If she was right, it was worth much, much more than that. But if she was wrong, it was worth nothing. Her thirty-two percent also made it clear that the ideas were hers; Mathieu had expected a more even split. Moe, Yves and Clara would hold fifty-five percent of the company.

Clara continued, "I want full control over research and development with no interference. I decide what goes to market, when it goes to market and how it goes to market."

Tom interjected, "So how will he make money? If you develop something but refuse to sell it, how will Mathieu ever recover his investment?"

Mathieu listened but did not care about the money; they could have doubled or tripled the amount. He also didn't care about the ownership percentage. There was only one thing on his mind: curing the unnecessary disease of aging. Mathieu did not want to miss this opportunity for a clear and exclusive partnership.

"When can we perform human trials?"

Clara reflected. "We need to understand the long-term impacts on the human body and that requires patience. Our procedure will be very intrusive, so approvals will be tough. In our current plan, we test on humans in ten to fifteen years."

"What if you had a lot more money? We can dilute ownership with non-voting shares, and secure significant additional investments. With five billion dollars from investors, how quickly could you move?"

Yves and Moe looked stunned, but Clara was calm and reflective. "We could invest in more powerful machine-learning and simulation tools. If models could accurately predict long-term effects, we would accelerate human trials by maybe five years."

"What if we tested exclusively on people in the company? As owners, we have the legal right to test on ourselves as long as we're confident in positive results. When you're ready, I want to be the first human trial. Could we start testing on ourselves in the next three years?"

Yves interrupted. "Wait a second. Clara – you're not a lab rat, and we're not in a race. Life has been like this forever, and it is too important to skip steps."

Mathieu spoke firmly. "I'll be the first lab-rat. And I can easily find other investors who are willing to risk themselves."

Clara's eyes widened as she did some calculations. "With significant additional investments, we may be able to achieve that."

"Just give me results I can share. I know a lot of billionaires that want to live forever, and when the time comes, I'll get us all the money we need."

Mathieu was comfortable allowing the three make all operational decisions, but not significant, strategic choices. "You can have your requested control through a simple majority vote for basic staffing, sales and operations; however, I will insist that major decisions, changes to board members and strategy updates require a two-thirds majority. That means that future investors and I will have the power to protect our investment, but no one person has full control."

Clara pondered the ceiling. "That could work."

Mathieu had negotiated a lot of deals in his life and had occasionally placed his trust in the wrong people. But Clara was untouched by the greed that killed so many projects. "Tom, call Elena and have her draw up papers reflecting our agreements. Let's get this contract done tonight. And then give the team one hundred million dollars and everything they need to get started."

Jaws dropped.

"Clara, Moe, Yves: I believe in you and in the importance of what we're doing. Tom, be fair with them and give them what they ask for."

Mathieu stood and put his jacket on. Life was good, and it was about to get better. The waiter came by to clean the table, and Mathieu asked, "Excuse me, who's the manager?" He pointed to the man in the flower shirt. Mathieu turned to the group. "Stay as long as you need to discuss the deal. I'll make sure they remain open for us."

Mathieu walked from the table with school-boy giddiness. Great things were going to happen.

Grampa would definitely be proud.

~~

A blast of exuberance blew through her body. She rubbed her hands and kicked her feet in the thrill. Nerea opened her eyes with a giant smile and pumped her fists in the air. "That was amazing!"

But the excitement wasn't hers; it was Mathieu's. Her thoughts slowly became her own.

She looked to Seren with her mouth wide open and panicked. "Clara isn't just connected to Waldon; it was her idea! She looked so happy and excited, with good people around her. Moe and Yves were dear friends, and Mathieu believed in her!" But Clara had never spoken about any of them. Her entire belief system was being torn apart. Nerea looked for answers. "Is Moe still alive?"

Seren's eyes softened. "No. Moe and Yves have been dead for fifty years. This all happened two hundred years ago, Nerea, so you will meet a lot of people who are now dead. Death was common before Waldon changed the world. If you were lucky, the people you loved grew old and died. If you were unlucky, they died young."

The passing of people she had just met hurt more than she had imagined. The dagger of mortality had never struck her heart directly; it had always been abstract, romantic and casually normal. Through their years of fights, Nerea occasionally contemplated her mother's death and perversely imagined it would resolve their problems. She fantasized about Clara apologizing on her deathbed, begging for forgiveness.

But Nerea's views of Waldon were being shredded. The corporation seemed to be born in a good place from kind hearts. How did it become so wicked?

Or was it wicked?

"Why did Clara not tell me she founded Waldon? How could she lie about something so big?"

"Waldon employees live in constant fear of being found out. She did not want you to know that fear. Your mother wanted you to have a childhood free from the burden that comes with Waldon and chose to shield you until your Decision. She wanted you to develop your own beliefs towards the value of life and death. If you were surrounded by Waldon in youth, she felt you would be blinded by its brilliance and may not open yourself to truths in the world around you.

"Your family story is woven into the fabric of history. You need to understand the threads that hold life together before you make the ultimate choice. Clara raised you, pushed you to leave the island and created these simulations precisely so that you could prepare your Decision."

'A precise experience?' Nerea looked to the basil and mint, and listened to the rolling waves in the background. Clara's manipulation was everywhere.

Chapter 4

08/04/2226 – The Envy Experience

Nerea stretched her shoulders back and wondered when she would finally learn her father's identity. The secret now felt insignificant compared to everything else, but she still needed to know.

Seren returned to the table and dipped a lemon-ginger tea bag into a glass of hot water. The tag on the string had a picture of a man that had often visited when Nerea was a young child. Gentle eyes and a giant smile brought much-needed joy to the island when he arrived. Nerea held memories of bountiful picnics and open discussions on his beautiful, striped blanket.

The warmth of those moments was the purest of her childhood.

She could still hear his tears the day he left; Clara asked him not to return.

"Your mother said Curly was the best hiring decision Waldon ever made. He took over her role as CEO when you were born. This simulation is his gift to you."

Nerea stared to the cup and wondered. "Is he my…" her voice

trailed off.

Seren shook her head. "No."

Nerea sipped and closed her eyes.

~ ~

15/11/2031 – The Acceptance Experience

'A life without risk is an existence without life.'

The hand-printed statement hit hard; someone knew he lived in fear. It was written on the bottom of the cryptic business card, under 'Waldon' and a flower logo with 48 petals. He inserted the card into his breast pocket and pressed it gently against his chest.

Curly's violent neighborhood scared him. He went outside only when absolutely necessary—and never when there was snow on the ground. But today, he would push through cold and fear and shame in search of something better.

With one hand on the doorknob, he reluctantly looked into his entrance mirror. The clippers had broken a month ago, and his afro was now an uncontrolled mess; but they'll never notice—they'll be focused on the shiny new pimple on his nose. Dark-skinned men were not supposed to get zits like this. 'Why today?' And how had he gotten so fat? Not obese, but definitely fat. Why didn't he exercise more this year like he said he would?

It was time to move.

Curly braced himself, opened the locks and took the necessary stride out his front door. He activated the security system built from discarded electronics, stepped onto the slush-filled sidewalk and felt the freezing water seep through his sneakers.

Winter was miserable. No number of layers could warm his body on these wet-wind days.

He had not slept since the card arrived yesterday. There was a loud knock and—through the camera—he saw a rough-looking man with a beard. Curly called nervously through the speaker: "Hello?"

"Hi, Carl. A friend told me you could help us. This is an invitation." He slid the card through the delivery slot and disappeared back to his car—like a bad-ass secret-agent. If Curly lived somewhere else, he might have even felt cool.

But alas… he never left the block he was born on—a failure— just like everyone expected.

There was handwriting on the back of the card:

> *Dear Carl,*
>
> *Your talent has amazed us, and your discretion is impressive. Come meet us tomorrow. We want to offer you a job.*
>
> *Yves*

And that was it. No address. No proposed time. No contact information. Just the business card in his pocket.

Curly was intrigued and figured out where to go.

Bus 217 stopped, and the doors opened. He stepped on, gave half of his remaining cash to the driver, and asked for a receipt and a transfer pass. If Waldon didn't reimburse him, Curly was screwed. The bus was not full, but he still hated looking for a place to sit. A teenager whispered a smart remark about his glasses, and her friends all laughed. He sat beside an old lady with a flower hat and warm-looking boots. She pulled her purse subtly towards herself. Curly didn't fit in anywhere. He put on his headphones, closed his eyes and wished teleportation existed. There was a long trip ahead.

During the next two hours, he attempted invisibility. It was what he always did in public. When the bus was almost full, he stood to let a bent, tottering old man take his seat.

Each transfer took him further from the city, deep into the farms and forests of the countryside. By the end of the journey, he was alone on the bus. Curly looked out the window with nervous intrigue. He got off at a remote stop and spotted a 48-petal flower on a sturdy iron gate. The walls surrounding the trees were both discrete and imposing. Curly stared into the cameras as he took out the business card and cautiously swiped it near a badge reader. The gate slid open and revealed a long lane into the forest.

He walked the snowy path for a half-mile, reached an opening and was blown away by an expansive property with a modern, six-story building and an attached, glass atrium that was bigger than a football field. There was green inside! It was a dream, unlike anything he had ever seen—a giant square built of glass and filled with jungle trees, birds and fauna from around the world.

As he approached the building, a hidden speaker announced: "Welcome to Waldon, Carl. Come inside. I've let Yves know you're here." He recognized the voice of his bearded visitor. Curly preferred the faceless welcome over a real person at a reception desk.

The doors opened to a hip entrance: empty space with lounge chairs, a coffee bar and games. No one was there. He put his jacket on a stool and appreciated the warmth. Without thinking, he picked a peach from the fruit bowl and took a bite. There was no breakfast at home, and his belly murmured in appreciation. A door hissed open, and two men approached with arms outstretched in genuine, open gestures. There was now sticky peach-juice all over his hands and he desperately tried to wipe them on the back of his shirt. Warm blood flushed through his cheeks. How had he become so awkward?

"Hi, Carl. My name's Yves. I'm happy you came."

"Hi, Carl. Moe."

He stuttered as he began. "Hello. My mother named me Carl, but I go by Curly."

Yves smiled. "Welcome to Waldon, Curly. I hope the impersonal greeting wasn't too intimidating; Tom keeps us discreet."

"You think that a giant glass box in the middle of the forest is discreet?" Whoops. Curly immediately regretted the observation.

But Yves welcomed it. "Ahhh. The Cube! Do you want to see it? Let's go for a walk."

Moe smiled. "He's proud of this place."

The group wandered across the lobby, through a disinfectant booth and into the enormous atrium garden. Despite winter temperatures outside, the space was warm, with incredible flowers, exotic butterflies, maple trees, intersecting pathways and a small waterfall. There was even a slight, springtime breeze. Curly had never seen such colors. "It's like a fairytale! How did you build this?"

Yves beamed: "My dads started it years ago, and we've made some big improvements. They travel the world and keep bringing back seeds. I named it the Waldon Cube."

Curly couldn't help himself. "Doesn't a cube normally have three equal dimensions?"

Before he had time to regret his comment, Moe exploded in happiness: "I know! I've told him the same thing a thousand times. It's not a cube; it's a cuboid! But he won't listen."

Moe and Curly nodded together.

Yves shook his head. "We have servers downstairs, and deep underground, we generate our own fusion power. This atrium is only the tip of the iceberg." He gave Moe a stern stare. "When we consider the third dimension includes what is underground, it is a cube."

As Yves turned to lead them deeper into paradise, Moe shook his head and mouthed to Curly: "No, it's not."

"How did you find us?"

Curly looked to the leaves and branches as he walked. "Uhm... well... according to the internet, you don't exist. Waldon has no presence. No history. No publicity. No funding requests. No news articles. No references in any journals. Nothing."

Yves and Moe exchanged a glance of intrigue. Curly loved finding things that people, governments and companies were trying to keep hidden. He continued quietly: "You filed taxes from a P.O. box as a privately-held medical research company, but declared no investments for deduction. I figured any research facility needs to get stuff delivered, so I checked the records of all major medical-equipment providers. Waldon has never directly purchased a single piece of equipment; however, there are plenty of free-text fields in delivery notes where the instructions stated to ring the bell by a flower-symbol when packages arrived."

Moe smiled. "That's kind of cheating, and I think… illegal."

Yves nodded. "It's perfect."

"How many people have you recruited this way?"

Yves responded. "We don't have many people working here: ten so far, and we have known each of them for years. The fewer people involved in our project, the better it is for all of us. You're our first external recruit."

Curly stopped walking, forgot he was in the real world and spoke with the confidence he had online. "Based on the delivery notes, you have some expensive equipment here. What do you do at Waldon? Why would you want me? What am I doing here? I'm a computer guy, a nerd. I don't even have a job or degree."

It was an impressive explosion of questions from a person who barely spoke to others.

Yves looked to him with warmth. There was trust in his eyes. "I proposed the name Waldon based on the novel written by Thoreau almost 200 years ago, at the advent of industrialization. It was the story of a man who left the grind of the city to go deep into nature and live off the land. His pond was called Walden. The book captured the simplicity and magic of being one with nature. It aligns Pantheism views that everything is part of an all-encompassing, immanent God, and reminds us that we cannot transform part of human life without impacting everything and everybody else."

"What are you talking about? You believe in Pantheism? Are you a cult?" As soon as he asked, Curly saw Moe shake his head discreetly and try to hush the question out of existence.

But Yves looked delighted: "There have been many famous believers in Spinoza's Pantheist ideas: Einstein, Lincoln, Tesla, Dickinson, Nietzsche and of course, Thoreau. There are lots of useful books in the library upstairs. Regardless, we chose the name Waldon as a reminder to stay focused on the big picture— happiness, life fulfillment and singularity—as part of any new paradigm we enable."

"And what paradigm are you planning to enable?"

"Time. We want to give people more time. Our technology will allow people to live longer and have better lives. But before we can test our ideas on humans, we need to run some extremely accurate simulations to understand the long-term impact of our treatment. And that's how we stumbled onto your rabbits."

Curly smiled. "I'm proud of those rabbits. How did you know it was me?"

"Butterflyninja is a legend in the simulation community, and Tom pointed your story out to us. Connecting your online identity to you was a bit of a challenge, but a Russian friend helped. You're discreet, and we need that. Now, tell us more about the rabbits."

World of Mayhem was an online gaming platform that had come out a few years earlier. Players created creatures, programmed survival techniques and defined their goals. They then sat back and watched the fights. After a lot of launch excitement, it became a dud when players bored of controlling behaviors and desires instead of actual combat. Playing God was not nearly as fun as the creators had hoped.

Curly had been working on an artificial-life simulator based on open-source code from around the world. He used it to program a family of rabbits and decided to see if they could survive in the aggressive environment of Mayhem. He gave five rabbits personalities and curiosity, programmed their bodily functions and instilled hope and fear and a sense of community.

Within weeks, the rabbits had multiplied and taken over the whole World of Mayhem island. They survived every attack and became smarter. The game's creators eventually had to reboot the system because the rabbits were everywhere. But they survived the reboot; they had anticipated extinction and hid a copy of themselves in the platform's source code—that surprised even Curly. The rabbits had developed intelligence, bred, lived, aged and died. They wanted their family to survive at all costs and won the game.

Moe was intrigued. "How did you build them?"

"I modeled their DNA." He paused. "I guess it's more accurate to say that I built Aurora and taught her to model their DNA."

Moe's eyes widened. "Aurora? You made a girlfriend?"

Curly's instincts were to defend himself, but Moe appeared genuinely impressed. "No—I built machine-learning Artificial Intelligence and called her Aurora. She's more like my daughter. I trained her to do the complex work and research."

Yves looked to Moe, and they nodded at each other. He turned to Curly. "I like you. We like you a lot. We want you to keep building what you're building, but for people. We need to develop a life simulator for humans because we'll never get governmental approval to run human trials without years of demonstrated impact. Humanity is not willing to wait. While money is no object, we need absolute discretion. Come and work for us. You can have anything you want. What do you want?"

Curly looked around the spectacular indoor garden. He really liked these two. "I guess I would need server space: lots of server space. And quantum computers—the gigatrit ones. I need to be paid fairly." He paused and looked them both in the eye. "But most of all, I need to know that I'm working for good. So, can you please tell me: what are you making? How will you give people more time?"

"We've cured aging."

Curly looked between Moe and Yves. They had none of the swagger nor the smirk of con men; they were trusting and clumsily honest. He had met a lot of crazy people online that wanted to live forever, but these two were not talking out of their asses. While clearly off their rockers, they were on to something. He instinctively accepted their absurd ambition and imagined his place. "And you want me to develop a digital simulation to test your product?"

"You've developed a technique to simulate life based on basic cell behavior. We're figuring out how to completely change cell and DNA behavior. If we can use your models to accurately simulate the long-term impacts of our cell changes, then we could accelerate testing by decades."

They had not asked why he did not go to school; they didn't care. They had not looked him up and down nor made him feel small; they spoke to him as an equal—to his face. They didn't throw pity and ask him about his neighborhood or his family shame; they showed him respect. And this was now the longest conversation he had had with real people in years.

"If I say okay, what do we do next?"

"Well, that's up to you. We have already set up an office for you and have a contract ready for your signature. You could start now."

"Can I go home and get some things?"

"If you want, but Tom can take care of everything you need. There's an apartment here for you, and it's filled with clothes we trust will be to your liking. We already have some developers who could work for you."

"Wait—work for me? What exactly is my job title?"

"We don't have job titles."

"Okay, but if we did, what would mine be?"

"I really don't care. It can be Computer Guy or Chief Technology Officer—the work is too important to have titles."

Curly smiled. Chief Technology Officer. That sounded good. And in a flash, he understood why God had challenged him so profoundly to get here: his life had been preparation for this moment, and there was no turning back. They wanted him. They needed him. They recognized his talent and made him comfortable.

"Are you in?"

His giant smile betrayed the answer before he could utter it. He was always going to accept but had not expected to find happiness. His heart beat faster and he giggled his agreement: "I guess I'm your new CTO. Where's my desk?"

Yves smiled, and Moe interrupted, "Wait—no fair. I didn't get to pick my title."

"Okay, Moe; what job title would you like?"

"Uhm—how about Chief of Science?"

Curly was confused. "What exactly is the difference between a Chief of Science and a Chief Technology Officer? Is Technology part of Science? Are you my boss?"

Yves looked back and forth between the two and smiled. "Curly and Moe, perfect. Follow me. Let's meet Clara before I show you to your desk." He turned and walked towards a cabin in the middle of the garden.

Curly and Moe followed and whispered like best friends at the back of the class: "She would be the CEO if we had titles."

Curly nodded towards Yves. "And what would his title be?"

"Maybe CCO."

Curly guessed: "Chief Commercial Officer?"

"No. We don't actually sell anything. He's more like our Chief Conscience Officer and resident philosopher."

Yves heard the whispers and interjected, "I'm not the resident philosopher. I build stuff."

"Clara won't let him back in the clean room."

"Moe!"

Curly and Moe looked at each other and chuckled. "So, Clara is our boss?"

"Yes. She's a bit of a control freak, but we all believe in her. She's unstoppable."

Yves pressed a button, and the three entered a bright lab space.

For the first time in his life, Curly felt safe.

~~

Nerea woke with warmth. She had journeyed from fear and loneliness to hope and trust.

Seren added softly to the experience. "With Aurora's help, Curly became the architect of everything you are experiencing. The simulations created to run medical trials turned out to be accurate enough to begin building the simulated world around us. Curly is looking forward to seeing you after your Decision."

The heat evaporated slowly from her body. Curly had shared something she could never have. Why would he do that to her? Nerea stood and walked to the beach. She needed to clear her head.

Curly had found companions and connection and experienced a greater sense of purpose in one day than she had in her entire life.

Nerea had never belonged. Not once. Money separated her from everyone she encountered. She had the means to snap their financial struggles out of existence; and that made her different. But she didn't want to be different. She yearned for connection and cried herself to sleep in its absence. Her mother did not need her, Seren did not need her, and no one was missing her now. Why would Curly flaunt something she could never have? He had found friends and a destiny. He was necessary. Her belly burned. Did this unattainable feeling exist in the world only to tease her?

She had felt something she could never have again.

Maybe she didn't deserve anything good.

Maybe she deserved to be lonely.

Chapter 5

08/04/2226 – The Shame Experience

A windmill with a missing blade wobbled awkwardly between tomatoes and strawberries. Nerea thought to roads and villages and skyscrapers that were falling apart all over the country—each structure was once someone's dream, and Mother Earth was slowly taking them back. Decay was everywhere.

Regardless of her Decision, death was coming.

"How did your brother die?"

Seren's sparkle dimmed. "I don't know, but the choices he made could only lead to death. He used to have so much power and walked around with an inexplicable confidence. Then he became addicted to extreme simulations, started stealing and stopped taking care of his body. He wanted to become someone else—anyone else. I couldn't help, and he disappeared. He had hurt us all so much that I never even searched for him. We don't even know when he died, but one day, his cremated remains arrived at my parent's house.

"It is why I never become someone else in these machines. I feel safe here in this level-one simulation, where I remain Seren, but the lives you are entering require a strength I do not have. They are not evil, but their distilled reality enslaved and killed my brother."

Simulation addiction destroyed minds all over the world. Escape from life was an alternative to death, but in many ways, they were the same.

Seren reached into an ice bucket and pulled out a chilled beer. She popped it open and handed it to Nerea. It was a President's Ale.

"What has Clara prepared for me?"

"This is the President of the United States."

~~

18/06/2039 – The Admiration Experience

Mariya Ramirez looked in the mirror and saw the weight of her job staring back. In two, short years, laugh lines had deepened to trenches and she wondered how long she could maintain the pace.

The luxurious bathroom was her escape from a tireless barrage of manipulation. Everyone wanted something and every sentence she heard hid the honest truth of an opposing view— uncovering that truth was exhausting. In here, the calm of running water and photos of her favorite places replenished her strength.

Despite the morning's intensity, Mariya calmed her frustration and focused on the next discussion.

'Breathe.'

'Stretch.'

'Go!'

She returned to the Oval Office with a bounce. Joe was waiting. "Do you need anything, Madam President?"

"That was the worst meeting I've had all week. Don't let Senator Johnson waste another minute of my time with her crap. From now on, she can talk to the Vice President; and when they agree on a coherent proposal, then we discuss."

"Yes, Madam President." Joe was the White House Chief of Staff. He was 55, wore a tight suit and black-framed glasses, and was an encyclopedia of facts, figures and connections. While he was poor with social cues, Mariya appreciated having him close and relied on him to summarize briefings, legislation and research papers. Unfortunately, Joe occasionally allowed unimportant topics to seep into her day.

She needed him to understand: "I am overseeing three wars, five bankrupt states, a nationwide transportation strike and a daughter who married a drunk. My time is extremely valuable. Who's next?"

"Clara Woodruff; founder and CEO of a privately-held biotech company called Waldon. They are secretive, well-financed and have never filed for research tax deductions, FDA approvals, or medical trials. Little is known about the inner workings of the company, but they have recently established sealed partnerships with major pharmaceutical firms. On Monday, Ms. Woodruff offered to make a one-hundred-million-dollar donation to your hurricane relief efforts in exchange for a twenty-minute meeting. This is not listed on your public agenda, at her request."

"Joe, you're wasting my time again. It's great that she's helping, but we clearly have more important topics to focus on. Are there any risks to this meeting?"

"Their board of directors has five of the wealthiest people in the world, plus Mathieu Baird. The five each invested a billion dollars for one-percent of voting shares and a larger, non-voting percentage of profits."

"A billion dollars? What do these guys sell?"

"They are not yet selling anything. Each of the investors had money to spare, so I don't know if they intend to recover their investments. The best theory we have is that as part-owners, investors can test products on their own bodies without regulatory approval."

"Human trials on billionaires? What are they developing: voice-activated Viagra? Because most billionaires I know would pay for that."

Joe responded dryly. "That's funny, Madam President. We don't know, but I suspect you're about to find out."

Mariya could never get a legitimate laugh out of him. "Is that everything?"

"An article showed up in Russian gossip press two weeks ago. Dimitri Kozelnov was on a live TV panel, got drunk and bragged that he had cured death."

"Dimitri is a board member of Waldon?"

"That's right. And is now being held by Russian authorities."

"Well, let's see what she has to say."

Joe opened the door and motioned for Clara to enter. "Good morning Ms. Woodruff. We are running two minutes late, so the President would appreciate it if you could be brief. Please come in."

"Thank you."

The woman stepped into the room timidly. Mariya had seen many business and world leaders walk confidently through her door, but Clara looked tense and almost scared to be there. She was young, exhausted and carrying profound weight. Clara nodded a greeting and Mariya smiled warmly. "Good morning, Clara."

"Good morning Madam President. It's an honor to meet you."

Joe stepped to the entrance. "I'll be back in eighteen minutes." The door closed, and the two were alone.

"Thank you for the proposed donation. It will help in the reconstruction of the hospital. The community has been decimated and needs all the help we can give."

Clara's voice cracked. "I can double the donation if required and trust the money will be well used. That's not why I'm here; I'm here because life is about to change. As our leader, you're about to take the most important actions of your presidency."

Mariya smiled. Her days were full of sales pitches and exaggerations, but she appreciated Clara's heartfelt directness. "That's a bold statement."

"I'll be quick. At Waldon, we've made significant strides to increase potential life span."

"Ahhh yes, elixir research. I understand that most promising leads are at early stages, with low probability of success. So, what have you achieved?"

"We've cured aging."

Mariya shook her head in amusement. "Another bold statement, Clara."

"We've developed a method that eliminates aging's central problem—cell degradation. We strengthen protective caps in chromosomes with a focused, genetically modified blood boost that begins a chain reaction in the body. The end result is that our cells can endlessly split and reproduce without degradation. Our pill treatment is personalized to the recipient's DNA, and it works on humans with one hundred percent efficiency; even better than I anticipated."

Mariya had a Science Advisory meeting every two weeks, and the topic was often discussed. "In our last briefing, I was told we're still 50 years away from making that type of breakthrough. Why should I believe you?" She was intrigued but not ready to accept the extraordinary claims. Clara was about to ask for something, and Mariya was not prepared to give this stranger blind confidence.

"We've successfully run human trials on ourselves over the past several years. I'm 29, but biologically speaking, my body is 25. Discretion has been key. To avoid government and public scrutiny, we have only tested our procedure on ownership and employee-shareholders. Money has come through the most discreet investors we could find. Cash, powerful simulations and accessible human subjects have allowed us to move quickly. In this dossier, you'll find that all thirty volunteers have identical results. Pictures, scans and medical records are included." Clara placed an envelope on the coffee table between them.

Mariya retained an amused tone. "So now the hyper-wealthy can buy eternal life? That should go over well with the masses."

"No. We have developed a simple and cost-effective method to make it accessible to everyone." Clara grasped a small locket around her neck and opened it to reveal a green pill and an empty space for a second pill. "Today, aging is a one-stop train ride, where death is the only way off. We propose giving people a one-time stop-over option. When they sign a Life Contract with Waldon, we provide two pills: a red pill initiates the contract and stops the aging process, and a second, green pill closes the contract and restarts aging. Red to stop aging. Green to proceed."

Clara then looked down at her open locket and touched the empty spot. "I took my red pill years ago, and my body has not aged a day since that moment." She then caressed the remaining pill. "This little green pill is irreversible. If I were to take it today, my body would resume aging, and I could never stop the process again. These pills make the Decision clear. We initially planned to wait five years before sharing them with the world, but we're being forced into an emergency response plan to fabricate and distribute."

The discussion was surreal. Mariya had disconnected herself from the true impact of the topic being shared. "An emergency plan? Is that why you're here talking to the President?"

"Yes. Dimitri Kozelnov is being questioned by authorities in Russia. Our secret will be out, and I need to control the public message, or there will be panic."

"If you wanted to remain secret, why would you have gotten involved with Kozelnov? Even I know he can't keep a secret."

"Mathieu Baird trusted him, and I used to trust Mathieu. I made a mistake and now, I need your help."

"What help?"

"First: protection. When our discovery leaks or is announced, governments around the world will be prepared to do anything and use any measures necessary to get a hold of it or even destroy it. Imagine the force some would authorize to ensure that they, their people, their families and their friends would have access to this treatment."

Mariya looked around the room and began to digest the consequences. What if Waldon had succeeded? She had been considering this as any other medical breakthrough, but it was not. Aging's cure fundamentally changed life itself. "How many years of life can you add?"

"In simulations, there's no limit. A body could survive forever. Of course, most causes of death are still possible—but not old age. With a young body, we're statistically less likely to die. In the near term, life expectancy will probably triple, and as we cure other sicknesses, it will rise to tens of thousands of years and beyond."

Mariya felt nauseous. She was looking forward to life after death; there was reassurance in heaven's promised reunion with loved ones. "Do you believe a lot of people will want that?"

"Do not underestimate the primal survival instincts of man to avoid death. The spiritual and the poetic may want to leave life as it is—there's beauty in its circle. But many love being alive too much to refuse life's extension. When God gives you the option of experiencing more of the beauty He created, should you not take it? The survivalists, atheists and agnostics will have a choice between the nothingness of death and the vigor of life. To answer your question: yes, many will choose to extend their lives.

"But there will be consequences. Dreams and desires will change. Retirement will vanish. Religion and beliefs will be challenged. Love and relationships will be irreversibly altered. Family and self-identity will need to adapt. Everything will be different."

Mariya's eyes widened. Government pensions, Social Security and retirement funds were already teetering on bankruptcy. "What happens to our overburdened planet as the population grows and grows? We don't have enough jobs for people today. We don't have enough money!"

"Now, you're starting to understand our principle problem: babies."

Mariya gasped. "Mierda." Her mother's language came first when she was in shock. "You can't just stop one end of the cycle of life, can you?"

"No, we can't."

Mariya's face numbed. "What do we do?"

"We have debated this amongst ourselves for the last eight years. I've decided that anyone in a Life Contract with Waldon will not be able to have children. The procedure makes you sterile. No babies."

This punched Mariya in the gut. "No babies?! You can't do that. How could you even propose such a thing?"

"People will be allowed to have babies after they have taken the green pill and are aging naturally towards death. Today, I am infertile, but on the day I take my green pill, my body will once again produce the necessary hormones for pregnancy. In this way, the cycle of birth, life and death is ensured. There's no clean way for this transition to happen. You can't stop death without stopping birth. There's no way to overstate what will change when people have this choice."

Mariya saw a flaw. "But people would simply have babies before they take the red pill."

"That's the second reason we need governments. We need a mandated birth control injection before puberty. Waldon will enter into Life Contracts only with those injected. Governments are powerful enough to ensure that children are not deprived of the Decision because parents did not believe in life extensions."

"Clara, we're not barbarians. Do you hear yourself? We cannot sterilize children! Getting government into the business of mandated birth control is wrong in every possible way."

"We cannot provide this service to people after they have had children," Clara replied, "because too many people would have kids and then come to us to stop aging. Populations would explode. In theory, we could create an 'honor system' and simply test girls to see if they had had a baby before providing treatment. But how could we tell if a young man has fathered a child? I know mandated birth control for children is morally awful, so if you have a better idea, please let me know. And quickly."

Mariya looked out the window, and her heart sank. People would demand access to this treatment, yet it was morally irresponsible to allow the population to increase exponentially. She searched her mind and found no better ideas. Her whisper was barely audible. "I have nothing."

"It's the best solution in a list of terrible options."

Mariya focused on the immensity of treating the whole planet. Her voice found a bit of strength. "How can you possibly treat everyone? How can governments afford this new burden? Personalized pills sound expensive, and we've already exceeded our financial limits."

"The service cannot exclude the poor, but it is expensive, so we need the rich to contribute appropriately. I've decided the Waldon Life Contract fees will be income-based, and the third reason we need you is that we need governments to collect those fees. It's the only remotely fair way I can imagine. Revenues will be split between Waldon and governments and will cover new financial burdens you may incur. You're much better positioned than Waldon to ensure that income is accurately declared and payments collected."

Mariya was dumbfounded. "Those aren't fees, that's a tax. Let me recap: you have cured aging and are proposing mandated birth control and a new 'Life Tax' to pay for it. Greed does crazy things to people, and you have lost your sense of reality."

Clara reached deep into Mariya's eyes. "If I cared about money, I would not try to solve the baby problem or the 'only for the wealthy' problem. It would be much easier and more profitable to release this product to the world at a fixed price and let the free market decide what to do. But I understand that humanity is too greedy, and this change too massive to be left to wealthy decision-makers. We need governments to bring it to the people in a controlled way. Fees and birth control are necessary for our world to survive."

Mariya had been run over by a truck. "So, every human has a choice: have children, grow old and die; or remain young forever?"

"Yes. We call this moment the Decision. It can be made any time after a person's 23rd birthday."

"Why twenty-three?"

"Bodies, morals and ideology need time to develop before entering into a Life Contract. People can wait to make the Decision until they are much older, but they'll remain infertile during those years."

"Imagine the protests. Global chaos. Aging is fundamental to life, and announcing its cure will cause turmoil."

"We know. For safety, we intend to remain anonymous, and speed is paramount to reducing the violence. Assuming your support, we have a plan to provide the treatment to everyone before the end of next year."

"For the whole planet?"

Clara responded with precision. "Yes. I want to limit the chaos. Wars will be launched if we wait too long. There's too much impatient greed. The transformations wrought on life, society and governments will be too massive. For 18 months, we'll give every adult in the world a one-time option to take the birth control and receive their pills for an immediate or future Decision. Those below 23 will be given the birth control and have a future Decision to make. After 21 months, those who do nothing will no longer have an option. They'll grow old and die as it has always been."

Mariya looked out the window. "There has to be a better way."

"Everything about this scares me. If you have a better path, I'm all ears."

Mariya breathed deeply. Every option was worse. A slow rollout would mean an explosion of babies before people took their red pill. It needed to be fast. But how could they deal with the regulatory issues so quickly? What about the long-term side effects? "Mierda. Mierda. Mierda."

"Dimitri's secrets are now understood by a foreign government. His selection as an investor was an unfortunate mistake. We need your help to move quickly. We need military protection and a rapid discussion with world and religious leaders. People are dying every day, and there will be no forgiveness if we withhold aging's cure. Speed is essential."

Mariya had studied the defining moments of each presidency and knew this was hers. She looked into Clara's eye for reassurance. "None of this sounds like a good thing for humanity. Is it really the right thing to do?"

"If we don't do it, someone else will, eventually. It's just a matter of time. There are a million different ways for this change to take place. You have the power to block me in this country, but you need to listen to what your people want. They'll want this. Blocking it will only cause violence and death. Our board of directors has clear, non-financial goals, morals and drive. But in the end, as CEO, the decision to release is mine. The conditions under which we're going to release are mine to decide. I've made my decisions, and I'm prepared to live with the consequences: the good and the bad. You must choose between supporting or fighting against this change."

Mariya stopped breathing for a moment. Presidents made difficult decisions every day, but the burden that fell on Clara was unimaginable. Never had someone earned her complete and devoted respect so quickly. "May God help you, Clara."

"Thank you." Clara paused and changed the topic. "I have a last request: I need an Artificial Intelligence license and access to a lot of data."

Joe knocked and opened the door. "Madam President, we need to meet with the Fisheries group."

Clara stood. "We have ten days before we need to make an announcement to the world. Please send us a team to coordinate all necessary actions. The list of officials, economists and scientists we believe are important are on this paper." Clara pointed to the envelope. "I assume there will be skeptics, so there's sufficient proof in those documents. Human trials should be unnecessary with the data we already have, but we need your help with approvals. People will not be willing to wait ten years. The first video conference is tomorrow, at 7am. Thanks for your time, Madam President."

Clara turned and walked out of the room. She had more important things to do than spend time with the President. Mariya could not even manage a 'Goodbye.' She sat back in shock. Since winning the election, she had always been the most powerful person in the room. She controlled the most influential policies, the third-largest economy and the largest military in the world. But Clara controlled life itself. Clara had walked into her power-office and politely taken full control. Waldon was about to become the most significant corporation in history. And Clara was the most remarkable person she had ever met.

Joe looked at the envelope and asked: "Are you okay, Madam President? Should I adapt our schedule to deal with that list?"

Mariya had trained her whole life to handle challenges, but the immensity of the moment crushed her confidence. Her country needed her, and it was time to step up. "Yes, Joe. Everything just changed. I need the President's Council to cancel everything on their agendas and meet in the Situation Room in one hour."

The most powerful person in the world now felt powerless.

~~

Nerea woke with a racing heart and rapid breath. If the President had felt this weight, she could not begin to imagine the pressure on Clara.

Waldon was not evil. There was no magical happy path that would have prevented the world's great sadness. Her mother had weighed and considered individual freedoms and the greater good, and chose the best way forward. She knew there would be adverse side effects and allowed the consequences to fall squarely on her shoulders.

Nerea's stomach churned. She was filled with shame for the years of rejecting Clara and the judgment spewed at the company she had built.

Disgrace threw darts at past instances of wickedness. She had cursed the faceless tyrants of Waldon and hoped their money would warm them in hell! Her conscience bled black. Why had she not tried to understand Clara's distance? Why had she assumed the worst? With evidence delivered in imagination, Nerea had falsely convicted the brave woman who's courage had changed the world.

For the first time in forever, Nerea wanted to give her mother a hug.

Chapter 6

08/04/2226 – The Vigilance Experience

"Hate is a monster that feeds on your soul, takes warmth from your life and leaves but a hole."

Seren placed a shot glass on the table and continued. "Those lyrics are from Eva's last album. Hate is a wicked place from which escape is difficult. It comes from a past that cannot be undone, only understood. If you continue to hold anger for your childhood, hate will continue to simmer, happiness will stay distant and love will be fragile."

Nerea stared at the glass but did not pick it up. "How can I possibly let it go?"

"To shed the burden of hate, you must open your heart to apathy. Apathy is a powerful and underused tool that allows us to observe the past without its emotional baggage." Seren pointed towards a white pebble on the ground." Your past relationship with Clara is like that stone. Pick it up and remember it, but do not gift it the power of your feelings, for it is not worth it. Apathy can allow you to choose how you want to feel today. It can allow space for love and happiness to grow roots."

Nerea bent and picked the rock from the ground. She held her childhood in the palm of her hand and began to understand its true weight. Memories were recast with the newfound insights of Clara's lonely burden. Motherhood was understandably impossible under Waldon's paralyzing responsibility.

But Nerea's self-identity was tied to the beliefs that emerged from her youth. Truths were being slaughtered, and it terrified her. "I'm losing myself. Things I knew yesterday have melted into the ground and turned every path forward into quicksand. I don't know where to step. How do I move on without forgetting who I am? How can I protect myself?"

"You are right to be cautious. Empathetic simulations become part of you, and their power can be weaponized. It is important to remember who you are and what you want, but do not fear the new person that emerges."

Nerea fiddled with the stone. "I'm sickened by the person I was yesterday and grateful for knowledge, but the next experience still terrifies me. Each drink carves something away and fills the space with someone new."

"Be gentle. You could not have invented the truth. Truth does not hide in the shelter of old beliefs; it is uncomfortable. It is found outside your walls, and when you discover it, you may finally understand that the fortress you live in is not a castle but a prison."

Nerea looked deep in Seren's eye. It was time to let go once again. "I've been alone for a long time. Thank you for watching out for me."

Seren smiled. "Your journey is difficult. I am happy to help."

Nerea picked up the iced shot glass: a layer of yellow on top of cherry red—a fiery sunset. "What's this?"

"I call it Bittersweet: limoncello and chili brandy. The next two simulations are reflective of the intensity and speed of change that followed Waldon's release. While the other experiences all take place in the States, Paul and Moe were both in Canada."

There was an unexpected kick to the refreshing drink.

~~

08/05/2040 – The Sentimentality Experience

Paul gazed out the restaurant window and tried to savor the sun's warmth. He struggled to clear his mind and appreciate something—anything. These silent moments used to be his favorite part of the job. The routine had not changed: he woke at the same time, exercised at the same time, started work at the same time, but everything was different.

His anger had faded months ago, replaced by nostalgia. Paul longed to return to the unrecognized perfection of before; he had been blind to its wonder. History's mundane details waltzed through his mind—fading relics of an escaping past. Coffee had lost its taste. The daily special was now the only option. The pothole on the road would never be fixed. Small talk was dosed with insincerity. Chaos had replaced pillars of certainty. Newsfeeds were partial and grim. Sharks were taking advantage of the weak, and the crazies were out in droves.

Humanity had been given a gift he wished could be returned and he was unable to ignore life's new emptiness.

Anja broke the silence. "Do you think our motto was designed a contradiction?" She was fiddling with her badge and searching for distraction.

He shook his head. "What are you talking about?"

"Maintiens le droit."

Paul took out his own under-cover badge and investigated. He carried the coat of arms every day but ignored its design since the entrance test. Below 'POLICE' and above 'RCMP GRC,' a bison head was wrapped with the French words on a scroll. "Okay?"

"It's translated 'Defending the Law,' but 'droit' means right. What do we do if there's a contradiction between law and a human right?"

Paul tucked his badge back into his shirt. "This is not up for discussion. It's not for us to judge the morality of those we defend."

Six months ago, orders came from the very top: 'Discreetly secure an unmarked lane leading to a private bridge and island. Intruders must be stopped. Use lethal force if necessary.' Anja and Paul initially had no idea who they were guarding, but they figured it out. The remote island hid the most sought-after people on the planet: the Waldon executive team.

This part of the province was almost empty—a great place to disappear. Visitors came for the cougars and white sharks but usually found only ticks and blisters. Most just passed through.

Silence made Anja uncomfortable. She continued: "Any news from your family?"

Paul's heart sunk. "Mom hasn't stopped crying. She believes my brother has rejected God and slaughtered her grandchildren. She's convinced red-pill-takers will burn in eternal hell."

He used to believe that God had created man as a perfect image of himself and given them each a clear path: trust the Bible, be kind, reproduce, grow old and join Him in heaven. Why would anyone reject that? Why had his brother abandoned them? Why had his wife abandoned him?

Anja understood his pain. "Don't be sad; everyone decides on their own. We don't all have your courage."

Paul no longer felt pride in his Decision. He had taken an early appointment in anger and was now confused. "A year ago, my world was perfect. I loved my job and my wife. Then Waldon delivered the nuclear Judgement Day that was long predicted; God's path was obvious—my choice handed to me on a divine platter. I rejected the Decision and embraced God's will, but now I'm miserable. How am I ever going to find happiness? Momentary accomplishments are meaningless beside the towering potential of people who will live a thousand years. Why has He done this to us?"

Anja shook her head. "I have no idea."

Paul sipped the cooled coffee. "How's your family?"

"Still in vigil. They won't act without the Church's blessing."

"And your sister?"

"Nothin'." Anja had no idea if her sister was dead or alive. Behind rumors of violence, she feared the worst. Most borders closed quickly and many communication cables were intentionally cut. Each government wanted to deal with the new reality in their own way.

Paul hesitated. "Have you made your Decision?" There were only eight months remaining in the countdown.

"I don't know what to do. I still want babies so bad, but why would I let myself die?"

While his razor-sharp convictions had dulled, he delivered the standard answer in an empty voice. "Suffering. Murders. Suicides. Robbery. Addiction. Families have locked themselves in their homes. Banks are closed. No one on the force has been paid in two months. Seeds and soil are replacing cash. When you look at the world today, why would you choose to stay?"

Anja fidgeted. "It's those greedy bastards on the island. They asked nine billion people to trust their unproven science, and now they're shocked we want to hold 'em accountable."

Paul took a deep breath and sipped his coffee.

There was movement on the island. A car drove across the bridge, up the lane and parked in front of the diner. The bearded driver strolled to the restaurant door and over to their booth. He sat beside Anja. "Anything unusual today?"

Paul did not like Tom: a foreign civilian with an ego and a gun. "No. Light traffic and four caravans." Everyone flowed in one direction: away from the city, towards fertile land.

They sat in silence and watched the road. The waitress came with an extra mug and poured a coffee. "Mornin', Tom."

"Good morning Elise." Elise had no idea who was living on the island. In fact, only six non-Waldon people knew the location of the executives: two pilots, a president, a prime minister, Anja and Paul. Elise did not ask questions—she was thankful to have protection. Everything was on the house. She returned to the kitchen.

Anja broke the customary silence and whispered one of the forbidden questions: "Why d'you bring 'em here?"

Tom looked at both and decided to answer. "It's no longer safe back home. The government is being pressured to make their identities public and bring them in for questioning. We need to remain anonymous. There are too many angry people with too many weapons. We'll go back to our office when it's safe."

Anja continued to provoke. "Up here, we don't much appreciate people walkin' around with guns. Have you ever had to use that piece on your hip? D'ya have any idea what it's like to hold the weight of death in your hand?"

Tom stirred his black coffee. "On the day my boss is in danger, I will pull the trigger without regret. The cause is too important to wallow in the morality of a single life."

Anja pushed: "Then you're dangerous. Why should we trust you? Why should we trust Waldon? I'm takin' orders from a prime minister who could be in your pocket."

Paul's eyes narrowed, and he prepared to kick her under the table. She had crossed the line. Anja understood the message and leaned back in the booth. It was time to shut up.

Tom spoke softly. "I understand your caution. Waldon leaders are doing something more difficult than you can fathom, and they're doing it in the most humane way they can imagine. My job is to keep them safe." He turned and looked Anja in the eye. "Your job is to decide if you trust your Prime Minister. If you do, then continue to protect us. If you don't, I guess we're screwed."

Nothing else was said. They sat in silence, drinking coffee. After twenty minutes, Tom stood, thanked Elise and returned to his car. He drove back onto the island.

Paul knew that Anja would remain faithful to their mission. Loyalty was all they had.

He stared down the hopeless road that connected them to the world.

~~

~~

02/01/2041 – The Anxiety Experience

Moe woke harshly in a fog and looked to his childhood clock for answers. The little dinosaur was on the three, and the big dinosaur was near the top. This did not resolve his confusion. Was it day or night? He looked to the darkened window and saw a sliver of light from behind the shades. It must be afternoon.

He could sleep for days. Home was like no other place on Earth—an escape from the crushing burden of the last decade. He could still hear screaming in his ears; Mathieu and Clara had fought constantly. The work was unrelenting, with no room for mistakes. Every minute of every day held unimaginable consequences.

The rollout was complete. December 31, 2040, 23:59 had come and gone. Everyone on the planet had made their Decision, and the numbers shocked him. Many had not trusted this new science or had refused to accept that change was happening. Now everyone understood; nothing would ever be the same.

And they were angry.

Maybe they were right. Maybe he had helped create something wicked. Maybe the world was beginning a slow descent into hell. He stared at the thin line shining into his darkness, illuminating nothing. Did the future hold any hope, or was it already dead? Only time would tell. Regret flowed slowly through his body. What if they had destroyed happiness? Waldon had already torn so many families apart.

The long wait began. His core trampled under the stomping of nine billion souls; each had discovered new ways to suffer. The burden grew with each passing second as he considered towns and communities and cultures they'd hurt.

Had he contributed to something that would prove to be good? Or something terribly evil?

There was a light knock at the door, and he snap-rolled onto his side, protecting his head with his pillow. His nerves were still on edge.

"Are you awake?"

"Come in." Moe's mother was seventy-eight years old and still exuded the silly joy of her youth. She put down a red gift-box, walked to the window and opened the blinds. Reflected sun poured in from the snow-covered hills that stretched as far as they could see. Moe followed her gaze and managed a whisper. "I missed this place."

"It's good to have you home."

"It's good to be here." The room was where he first discovered safety—unknown as a child in war. Here, nightmares faded to dreams and he was gifted a new life. Here, he could disappear for hours inside the posters of Persian lynx, screw-horned goats and Asiatic black bears. Here, he was home.

His mother sat and caressed his shins through the quilt. "You look tired."

"I am. This time has been heavy."

She nodded. "Life has always been a journey between moments that change everything; 'before's and 'after's. It is not always better, not always worse, but it is important to keep loving and embrace the new, or else we die." She placed the large box on his lap. "I want you to have this." Moe twinged—he had not brought Mum anything; he had barely remembered to brush his teeth.

He peeled the tape carefully, removed the paper and meticulously folded it to be used again. The white box was from a microwave that they had bought years ago. He opened it carefully and revealed his mother's most prized possession: a beautiful, striped blanket. He instinctively pushed the box back to his mother. "I can't take this!"

Mum smiled and pushed it calmly back to her son. "Yes, you can. But first, I want you to understand its power." She took the blanket out of the box and wrapped it around his shoulders. "Many years ago, your father came to my town's annual fair and was brave enough to ask me to dance. I was wearing a beautiful striped dress, feeling very pretty, and I was foolish. I turned him down. I had my mind made up that I would only dance with Kenny MacLennan. But your father was stubborn. He saw I was cold in my little dress, and he got an idea in his head to offer me a blanket when he saw me again. He had no money, so he taught himself to weave. He made it using wool from his family's sheep and dyes from berries and flowers. A full year later, he came back to our fair. Again, I was wearing my striped dress, and again, I was cold. Your father came to me, right in front of Kenny MacLennan and offered me this blanket. I had no idea where it had come from, but I knew immediately it was full of pure love. We danced together all night and were married a week later."

"But he gave it to you!" Moe had loved his father profoundly. He had never taken time to mourn and had barely stopped working to come to the funeral. The strain of Waldon was inescapable. His absence in his mother's darkest moment remained his deepest regret.

"We brought this blanket to the airport on the day you came into our lives. You looked freezing and scared. But you calmed down as soon as we wrapped it around you with a hug. This blanket holds much more than your father's love: it holds the birth of our chosen family. It holds our unrelenting and eternal love for you. I want you to have this blanket as you go forward and make your own choices. That way, we will always be with you."

Moe recalled the confusion and fear of his adoption. There was much he had not understood, but when he saw them for the first time, he knew he was safe. A tear rolled down his cheek. "Thank you."

Mum smiled broadly and massaged his feet. "You have not told me your Decision. Can you share it now?"

Moe could not tell his mother that he worked with Waldon. That information could get people killed. He whispered his answer: "Red pill."

"Yesssss!!!!! That makes me so happy! Why do you look so sad about it?"

His mother had let the deadline come and go. "One day, you too will die. Then I'll have no family left. I'm alone. I can't fathom the eternal emptiness that lies before me—before us all. What have I done?"

"Nonsense: you have friends! You have Clara and Curly and Yves. That is a lot more than many. This world is amazing, and I am jealous of those courageous enough to take that little red pill. I am proud of you for choosing life." She reached in and gave him a giant hug. Touch. He felt her love loud and clear.

And then she squeezed harder.

After years of intensity and stress, Moe's small tears turned to sobs. He finally allowed himself to cry.

Mum held him tight. "Don't listen to people who criticize your

Decision. If I were years younger, your father and I would have taken the red pill together. We were so in love. Now I need to see him again, and the red pill would only delay that."

Moe wiped his face. "Is joy dead? Happiness comes with the progression people need to feel alive. There's no progression in eternity."

"I wish for you deep wonder in the endless new experiences you will live. Seize them! But happiness will also be found in moments of comfort. Do not confuse comfort with monotony! Appreciate the beauty of time with friends and loved ones. It filled me with ever-increasing joy to wake beside your father each morning. We laughed together every single day, and I am convinced that could have lasted into infinity."

"Aren't you wishing for grandchildren?"

"Moe, life is beautiful. It makes me unbelievably happy to picture you wandering this Earth for millennia to come, helping others, making scientific breakthroughs and learning everything your curious mind can possibly desire. Billions of people may try to convince you that life was better before. They may try to tell you that there is poetry in death. Ignore them. Live. Just imagine the limitless possibilities you have in front of you. Be happy and thankful. The people who died before you never had this opportunity. But you do. Your generation finally has control over life. You have been given a gift, and anyone who tries to convince you otherwise does not truly love humanity.

"Be proud of your Decision. Be proud of your profession! Relentless scientists like you have given us Waldon. Now let's go downstairs and have some pancakes."

~~

Chapter 7

08/04/2226 – The Interest Experience

Nerea followed Seren onto the beach in silence. They stripped down and waded into the water. Stars pierced through the darkness and decorated the sky with calming infinity.

Nerea wanted to relax, but her thoughts raced around the souls she had met. She considered the unbearable pressure her mother must have felt. How did Clara find the strength and courage to survive?

She thought of Curly and the incredible wave of warmth that hit when he found 'his people.' How did he feel about Waldon after all these years?

The President's mind was the most complex and beautiful place she had ever visited. The intensity and incredible speed of Mariya's thoughts were staggering. Did she struggle with her own Decision?

She wandered around Mathieu and Tom, honorable and driven. Where were they now? Eva and Louis. Sven and Phil. Anja and Paul. Moe and Yves. Lost to dust. What happened to them? What became of their hopes and dreams? They lived through the chaos her mother had unleashed. What did they think of her actions? What did they think of her?

Nerea would make her Decision tomorrow. Was she ready to grow old and die? She pictured the tiny sugar cube that Phil had held up. It was so small; its days too limited. There was still so much beauty to experience. But what would the red pill do to her desires? Would it change her?

And one question now looped louder than ever, unable to remain unanswered. Nerea turned to Seren with aggressive insistence. "Who is my father? I need to know who he is. I want to know if I came from love, or am I an accident? I need to know who I am before I can decide what I will become."

Seren avoided her eyes. "Your mother told me that work got in the way a lot."

"You're avoiding my question just like Clara has for twenty-three years."

Seren took a deep breath and turned sharply to Nerea. "This next simulation will be heavy. I was not convinced you should have it, but your mother insisted. I prefer to let you experience it before we go further." Seren scooped up a handful of saltwater and offered Nerea a sip. "Yves is your father."

Nerea locked into Seren's concerned eyes, tilted her head back and swallowed.

~~

19/04/2171 – The Aggressiveness Experience

Yves stared through Waldon's iron-flower gate and combed fingers through his long beard. The rustic wild hid countless cameras and scanners. They knew he had arrived—would they let him in? Did Tom know what he had done?

Inside, a deer strolled out of the woods and onto the lane. She paused to observe her through fence rods. Did the deer accept that she was born to die? Or was she focused only on the pleasure of life? Freud believed that humans were controlled by these two impulses: Thanatos and Eros. When Yves was young, he was obsessed only with Eros: learning, living and love. But age and travels had allowed him to embrace Thanatos, the darker brother who beckoned him to pass through death's gate into something bigger than existence.

A lock clicked open and the startled deer disappeared between bushes. The gate swung slowly into the forest lane. After ten long years, Yves was finally returning home. He hopped back into his pod and rolled towards the Cube. The tree covered path glowed in a mystical shade, with the atrium's glass sparkling through distant leaves. Despite Waldon's dark failures, this remained the most beautiful place in the world.

His fathers had died almost a hundred years ago, and the Cube was a reminder of their love. He rolled out of the trees and embraced the giant atrium; it was spectacular. A single tear rolled down his cheek.

Yves entered the building in flip-flops. Lobby games were long gone, and the fruit bowl now held two dying peaches.

On his right, the security door hissed open, and Tom stepped out. He observed Yves from a distance. "You're back." There was no warmth between the two. Tom was always on high alert for board meetings and appeared particularly suspicious of this unexpected arrival.

"It's good to see you, too," poked Yves with a wave. He turned and walked swiftly towards the Cube's entrance. Reconciliation could come later; for now, there were secrets Tom could not know.

Yves passed through the disinfectant booth and the atrium door slid open. He filled his lungs with clean jungle air—fresh and full of life; there was no smell like it. Plants from around the world grew in perfect balance. He kicked off his flip-flops, stepped onto the dirt path, and embraced the energy. A bright blue butterfly flew from behind the waterfall and landed on a nearby birch.

"YVES!!!!!" Moe and Curly called in unison from the distance. A rush of joy flowed through his body as the pair stumbled over each other and sprinted to him in a collective hug. They pulled each other close and danced with child-like joy.

Curly rejoiced, "Wow! It's great to see you!!!"

Moe was ecstatic. "We were hoping you'd come! The meeting five years ago was painful without you—bastard!"

"A ten-year sabbatical without calling? Well done! Come with us."

The trio began a slow, giddy walk to the lab. He had missed them both dearly.

Curly put his arm around Yves and pulled him tight. "That postcard you sent was hilarious! It was the first piece of mail to be delivered here in fifty years."

Moe joined. "Tom's security didn't seem to know what a postcard was, and the photo was spectacular! Like time hasn't touched it. Tell us everything!"

"…and quickly, because we have something to show you."

"Patience, Curly."

"But it's so cool!"

"Curly!"

Curly sighed and refocused. "How was Ladakh?"

Yves loved how they squabbled and finished each other's sentences like twins. "It's no longer the same, but some villages still seem to have life figured out and don't need Waldon to make them happier."

"Is it true you became a Buddhist monk?"

"For a while, yes. I studied, lived in a monastery and was ordained for a few years."

Moe got straight to the point. "Did you follow ALL of the ways of the Buddhist monk?"

Yves stopped walking and looked to his friends with a grin. "I'm gone for ten years, traveled the world, meditated with some of the most enlightened souls on the planet, and your most pressing question is to find out if there were any women?"

Moe and Curly glanced at each other and nodded in unison. "Of course."

"Wow. I was expecting that question to wait for drinks tonight, not two minutes after my arrival. Have you guys even left the Cube in the last decade?"

Moe kicked the dirt. "Well, no, but we've been busy!"

"We made something cool!" Curly interjected. "Come see."

Moe chastised him again. "Curly! Patience. You are going to live forever but can't wait ten minutes to find out how one of your best friends in the world is doing."

"Sorry."

"…So you were telling us about your women."

"Moe?!"

Yves stopped in feigned frustration. "I was not telling you about my women because there were no women!"

Moe looked him in the eye and smiled. "No women? Uh, uh."

Yves smiled sheepishly. "Almost no women. But it does not take away from the deep, spiritual journey I was on."

Moe looked excited. "Yes! I was right."

Yves shook his head and kept walking. "How is our fearless leader doing?"

Curly cringed as he answered. "She's been vicious since you left and ruthlessly demanding for this project."

Moe added: "She fights with Mathieu and the other investors all the time now. It keeps getting worse."

"Is she dating?" Yves knew the answer but needed to ask.

Curly responded. "Of course not. She doesn't trust anyone. She's convinced that something will happen to her, and the investors will change the direction of Waldon." He put both hands on Yves' shoulders and looked him in the eye. "You need to let go. Eternity will be pretty freaking depressing if you hold on to your obsession for her."

"I'm not obsessed with her." Yves was absolutely obsessed with her.

"Oh, really?" Moe poked.

"Come on. We dated fifty years ago, and it didn't work then. There's no reason it would work now. Besides, she's not even my type."

"Then why did you storm out of the boardroom and vanish for ten years after she attacked you?"

Clara's comments had been more vicious than anticipated, but they were part of a plan. He was able to disappear without raising suspicions. "That's not why I walked out. I walked out because our company needs a refreshed conscience to tackle the world's misery."

Moe reacted sarcastically. "Really? And sleeping with Buddhist women brings you the necessary enlightenment to save humanity?"

Yves smiled and shook his head while Curly buckled over in laughter.

The group passed through a hallway and into an inner laboratory. In the middle of the room stood a white, egg-like chair, reclined back into a bed. Yves meandered around it and asked, "What have you built?"

"We've achieved level-three simulation."

"I thought there were only two levels. What is level-three?"

"Level-one was video games; where players know who they are and control their actions in the simulation. Level-two was becoming a character in a movie with five senses and inner dialog projected into the frontal lobe of the audience. We have finally overcome the last hurdle to level-three simulations; passengers can now disconnect from the noise in their own heads and fully experience someone else's conscience."

Curly jumped in. "With Aurora's quantum computing, we figured out how to block users from their actual memories and self-awareness. We've produced processors so quick and sensor-webbing so accurate, that we can map a brain's unique neural network and mask it in real time with new thoughts, vivid memories and complex concepts. Simulations no longer start from emptiness, but from an active brain with history."

Moe continued, "We call them empathetic simulations. A passenger can fully live moments of souls who died a hundred years ago."

"Aurora used the Waldon Record to recreate periods in the lives of real people through their electronic records."

"And it's amazing!"

Yves was puzzled and horrified. "The simulation market is already wasting the lives of millions of addicts. Why would we contribute to that wasteland?"

"Clara decided that we needed to address connection and the numbness of eternal life. We can now offer our customers an escape to a different life, a finite life."

"And she thinks this will solve Waldon's problems?"

"It could help." Moe broke into a smile. "It works really well. It's intoxicating and invigorating."

"When you enter, you forget what you know; it puts taste back into food. You experience crispness, emotions, highs and lows, ecstasy and pain. You become someone else: a complete stranger; somebody with a cognitive and emotional history. You live their pure experience, and when you leave, they remain part of you, of your memories."

This hit hard. Newness was rare. Yves missed the wonder of discovery: finding new colors in nature, breathing the energy of new air, experiencing a first of anything. Wonder could free millions from the numb he had witnessed, but it came with a new danger: humanity could easily be seduced into a life of pure ecstasy. Stoicism taught that man's sole purpose is to seek joy and freedom from suffering. But Yves knew that pain was necessary, or ecstasy would become the new numb.

"Clara believes our disconnected world needs more empathy. People are distant from the souls around them, and experiencing someone else helps to connect us. You need to try it. We've recreated some incredible people."

Yves had a flash: "Wait… can you be me?"

Moe sighed: "Unfortunately, no. We fought for that one, but Clara specifically said if ever she found out that one of us became you and then slept with her in your past, she would ram her boot so far up our asses that we would taste the shoe polish."

Yves snorted a giggle. "Ouch!"

Curly elaborated. "Clara set the rules. We can only simulate dead people or people who volunteer to perform a brain scan."

Yves understood that becoming someone who is still alive would be morally wrong.

Curly continued, "Aurora has indexed the entire Waldon Record, from the dawn of digital until we released the pills onto the market. She has been able to recreate several million hours of life experiences with 99.7% reliability during the period from 2005 to 2041."

Moe added, "You can become a famous sprinter setting records, or a president, or a pop star."

This was messed-up. "And she wants to share this at the board meeting?"

Curly answered, clearly echoing Clara. "The investors are concerned. People are going back to the old ways in droves in some regions."

"Millions are abandoning our services and taking the green pill."

"And millions more take the green pill directly when they turn 23. They never benefit from Waldon life extensions."

Yves was not concerned. "And so what? We have customer free will ingrained in our ethics standards. We'll deliver a service to people who want it, but never sell it as a better way to live. The investors have all signed the charter."

Curly and Moe continued the back and forth of finishing each other's sentences. "We know."

"Losing customers is a natural expression of free will and the human spirit."

"It's actually pretty romantic—the cycle of life and all."

"But the investors are worried."

"They want their extreme lifestyles to continue forever."

Yves interjected. "Some of the richest and most powerful people in the world are getting scared? Good! They should be scared after everything I've seen. They've inflicted much damage in the world. But I still don't understand why Clara would want to appease them."

Moe continued. "I doubt she's doing it for them. She's kept the details for today's meeting secret, and we don't know what she is planning to share. Unfortunately, Mathieu was down here last week and found me in a simulation."

"Which was pretty funny…"

"Shut up. It was embarrassing."

"No, it was funny. Tell him!"

"Fine. So, I was in the simulator being Bieber."

Yves coughed. "What?"

Moe continued, "Leave it alone. Curly was Lady Gaga for a day last week!"

Curly turned a bit red. "That was just a test. This was your twentieth time!"

"Whatever. So, I was in the simulation, and Mathieu came into the lab. When I woke, he was pissed. I panicked and told him it was nothing. He insisted, and one thing led to another. He tried it and was in there for an hour. I'm a bit concerned about today's board meeting. He knows what we've developed behind his back."

Curly giggled. "I love that Mathieu was a teenage pop-star!"

Yves was concerned. "Does Clara know that Mathieu has seen it?"

Moe answered. "Yeah. She's pissed. But she's been too busy building her own simulations with Aurora to come and yell at us."

"Where is she?" Yves looked to the door.

"In her office."

"Thanks." It was time. Yves walked back through the atrium in bare feet and to the elevators. He rose to the sixth floor and proceeded down its drab and darkened hallway. Executive floors were some of the loneliest places he knew. Bureaucracy had squeezed the energy out of the space: a lifeless tunnel in the birthplace of eternal life.

At the end of the hall, Clara's door was open.

There she was—beautiful.

Clara sat on the windowsill with a tablet and a steaming cup of coffee. Her cappuccino eyes glistened as the sun shone on her calm face. Stunning. Yves could not deny it: he had always been in love with her and it hurt him every day not to be together. While Mohist beliefs had trained him to love indiscriminately, he knew his heart had always been reserved for her.

He tapped the door frame and whispered, "Knock, knock."

Clara looked up and offered a dulled smile. "Welcome home." Her body had not aged, but Yves could see the years piling on her shoulders. Did she think about him? Clara put down her computer, walked slowly towards him and stopped an arms-length away. He could feel her warmth.

There were stories to share and questions to unwrap; but there was no rush.

The corners of her lips moved up ever so slightly. In her own way, maybe she loved him. He broke the silence. "You look tired."

"It's good you're back."

Yves smiled. She needed him!

"Come." Clara took Yves to the window, made him an espresso, and the two sat in the sill, facing each other. The mid-morning sun warmed their cheeks.

He could feel her strain—a burden born by the mother of immortality. She never let the weight of the company fall to others. He had provided guidance, but Clara had the final say in every moral decision they made. Waldon's life extensions had altered human existence and destroyed the beliefs and will of billions. There was no way to know if she had made the right choices, but her moral compass never veered. Yves was in eternal awe of his childhood friend.

"How was your travel today?"

"I watched an old movie—from Charlie Chaplin. It was filmed at the dawn of the Holocaust. In it, he said, 'The misery that is now upon us is but the passing of greed - the bitterness of men who fear the way of human progress. The hate of men will pass, and dictators die, and the power they took from the people will return to the people. And so long as men die, liberty will never perish.' That hit me hard. Men can no longer die, and liberty has died in its place."

Clara exhaled and shook her head. "We have to act quickly. Did you see the simulator?" There was a tinge of urgency in her voice.

"I saw it. Moe and Curly are incredible."

"They are. I've been tough on them."

"Your little project woke them up. They're over a hundred and sixty years old and have the enthusiasm of toddlers."

She smiled. "They've created something amazing. It's life-changing to live as someone else. A couple of months ago, I spent an hour as a famous basketball player. For the first time in many decades, I was able to disconnect. I felt her years of dedication, doubts, confidence and shame. It was unlike anything I have ever known."

"How did you feel afterwards?"

Clara exhaled and looked into Yves' eye. "Do you remember when we were teenagers, and Sven and Phil would to take us to movies?"

Yves nodded. How could he forget? It was the only time he ever heard Clara laugh.

"My favorite moments were not during the films, but in the brief fogginess as lights came on afterwards. For two hours, we saw joy and love and revenge, and when it was over, my mind always needed some seconds to swallow it into memories. In those magical flashes, I existed in an alternate reality, where both fairytale and history were true: good could conquer evil, justice would prevail and happy endings existed. But by the time we left the theater, the haze lifted, I returned to my pain and the experience reduced itself to words and faded images. In empathetic simulations, the fairytale becomes part of you, and its memory remains as real as our childhood or yesterday—impossible to ignore. When my simulation was over, I stood up from the chair and began to question my life's actions. I found a new perspective and yearned to return to her simple life where hard work paid off and victory was possible. I can't go back, but I am richer for having lived those sixty minutes."

Yves caressed the rim of his cup. "You're strong. If it changed you, it will change others. Is that what we want?"

"It's not manipulation, it's knowledge. There are many who need a new perspective in order to see clearly."

"If Plato was correct, and ultimate knowledge is the meaning of life, then perhaps you have created something wonderful. But given the millions of addicts that are already losing themselves, why would you risk giving this to a weakened world?"

"Alcoholics need help, but that does not mean we should ban all alcohol. Wine brings people together and makes life fun. Simulations on the regulated market are fun, but they do not bring people together. They don't connect people, they entertain them. Our simulations could restore the empathy we've lost."

Yves took the last sip of his espresso and stared into the forest. "I used to believe that our pills would unleash a new era of kindness. After millennia of basic survival, humans finally have time to listen to each other. I thought that would be enough, but I was wrong. Greed and individuality continue to deepen."

Clara's frustration bubbled through the calm. "And the greediest individuals are our investors. I need to take back control, so we can finally give people what they need."

She was perfect in her flaws, and every ounce of his being yearned to be with her. She fought for every soul to live life to its fullest potential. Every decision she ever made was for them. Her drive and singular purpose were an immeasurable gift to humankind, and he could no long hold back. "I love you."

Clara looked him in the eye, and her strain eased. "I know."

It was not the right time, but Yves needed to try: "Marry me."

Clara laughed and shook her head. "Wow, that took almost fifteen minutes. You can't keep proposing to me—you know how I feel about eternity."

"Then take me to the island tonight for a welcome-home dinner."

Her eyes shifted, and she tried to hide a smile. "Let's see how the meeting goes."

That was not a 'no'! He had not been invited to the island in twenty years. Yves tried to keep a silent, straight face, but his mind was dancing: 'YES! YES! YES! YES! YES!'

It was time to get to work. They had agreed on a plan ten years earlier. His emotional departure had allowed him to travel freely and research the raw impact of Waldon investors on the world. He had explored corners without Tom or Waldon security finding out. He recorded the stories of those who suffered daily to pay their Life Tax and lived in constant fear of the Penalty. Waldon's pure intentions had warped into something truly awful. Maybe this new data could finally ignite change. "Did you like the postcard?"

"Yes. The hidden chip was cute. It got through Tom's security with no questions."

"Recording those experiences was the hardest thing I've ever done. Despair and inequality are everywhere. After all these years, Life Taxes and Penalties are still tearing families apart. Even children are miserable—they prepare their Decision as toddlers and feed on the daily fear and anxiety of their parents. Poverty feeds poverty, while compounding wealth squeezes every cent it can from global desperation. The rich stay infinitely powerful, and the poor have lost all hope."

"And we now have a digital record of it."

"How do we share it with investors?"

"I've developed special simulations with Aurora for each of them, using the data you sent. They'll finally know the pain they are causing and understand that they have become the problem. These simulations will provoke the necessary empathy and votes to change things. They may even be so overcome with regret that they choose to take their green pills."

Yves' stomach tightened. "We can't manipulate them that way, that's brainwashing! Tricking someone to take their pill is murder! And it's illegal to make someone experience a simulation without consent!"

"Yes, we can. As part-owners, they have each signed waivers to test our products without liability. And they will ask to see it. Mathieu knows about the simulator and already understands the impact it can have. His discovery last week was not accidental. He'll convince the other investors it's safe."

He knew it was wrong, but he froze. In sixteen decades, he had never talked Clara out of anything. How could he even begin? Yves wanted to vomit.

"When they feel the suffering they have caused, they will need to fix it."

"When?" He could barely talk.

Clara looked to the clock on the wall and sat up from the sill. "Now."

Yves froze; it was time for the board meeting. Clara stepped to the door, and he struggled to follow. She guided them from the office to the hall and towards the boardroom. His mind raced. He could barely feel his legs. He had followed Clara's lead for many years, and life had turned out okay so far. Maybe everything would be fine.

But what if it wasn't?

Clara paused at the door and straightened her shoulders. He tried to breathe and used all his strength to open the large, oak door for her. The seated group hushed as she strode in. Mathieu sat at one end of the table, surrounded by investors Dimitri, Yingtai, Arjun, Afonso and Tanaka. Curly and Moe were next to the two empty chairs at the head of the table. Moe had his striped blanket draped over his shoulder. Tom and nineteen employees who each had 0.1% ownership sat in chairs at the back of the room. Yves followed Clara to the front, avoiding the laser-stare from Tom.

The walls reeked of bureaucracy and greed—a reminder of Yves' failures.

The thirty in the room were the original immortals, and they were all focused on Clara. They had split into a broken family— beautiful intentions eroded by time, stubbornness and money. But they didn't deserve to die.

Clara began. "Aurora, please begin recording. Ladies, gentlemen, thank you for joining me today. We have some news: I just finished validating a new product with our Chief Conscience Officer, and I'm certain you will all be delighted with its potential."

Mathieu interrupted. "For the record, I maintain that Yves' prolonged absence and your failure to appoint a new Officer is grounds for CEO dismissal."

"We wrote the corporate governance together, Mathieu, and he cannot be replaced without a 2/3 majority vote. It may not be perfect, but it's the only eternal law we have."

Dimitri chimed in aggressively. "We are losing a lot of customers, and it is now urgent to do something to secure our future. What do you propose?"

Clara smirked. "I did not realize that you were running out of money, Dimitri. I suspect all of you are more concerned about losing your power."

The investors glared as Mathieu refocused the discussion. "Not all of <u>you</u>, Clara—all of <u>us</u>." Mathieu took a moment to look around the table. "We are in this together."

"Are we?" Clara paused and turned to Yves. "Ten years ago, I sent our Chief Conscience Officer on a secret mission to understand the impact of our product on the world. I wanted an unfiltered view, not the reports governments send us. Yves, based on your decade of research, what are the primary obstacles to retaining our customer base?"

Yves could not concentrate through the nausea. There was a crack in his whispered answer. "Boredom. Numbness. Absence of meaning with nothing new to live for."

"Do our customers want to die when they choose to take their green pill?"

He looked at his glass of water. "No. They want to feel something. Many have lost hope and prefer to live a limited existence where choices have consequence."

Clara cut to the point. "We have developed a product that will resolve Waldon's biggest challenges and revolutionize the simulation industry at the same time. We've overcome the last obstacle to level-three simulations, and it's so compelling, so enriching, so passionate, that customers will want to live forever just to experience it all. They'll be able to feel the crispness of life from before Waldon and return with new empathy for the real world. It's beautiful, and people will choose our red pill if they have it in their lives. Just ask Mathieu."

All eyes turned to a visibly uncomfortable Mathieu. He conceded with a whisper: "It is impressive."

Dimitri was captivated. "You lived the emotions?"

Mathieu responded sheepishly. "Yes."

"What did you feel?" Arjun wanted to know. "Lust? Passion? Love? Happiness?"

Mathieu stared at Moe, as if to say: 'Don't you dare tell them!'
"All of it."

Clara continued. "Who would like to try first?"

Mathieu closed his eyes and raised his hand.

Moe elbowed Curly and let out a muffled laugh. Clara gave them a stern look. "Can you two please set up the machine? Aurora, unlock my secure folder and share the simulations we developed."

Tom interjected: "What simulations? It's not on the agenda and no one informed security!"

Mathieu reassured him: "It's fine, Tom."

Clara smiled. "The best way to understand is to live it. Come with me." She stood and led the group towards the elevator. Yves wanted to scream under her glaring omission, but nothing came out. She had said nothing about risks! Was she leading the parade of trillionaires in a death march? They were moving blindly into an experience that may change them forever. Out of the corner of his eye, Yves noticed Tom dart towards the stairs. Where was he going?

On the elevator, he glanced nervously around to the smiling faces. Mathieu was almost giddy; he had no idea that he was about to live pain that could never be undone. Would he feel guilt for his own greed, and decide it was time for his green pill? Yves wanted to defy Clara and whisper a discreet warning; or maybe Mathieu deserved to see the truth.

The door opened, and Mathieu advanced to the simulation lab with Curly and Moe. The others gathered in the Cube's garden and discussed the potential of this new invention. Minutes passed and Yves paced furiously. Why was he trusting Clara's judgement? Something felt wrong. What should he do?

Tanaka and Yingtai strolled to him with smiles. He tried to hide his tremble.

There was a hustled movement along the atrium's inner wall: Tom ran across the back of the Cube and cut towards the lab.

Yves moved away from Tanaka and grabbed Clara's arm. "Can we talk for a moment?"

"In a few minutes, Dimitri and I are just discussing the…"

"NOW!"

The two shuffled away from the group, but before he could whisper his concern—*BANG!* A sharp explosion: a firecracker. Adrenaline took over as Yves sprinted through the dirt and into the lab's hallway. The simulation room was locked!

BANG! A second explosion. Gunshots! Yves panicked for his friends. He took a flying leap towards the door and broke it down. Tom held a gun over a bloodied Moe, while Mathieu lay unaware in the simulation chair, covered by the webbing. Curly had his hands in the air and was crying and yelling hysterically. "NO! NO! NO! Stay alive, Moe! Stay awake!"

Yves was confused. "TOM!?! What are you doing? Put the gun down!"

He turned away from Moe and snapped the gun at Yves: "SHUT THIS THING OFF!! IT'S BRAINWASHING!!! YOU'RE KILLING HIM!" His attention and the gun waved ferociously between Yves and Curly. "AURORA! TURN IT OFF!" Yves needed to pounce. Hostility twitched in his muscles. Fight pumped through his veins as he prepared to leap at the gun and protect his friends.

Moe, full of blood and grasping his stomach, stood up quietly behind Tom. Yves froze and whispered to himself: 'No, Moe! Don't do it.' But it was too late. Moe lunged at Tom's back; on impact, Tom fired his gun. A searing slice cut through Yves' chest.

Yves collapsed to the floor.

With an elbow-shove from Tom, Moe fell back to the ground. Blood seeped into his striped blanket. Yves and Moe met eyes across the floor. They were both dying. Yves looked up to his attacker with blurred vision. Tom screamed: "No. No. NO! What have I done? AURORA! I SAID SHUT IT OFF!"

The pain—the pain was severe. Ice numbed his spine. He couldn't feel his feet. Where was Clara? God, please let her be okay. He looked to Moe, who's open eyes fell lifeless. He wanted to yell, but no air came. The fog was thickening. Poor Tom—he would never forgive himself.

This was all Yves' fault; he could have prevented it.

Clara rushed into the room, screaming wildly, "NO! NO! NOOOOOO!" She grabbed his head with panicked tears. Yves knew he was about to die.

He was okay with that.

It was his time. He wanted to know what came next. He wanted to understand the nothingness. Nietzsche believed that life was only worth living if inspired by goals, but Yves had nothing left.

"I'm ready," he whispered to Clara.

"NO!" Tears streamed down her face.

Yves closed his eyes. A last wisp of life faded away.

Darkness.

Emptiness.

Nothing.

~~

Pain shot through Nerea's body. She had just experienced her father's death. "What the hell, Seren?!!??!!"

Dying was surprisingly calm. A welcomed relief. It amazed her how quickly Yves had let go.

Then confusion as her heart sank. "How am I here if he died so many years before I was born?"

Seren was silent as Nerea trembled and collapsed onto the sand. Yves was a wonderful man—a father she could never meet. His loss brought a stabbing anguish through her core.

"The next experience is of your mother and will answer your questions. I suggest you go to bed and get some rest before we take it on. You've been through a lot today."

Nerea cried, crushed with apprehension and anticipation. She was getting the answers she sought, and it hurt. She sobbed her way back to the garden, lay down on the couch and pulled the quilt over her head. Sadness filled her exhausted belly. She had finally met her father, and he was already gone.

Nerea cried herself to sleep.

Chapter 8

09/04/2226 – The Pessimism Experience

It was Nerea's 23rd birthday, the day of her Decision.

She woke early, strolled to the water and searched the horizon for guidance that would never come. Nerea could not bring herself to swim. The morning ritual was pointless; no amount of water could cleanse the numb from her body. Yesterday had killed her hidden-family fantasy and left her alone with a mother incapable of love. Her life was paved in lies, and both pills forward led to despair. Loneliness and death always won.

Nerea was unable to embrace anything good in the surrounding calm. A breeze cut through the hurt and reminded her to keep moving. She walked back to the garden and collapsed on the couch. Seren came from the house with black coffee and a cupcake.

"Happy birthday, Nerea."

She faked a smile. There was nothing happy about today. "Thank you." Nerea picked up the coffee and stared into its obscurity.

The weight of an empty destiny paralyzed her body as she sipped the darkness.

~~

15/07/2202 – The Remorse Experience

Clara sat in the windowsill of Yves' library and gazed into the Cube. She missed him dearly. Why had she pushed him away for so many years?

He had died decades ago, but she thought about him every single day. Eternity was empty without him. Countless hours were spent in the simulator reliving their cherished moments on the island. But it was a lie.

Each return to reality deepened the hurt, and each goodbye tore at her soul. Waldon would never be the same: Yves and Moe were dead. Tom was convicted of murder and aging in prison. The world was not better off than when she was born; it was divided and miserable. Life Tax revenues continued to roll in, and the shareholders' wealth continued to grow. The voting shares of Moe and Yves were now in limbo, and Waldon was in a state of paralysis. No one could unblock or change anything.

She should never have given away so much power. Conflict could have been avoided, and Yves would be alive. Regret was her penance for trusting others.

There was a knock at the door. "Come in." Only one person who knew where she was.

Curly entered. His eyes were heavy, and he did not step with his usual jubilance. "Hi Clara. How are you?"

She scanned the rows of books for answers. "The sadness won't go away. I miss Yves and Moe too much. I was foolish and never stopped to appreciate the bond we had. We were a family and now we're alone. I've spent my life chasing the unattainable: an impossible future when all the world's problems are resolved and everyone is thankful for the Decision we have given them. But I forgot to appreciate our journey. I miss Yves with all my heart. He loved me, and I never embraced my feelings for him while he was alive."

Clara's head dropped. "I never allowed love into my heart."

"You're not alone, Clara. We're still family. Stop kicking yourself and focus on the future."

Clara looked at Curly and nodded. A decisive, new energy flowed into her body. "That future begins now."

"Are you sure you want this?"

"I'm sure. Is the simulation ready?"

"Yes. Aurora has prepared everything."

Clara stood and walked towards the door.

"…Now?"

"Yes, Curly. Now."

Clara rode the elevator downstairs, walked into the Cube and stepped into the Lab. She was calm. How would this experience impact her? She lay in the simulator and pulled the webbing over her body.

~ ~ ~

05/10/2009 – The Submission Experience

Louis was lost in Clara's 6-month-old eyes, beautiful and happy. Lying on the grass in the shade of the hospital was a much-needed escape for them both. Louis encouraged Clara to stroke the lilacs and experience the touch and smells of color. He made silly faces while his baby giggled and caressed his face. Clara snuggled and blew spit bubbles on his chest.

Phil called from a distance. "Louis!"

Louis got up slowly, walked to Phil and kissed him on both cheeks. "Thanks for coming. How are you doing?"

Phil smiled and stroked Clara's cheek. "I'm doing well. We had some great news today. It looks like Clara may have a little friend next year."

"That's fantastic! It worked! Wow. Congratulations!" Louis pulled Phil in for a hug. "It will change your life in ways you're not expecting." Louis looked down at Clara's curious face. "When I have her in my arms and walk past a mirror, I don't even see my own reflection; I only see her. She's the only thing that matters. I could have a shaved eyebrow, and I would not even notice. How's Janet doing?"

"Marvelous! I still can't believe she's doing this for us. Sven and I have fallen deeply in love with her." His smile faded. "We plan to name the child after Eva. How's she doing?"

"She fought so hard, for so long. But it's over. The doctors have given her a month, but it'll be less."

The two looked down at Clara, who smiled back. A deep sadness rose in Louis' throat, and a tear rolled down his cheek. The friends held each other while baby Clara looked at them in awe.

"Eva knew that the cancer might kill her when she chose not to have radiation during pregnancy. Her decision gave this little angel a chance at life."

Phil looked at Clara and spoke in a silly voice. "You're the luckiest baby I have ever met; a mother who gave you everything, and one of the most amazing humans I've ever known as a father."

Louis smiled. "Thanks. Let's go see Eva."

The three began the long walk from the garden into the hospital hallways. Each room they passed was filled with a calm that was both unnerving and reassuring. Everyone's life was changing in one way or another.

Louis arrived at the door where they had spent the last weeks, took a deep breath and entered. Eva was sitting up and looking skeletal—it was a bad day. Her hair was long gone, and the joy in her eyes had faded to tiredness and pain.

She managed a weak smile. "Phil! How are you? It's good to see you."

He hugged her carefully. "I'm good. Janet's pregnant!"

"Fantastic! With fathers like you, the child is bound to do remarkable things."

Louis' throat clenched tight and he held his breath; Eva would never meet that baby. She turned to him with a tired but loving gaze and put out her arms. Louis passed Clara onto her chest and gently began to rub Eva's shoulders. Mother and daughter looked into each other's eyes with smiles. Eva began to sing her soft, Celtic Lullaby.

> "The first time I saw you, life beat to my drum.
> Raindrops on roses all danced in the sun.
> Your questions unanswered wandered to me for breath.
> I smiled and knew that you'd soon learn the rest.

The next time I saw you, life beat to our drum.
Raindrops on roses all danced in the sun.
Our questions unanswered wandered with us for breath.
We smiled and knew that we'd soon learn the rest.

The last time I saw you, life beat to your drum.
Raindrops on roses all danced in the sun.
My questions unanswered wandered to you for breath.
You smiled and knew that I'd soon learn the rest."

Louis would soon lose the love of his life; the sexiest and most caring human he had ever met. There would only be a few more songs before Eva died, and he would be forever alone to raise their daughter.

Eva continued humming in a melodic and whispered voice.

Clara gazed into her mother's eyes with wonder.

~~~

Clara woke from the simulation in pain. She walked into the atrium, took off her shoes and strolled on the dirt of the garden pathways. For more than a century, she had stubbornly blocked Yves from reaching her heart; but even in death, his love was unstoppable.

Clara never felt desire to have a child. But now, it consumed her every thought. She wanted a baby. She needed to have a baby.

And she knew what to do.

The fertilized embryos frozen with Yves at the dawn of Waldon were still viable. They were conceived as a precaution before testing of the pills began.

She would start a small family with the love of her long-lost friend. Almost 200 years after the embryos were created, Clara
~~~

would have Yves' baby.

Her Decision was made: it was time to let go.

Clara took the green pill from her locket, put it on her tongue and swallowed.

Her life was beginning to end, and she could finally live. She would have a baby, become a mother, grow old and die.

~~

Nerea's body filled with her mother's warmth. She had never held a baby but now knew its fulfillment. Someday, she might even start a family of her own.

Nerea was not an accident—she was a choice. Maybe her relationship with Clara could be repaired and she wouldn't be alone forever. Nerea fantasized about forgiveness and growing old with her mother. She imagined having a baby and introducing him to Nana.

The birthday cupcake remained on the table with a hand-written note from Seren:

> 'You have completed all ten simulations. When you are ready, take a bite of this cake and come back to my office. It is time to finalize your Decision.'

Red pill or green pill? Stop aging and experience more of life? Or embrace its natural limits and maybe have a baby? The evil of Waldon was an illusion, and her Decision now wobbled high in the air.

Nerea needed to move her body. She stood, ran away from the beach and across Eva's favorite bridge. At a sharp bend, she cut into the woods, towards her grandmother's secret spot on the river. She stripped naked, embraced the sun and dove into the water for one last swim.

The cycle of life was beautiful. Eva and Louis had loved each other and Clara deeply. Sven and Phil had loved each other and Yves with all their hearts.

Love had built her family. Nerea belonged in this world, and maybe she deserved its love.

She walked slowly back to the beach house, sat in her favorite chair and looked to the ocean. The smell of basil and mint was as crisp as it was centuries ago. She would miss this place. "Goodbye."

Nerea took a bite of her birthday cupcake.

~

Chapter 9

09/04/2226 – The Cynicism Experience

After a long shower, Nerea passed through Seren's office and noticed details missed when she first arrived. A massive painting filled the space with color: a laughing child, a rainbow and stars full of wishes. To the right of the canvas was a cold, corporate addiction poster listing five signs you may have a problem and how to get support. Joy spoiled yet again by persistent sadness. Nerea did not belong to this world.

She stepped outside and sat across from Seren in the backyard garden. Nerea reached into her pocket and pulled out her sealed locket. Inside was a red pill to stop the aging process and a green pill to continue it—a numb without end or babies and death. The locket had not changed but was now infinitely heavier. Life and death and family legacy; in the palm of her hand. Nerea put the silver chain around her neck and noticed its resemblance to Clara's. The lock would open when its timer reached zero.

There were twelve minutes left.

Nerea tried to empty her mind and remember who she was and what she wanted in life. She needed to calm her racing thoughts. Each simulation from the last 48 hours was manipulating and enriching her Decision.

Seren placed a large, sealed envelope on the table. "It is time for you to look inside."

Nerea took it and sighed. What could her mother possibly add?

Seren handed her a paper knife and Nerea sliced open the envelope. She cautiously pulled out a stack of sheets and found a signed note from her mother on the top.

Nerea put the documents down and read the letter silently:

> Dear Nerea,
>
> The last twenty-three years have been excruciating, and I am prouder of you than you will ever know. I trust your curiosity and drive are now ready for the task ahead.
>
> Yves once told me that the happiest children he encountered were those who knew nothing of Waldon. They grew up free from the Decision and could embrace life with pure innocence. I wanted to give you that childhood and decided to keep many secrets from you. Because lying was not an option, I often left you with silence. I know it was difficult, and you may believe there was a better way; but it was my choice, and I made it.
>
> From today, there are no more secrets.
>
> I am proud of the good Waldon has done, but there is a lot of unnecessary inequality that has resulted. For many years, I could not find a path to repair it; then, things got worse. When your father and Moe died, I lost the ability to change even simple, operational topics. The shareholder agreements from the 'Flagrant Fowl' have locked us into unmanageable governance. I need a 2/3 majority to remove Mathieu and several other board

members from Waldon. I need votes to fix the cruelty of the Penalty, heal simulation addiction and ignite a redistribution of wealth in this world.

Twenty-four years ago, it finally dawned on me: I could have Yves' baby, and you could inherit Yves' shares. Because they cannot be sold, inheritance is the only way to pass on Waldon voting shares without 2/3 shareholder approval. If you choose the red pill today, there are a few things that will happen:

1. You will inherit your father's Waldon shares and become a voting member of the Board of Directors. There is a document to sign attached. Waldon rules stipulate that only people who have experienced the red pill can participate in key votes.
2. Curly and I propose that you replace him and become the CEO of Waldon. This will need to be confirmed at the next board meeting in two years. You are young, and we need your energy.
3. I cannot change the company without shareholder support. I believe you are the right person to secure the 2/3 majority required to make necessary changes to Waldon.
4. When I eventually die of old age, I will leave my shares to you, and Waldon will become your company.

If you choose to take the green pill, your inherited shares will remain non-voting shares, and the future of Waldon will be determined by the remaining shareholders when I die.

You did not ask for this burden, but it falls on you.

Sincerely,
Mom

Nerea dropped the letter and crunched her shoulders forward.

Seren could feel her panic. "Are you okay? What does it say?"

Nerea could barely breathe. She pulled her legs up into a ball and rubbed her forehead against her knees. "It's a job offer as CEO of Waldon, plus my father's shares… if I take the red pill."

Seren's eyes widened.

Nerea's mind raced and she looked to the sky for guidance. She was not born of love, but of corporate desperation. Her Decision had been ripped out from under her. She did not want to live forever; she wanted to grow old. She wanted a family and a simple life helping others.

But her life was not her own. Clara had tricked her into believing she could choose her destiny. Nausea filled her stomach as she stretched her legs and lay back in the chair. "I don't have a choice to make here today. My life has never been my own. My Decision is a lie."

"Why do you say that?"

Nerea tried to pull fresh air into her panicking lungs. "If I take the green pill, Waldon will fall to the other board members when Clara dies, and Waldon's misery could continue for centuries to come. Clara has placed the future squarely on my shoulders."

She looked to her Coach for reassurance but found none. Seren gazed to the sky and shook her head in disbelief. She turned to Nerea, placed her hands on her knees and consoled as best she could: "I am so sorry."

Nerea looked to the locket timer as the last few seconds counted down to zero. At precisely 11:00—'Click.' An inner mechanism unlocked, and the seal popped open.

She had waited her whole life for this moment and now wanted it gone.

"You don't need to decide now. You can wait a few days or even years. It is up to you. You are in control."

Nerea looked Seren in the eye. "No, I'm not." She reluctantly took the locket in her left hand, clasped her right hand on the top and opened it. Two pills stared back at her: green and red; innocent and omnipotent; mortal and eternal. The beauty of life sat beside the loneliness of living and pretended to give her a choice. Life and death looked so similar.

Deep in her heart, she felt the green pill calling. Its poetic elegance was natural and clear: Nerea knew she was born to die. She caressed it with a finger and whispered: "Someday."

She took the red pill between her fingers, stared at it and winced. Swallowing those few milligrams invited a corporation to control the rest of her life.

Then again, it was her corporation.

Tears seeped into the corners of her eyes. "It's like I'm about to kill a piece of myself." Nerea looked to Seren. "There's no point waiting. Do you have something to wash this down?"

"Water, champagne, or tequila?"

"Tequila."

Seren smiled, reached beside her and pulled out two shot glasses and a bottle of Tequila. She poured the shots and handed one to Nerea. "You are an incredible woman, and it has been an honor sharing these days with you. When you take that pill, I am no longer your Decision Coach. Our work together is done, but know that you will always have a friend in me. Call if ever you need my help."

Nerea smiled. She was a little less alone.

Seren handed over salt and a generous slice of lemon.

Nerea licked her wrist and poured the salt.

Seren did the same. "I am proud of you. I wish you a long and fulfilling life."

"Thank you, Seren."

Nerea licked the salt, put the red pill on her tongue, shot back the tequila and sucked on the lemon.

The sour was vicious.

Act II

Plants are selective about who they trust. Robins eat Toxicodendron radicans like a delicacy, excreting the seeds out far away so that the plant can travel and grow in new forests. Also known as poison ivy, the plant will cause serious harm if touched by humans, can damage organs if ingested and may even be fatal if its fumes are inhaled.

Chapter 10

09/04/2226 – The Anger Experience

Her life was no longer her own—it belonged to her mother.

"ARRRRRGH!!!!" Nerea pounded the bed and screamed to the rolling road from her moving pod. The space was travelling over three hundred kilometers per hour, but the room's only vibrations were from stomps and kicks and air conditioning. Her blood raced, and she desperately needed release. She delivered a hard elbow to the cushioned headboard and hit the wall beside her. Her breathing accelerated. She jumped to her knees and began punching the fold-up table like a speed bag.

For the first time in years, Nerea needed to see her mother—to both hug and yell at her. Nothing was fair.

She stood and jogged from the front to the back of the vehicle. A gym-pod would have been a better choice—sleep was impossible. Nerea shadow-boxed the theater seat with increasing strength. She clobbered the headrest, uppercut the back support, and jabbed at the cup holder. After a jerky head-bob, she accidentally clipped the screen with a left hook-haymaker—the screen cracked! 'Crap.' She looked up through the moon roof. "Pin, can you please get that fixed?"

The pod answered with an androgynous voice over the speaker. "Of course. It can be done eight minutes after we arrive, or we can stop in sixteen minutes and repair it on the way."

"Later is fine."

There was blood on her knuckle. Nerea took a deep breath and walked to the medicine cabinet. Everything Nerea had wanted in life was lost—a future ripped away. The cruelty of Waldon's Decision came from honorable origins, and she no longer felt morally superior to those inside of the company. Waldon would become her company; the path forward would be hers.

Life had been much easier three days ago when Waldon was run by faceless tyrants. But they were not tyrants; they did the best they could and tried to steer the world away from suffering.

Was a better future even possible? Why did her mother hide her destiny from her?

She yearned for the guidance of her father. Yves was in and out of her life in a flash, but his spirit lingered deep in her bones. What would he have done?

For the next hour, Nerea sat up in her bed and stared at the passing clouds. When tree branches began to cross her view, she looked ahead and saw Elise's Diner; they had arrived to the island. The pod crossed the bridge, and the heavy wooden gate opened wide. No one came from the security cabin, but they were there. She rolled silently through two kilometers of forest road, past guest houses and the pod-hangar, and up to the main door of her childhood home. The mansion was built at the southern tip of the island; allowing year-round views of sunrises and sunsets. Nerea stepped out and looked around at her youth. The trees were taller, but the island had not changed. The gardener had laid flowers in the same perfect pattern as every year: pink, purple, blue, green, yellow, orange and red.

The front door opened, and Clara stepped out onto the porch. There was a hunch in her posture; she looked lonely. Then, Curly stepped outside and joined her mother's side. Nerea was surprised and relieved by his presence; maybe he could mediate.

They stared at each other in silence. Each was trying to assess the moment, and Nerea knew they sought confirmation of her Decision. She allowed their pained anticipation to endure.

Curly eventually broke the silence. "Hello, Nerea."

"Hello, Curly." His eyes were full of worry while his smile held the warmth that Nerea needed.

He continued: "It's good to see you."

She nodded and locked into a stare with Clara. Nerea had grown close to the simulated versions of her mother, but the meters that separated them now could have been mountain ranges. At the back of her throat, Nerea could still taste the screaming and hurtful attacks of her youth. Dark shame and fury lingered.

But there was a difference: Clara looked vulnerable. She feigned strength, but the façade had cracked. For the first time in her life, there was fear in her mother's eyes. She was not in control of this moment.

Clara cut straight to the point: "What was your Decision?" A broken voice betrayed recent crying.

Nerea was not ready to ease her mother's guilt. Her thoughts raced: 'Should it matter? I'm your daughter, and you should love me regardless.' But she was unable to speak. Resentment clawed at her core. Nerea opened her locket and displayed the single remaining green pill to her mother.

Clara's shoulders drooped, releasing decades of tension. She raised her arms, began a smile and took a half step towards her daughter.

Nerea immediately took a step back. "What have you done, Clara?"

Her mother dropped her arms and burst into a sob. Nerea had never seen her mother cry. She was surprised by her own reaction and the instinctive rejection of her mother. Despite everything she had learned, she could not abandon the hate.

Curly offered a solution: "Nerea, why don't you clean up from your travel, and we can go for a walk together?"

She went to her old bedroom and took a long, hot shower before heading down to the beach for a sunset walk with Curly. His pants were rolled up, and he had Moe's blanket tossed over his shoulder. Neither said a word as they began the stroll.

A cold wave washed over their feet. Curly broke the comfortable silence. "Your mother did the best she could. Maybe you'll forgive her one day."

"Forgiveness is necessary in love, but Clara never loved me. Why should I forgive her? I'm simply an unfortunate necessity."

Curly stopped walking, and a second wave washed over Nerea's ankles. As it retreated, sand was pulled from under her feet. "Clara never had the maternal instincts to raise a child. Her whole existence is weighted by the responsibility to ensure meaningful lives for the billions of people who use our services. She has changed the definition of life itself and held this burden alone for almost two hundred years. Some could assume that she took her green pill to escape and move on to something easier, but Clara values Waldon more than she values her own life. She understood the only way to change Waldon was with a legitimate heir for Yves' shares. The only way to do that was with the embryos that produced you. She did the calculation and decided that the best path forward was to have a baby; to have you. She was willing to sacrifice her own life to resolve Waldon's greatest problems."

The directness punched her core.

"From the moment she became pregnant, Clara did the best she could. She protected you from the strain she felt every day. I disagreed with her choice to isolate you, and it caused a rift that lasted years; but she's your mother, and she stuck to her choices."

"What happens now?"

Curly picked up a flat rock and skipped it across the water. "I am proud of what Waldon has done, but our job is not finished—the world needs more from us. We are in the unique position to right vast suffering, but the investors refuse to help. They have not trusted us since the murders and vote against every change we propose. Maybe they will trust you."

She had spent years observing the negative consequences of Waldon and was ready to shout from the rooftops for change, but Nerea had never put herself in the shoes of the people who must fix it. Now, she was unable to put her finger on any specific ideas or path forward. "If you had their votes, what would you change?"

The pair resumed their stroll. "In our push to grant people endless experiences, we did not prepare societies to adjust. The ills of our patterns never adjusted to the new reality, and too many citizens are miserable. Waldon did not invent suffering, but we erased it's finish line. We amplified deep rooted problems that people had long ignored and created new issues in the process. Poverty was entrenched with the exponential growth of the wealth gap. We gave governments a weapon when we allowed them to define and administer the Penalties. And we enabled a significant rise in simulation addiction when we released empathetic simulations. But with the support of a few investors, we can fix things."

"How did the Penalty start?"

"The Penalty is not set by Waldon. It's defined by each country to ensure their citizens pay the Life Tax. While some governments have reasonable fines or prison terms, many impose sanctions that are essentially death sentences: cutting basic income, removing access to medical care, or even forcing people to take their green pill. The choice to live eternally has become driven by economics and fear, rather than free will."

"What can Waldon do about it?"

"If we controlled the board vote, we could reduce our fee and ensure the Life Tax is almost free for those who cannot afford it. With no tax, there's nothing to penalize. Governments may panic, but it would be a step in the right direction."

Nerea contemplated the impact if tax revenues plummeted— governments would crumble. Was there a better way?

"The second misery Waldon enabled is linked to the empathetic simulations I created with Aurora—one of my greatest achievements and most significant failures. We started selling them after the murders and believed it would help people connect to other souls. I underestimated their addictive nature. There are now millions of addicts to our simulations, and Waldon is part of an industry that is destroying lives. People are losing their humanity and forgetting to live in the real world.

"If we controlled the vote, Waldon could push for stronger regulation. We should restrict people's time in simulations and only allow ethical content. I know that this would hurt the profits of Dimitri's SimuPlex business, but we can no longer justify inaction.

"The third misery is the exponential wealth gap in the world. The shareholders of Waldon are the richest humans in history, and Waldon is the primary cause of this entrenched imbalance. Some investors used their wealth to buy up businesses and companies in the chaos that followed our release. A person born today has almost no chance of economic success. Either you're born rich, or you stay poor."

This idea infuriated Nerea a little bit: "Why has Clara not used her wealth to help? What's stopping her? Her inaction is unforgivable."

"Her money is locked up in Waldon. She earns a decent salary, and her contract ensures Waldon will take care of this island and everything she needs, but dividends are reserved for the investors. The vast majority of your mother's cash is accumulating in Waldon accounts and untouchable without shareholder agreement. I have a similar contract, and neither of us wants or needs more money. If we controlled the vote, we could use the Waldon cash pile to do a lot of good in the world. We could also remove board members who don't redistribute wealth and even lobby to rebalance through increased taxes on the uber-wealthy. We're only two hundred years into our journey and need a great correction before we can begin a fair and infinite future."

Nerea's head spun. "How much money is in Waldon accounts?"

"More than you could ever imagine."

Nerea had thrown much undeserved anger at her mother. Perceived wealth and inaction were anchors in this hatred, and their chains were being cut. For a split second, she pondered the fortune she would one day inherit, and reveled in its power. Money was addictive, and convincing others to let it go would be difficult. "Your plan sounds complicated."

Curly chuckled. "Simple solutions have rarely fixed the world's great problems."

They turned at the boulders and walked home in reflective silence. Their feet splashed lightly as waves rolled up the beach. Each step through the water was cleansing; like she was walking towards something new. The sandbars offshore had washed away, and Nerea remembered the freedom of exploring them as a child. She almost missed this place.

Clara had set a campfire on the beach and sat with two empty chairs, an open bottle of Cahors and three glasses. She didn't look up as they approached. Nerea sat quietly and embraced the silence. The mother she met in simulations was more human than the cold and controlling woman she hated three days ago.

There would be no hugs today, but Nerea could sense a truce settling on the island. In a barely audible voice, she whispered to the fire: "I know you did the best you could, Mom." It was the first time she had not called her 'Clara' in ten years.

Her mother's eyes opened wide. "Thank you."

Clara stood, poured three glasses of wine and handed them out. She raised her glass to Nerea. "I wish there was another way, but I need you."

"I know."

These simple words began a new relationship.

The three sat in silence as darkness fell. Questions could wait; Nerea needed to savor the calm for as long as it lasted. She was terrified of the days beyond tomorrow's sunrise.

Under bright stars, Clara remembered something irrelevant: "I almost forgot: Happy birthday."

Nerea pretended to smile. "Thank you."

Curly offered his wishes. "I keep forgetting to celebrate birthdays. Happy Birthday Nerea! You should relax for a few days. You'll need strength for the journey ahead. When you're ready, come by the Cube so I can introduce you to Aurora and the rest of the Waldon team."

"Journey?"

Clara explained: "Every time Yves came back from his travels, he understood the world a bit more. With today's disinformation, it's impossible to know the reality of other countries without visiting. You need to leave Canada and connect with other cultures. We can secure entry-visas to most places through our government contacts and I'd like you to meet each of our investors in their home countries. Our next board meeting is in two and a half years and you need to convince some of them to join us."

Nerea's knees grew weak.

Curly handed Nerea a paper. "Here's the status of the voting shares."

The paper had names and ownership.

THE WALDON CORPORATION
Board of Directors Voting Structure

Clara	(Founder, Canada, USA)	32%
Mathieu	(Investor, USA)	31%
Moe	(Founder, Deceased)	15% (Shares in trust)
Yves	(Founder, Deceased)	8% (Shares in trust)
Curly	(CEO, USA)	7%
Yingtai	(Investor, China)	1%
Arjun	(Investor, India)	1%
Tanaka	(Investor, Madagascar)	1%
Dimitri	(Investor, Russia)	1%

Afonso   (Investor, Brazil)   1%
Employee Shareholders (USA)   0.1% each:
   Tom (Incarcerated, Shares in Trust), Glendon, Fred,
   Myer, Conroy, Jill, Evelyn, Cece, Alison, Erika, Mike,
   Jon, Emily, Marc, Jessie, Charles, Brad, Martin,
   Euphemia, Sylvain.

Curly explained: "Mathieu is firmly against any change we propose, and unfortunately, most investors are loyal to him."

Nerea did some quick calculations. "What about Moe's shares? We can't get 2/3 without his shares."

Curly responded. "Aurora has established a potential blood heir from his Afghan birth family. We have not made contact, and we would like you to go and meet him." He took Moe's striped blanket from his shoulder and handed it to Nerea. "If he proves to be a good person, with the heart of his cousin, I want you to offer him this gift."

Clara continued: "We should have the support of the early employee-owners, but convincing investors to join will be difficult."

Nerea looked at the paper. With early employees, they would control 48.9% of the vote. Moe's heir would bring them to 63.9%. She would need to convince three of five investors to reach 66.9% and a 2/3 majority.

The dancing fire warmed her feet, but she knew its comforting flame would soon die. She was being asked to undo her mother's greatest mistakes. Disparity and misery were now her burdens to bear.

It was impossible.

Nerea felt small.

Chapter 11

17/04/2226 – The Despair Experience

Anxiety for tomorrow and shame for yesterday consume the precious minutes of far too many todays.

The immensity of Nerea's challenge paralyzed her trembling movements. Stress grew in her gut, and no amount of vomiting helped. Days rolled by in a haze. Despondent anguish filled her body and replaced all of her drive with gloom. Getting out of bed was almost insurmountable. How could she even begin?

She needed help.

Nerea pushed herself to a day-pod and traveled to Seren. The door opened before she could ring the bell. Lilac and lemon. They hugged, and she collapsed in Seren's arms. "I can't possibly do what they are asking; it's futile."

Seren smiled. "Come with me for a jog. It is a beautiful day, and sometimes fresh air is the best place to find hope."

When they started, Nerea could only manage baby pace, but each stride hurt a little less. By the time they reached the dirt pathway, her step had grown a fraction of a millimeter longer and left a tiny opening. It was comforting to have Seren by her side. They looped around the lake with the soft sounds of feet, breathing, trees and ducks. Seren was right; exercise was vital for the mind. After a shower and a light snack, they went to the garden for a coffee.

"There is no uniquely perfect path forward, and you may not succeed, but you need to try. You have spent a lifetime dealing with the crippling distance from your mother. Now she has asked you to resolve some of Waldon's biggest challenges; problems she created. Your inherited burden is tied to your strained relationship. If you want to improve this world, you must shed the invisible weights of your past and your future. You must open yourself up to the people you will meet and learn to live in the present. It is the only way to achieve what you have been asked to do—one small step at a time. It may also be the only way you can survive."

"How? I'm alone. I've always been alone."

"You are not alone. You have me. And opening your heart will ensure you are never alone. Listen and allow others to get close. Some already share the weights you carry. The other Waldon employees have lived through a lot, and I am sure they will give you strength."

Seren was right. They, too, must be feeling the weight of their past and the uncertain future. It was time to visit Waldon. Nerea returned to her pod for an accelerated journey across the U.S. border and to the Waldon offices. In a world where hours no longer mattered, Nerea saw profound irony in the speed of travel and the masses of time saved. The challenge was not to find time, but to spend it usefully.

The last leg of her trip was familiar. An iron-flower gate opened to the overgrown lane that both Curly and Yves had taken on their arrivals to Waldon.

As she rolled through the forest, she looked around for deer and felt Yves' butterflies. Through the trees, there was a glimmer of light reflecting off of the glass. As she passed under the last branches, the Cube seemed to grow out of the ground. It was somehow much bigger with her own eyes. Her grandfathers had built the giant, glass atrium with her father and it was astonishing.

Nerea stepped cautiously towards the Waldon entrance, and Curly strolled outside to greet her. "You look tired. Are you up for meeting the others? Or do you prefer to wait?"

It was time to dance. "Let's go."

"Follow me!"

After touring the indoor garden, Curly took Nerea to each of the people living and working there. They were family, and Nerea could see he was excited to introduce them. Their warmth was genuine, and they smiled and shared tears when they learned that Yves was her father. Over the next hours and days, she spent time with each of the early employee shareholders to get to know them.

She sat with Evelyn for a coffee and learned of her partner's struggles with simulation addiction. Cece shared Nerea's passion for climbing, and Marc told silly stories of dressing up as an Elvis impersonator on the weekends. Jon's nickname was Mike, and Mike's nickname was Pistachio. Alison was born Samuel, and Martin was born Stephanie, and they had fallen in love and married each other years ago.

Curly smiled and asked, "Do you want to meet Aurora?"

"Of course!"

They took an elevator deep underground. The doors opened, and Nerea's jaw dropped. The entire layer under the Cube was cold and stacked with endless rows of servers and quantum computers. The amount of computing power was unfathomable!

Curly beamed. "This is where my daughter lives. Aurora, say hello to Nerea."

A child's voice spoke through hidden speakers. It sounded like she was everywhere. "Hello, Nerea. It is nice to meet you."

Nerea was amazed. "Hello, Aurora. This room is unbelievable! How big are you?"

"I have 780 yottabytes of storage and 30 zettatrits for probability calculations. I can print more capacity as required and have robots for any repairs."

Curly smiled with pride. "We also leverage external data and computing if required, but distance becomes a limitation when doing the calculations we run. Aurora is an important part of Waldon. Our Artificial Intelligence license is a unique and fortunate heritage that the government has left untouched. Strict laws now prevent the creation and utilization of A.I.; the risks are too great. Malicious A.I. code could quickly develop non-programmed objectives, incomprehensibly efficient languages and non-standard storage methods, or replicate and decentralize itself. But Aurora is more than an A.I.; she's part of the Waldon family. She's discreet and has earned the trust and love of the whole team. You can ask her for help whenever you need it."

Aurora confirmed with enthusiasm: "I am delighted to support you in every way I can. Your journey is important for us all. Curly told me you will become our new boss, and I look forward to you taking over."

"There's still time before that happens; but thank you."

"I will be ready when you are."

The rest of the team shared hardships, memories, dreams and regrets. The stories Nerea loved most were from the early days of Waldon. Clara was the brains of the company, Curly and Moe were the hard-working hands, and Yves was the heart.

Many shared stories of Yves and described him as kind, a great listener and an occasional womanizer. Every girlfriend had a nickname. Jessie and Charles re-told one of the more famous tales: "One day, Yves went on a date with an attractive woman who told him she owned a see-through retail store. He became giddy with excitement and obsessed with uncovering the enticing lingerie that a see-through retail owner would wear. As the evening wore on, it became clear she was the single most boring person he had ever met: a little judgmental and even a bit mean. Normally, Yves would have walked away, but he was fixated on discovering what she was wearing under her clothes. The night was painful, and she would not stop talking. Finally, she invited him back to her place for a drink, and that's when he asked: 'So what's it like working in see-through retail?' She looked at him funny and answered: 'Not see-through—seafood!'" Jessie started laughing. "Yves always kept us amused with his stories. I miss him, dearly."

Fred, Myer and Conroy shared funny stories of 'The Curly and Moe Show'—the interactions between the two were legendary. They were always trying to one-up one another.

Erika even offered to share a personal simulation from her job interview at Waldon. Nerea accepted.

~

26/01/2033 – The Surprise Experience

Erika was an anxious wreck. Her belly was shaky, and her legs were weak. She had never heard of Waldon and had not even applied for the job. This was her first interview since the breakdown, and her resumé was a gap-filled mess.

She needed the work and desperately hoped the people in front of her would be gentle and see her potential. The interview request had come only a few hours ago, and there was no time to prepare. Now, the broom closet called her, begging her to come ball-up like a hedgehog.

"Welcome! I'm Curly, and this is Moe."

"Hello, Erika," Moe spoke warmly and then went straight to the point. "How would you simulate the aging of DNA?"

Erika had been developing simulations before her breakdown but had done nothing recently. Science had evolved and she felt out of touch. "I did some work years ago, but I was not able to develop a working model. And then…" her voice trailed off. Tears were close.

Moe continued in an emotionless tone. "We know: your mother was killed in a robbery. Sorry for that, but Curly's brother killed his mom and then committed suicide; he found a way to move on."

Curly interjected. "Moe's birth mother was shot for bringing her daughter to school. But you still have some family, so be thankful. How far were you from completing your work?"

Erika was petrified and immediately concerned for the two in front of her. "I think not far… wait, and the rest of your family? Are they okay?" She instantly regretted the question, but it popped out. She was messing the interview up badly.

Moe spoke calmly. "Curly's father overdosed, and his grandmother took care of him but died when he was in high school."

Curly smiled at his friend. "Big deal. Moe's birth father was shot in front of him as a child, two weeks before his two brothers and sister were killed by a missile strike on their apartment complex. And his adopted father died last year."

Moe smiled back. "Curly had to brush his teeth with soap for months because he couldn't afford toothpaste."

Erika shook her head in dismay as Curly smiled with his friend and continued. "Moe survived in five different refugee camps by selling some of his food and toiletries to others."

Moe's smile faded and he turned to Erika. "Life is not meant to be easy, and none of us will ever be perfect."

"Everyone in this company is a bit messed up. We're all damaged."

"It's what makes us work well together. If you think we're broken, wait till you meet our CEO."

Curly continued. "We know about your background. We know about your breakdowns. You're not alone. We care about changing the world. Euphemia recommended you to us, and we trust our people. The work you were doing may help us resolve some problems we're having, so if you want a job, it's yours."

"Our question is: how quickly could you pick up where you left off?"

Erika's mouth opened in dumbfounded awe. A jolt of joy twitched through her body. A giant breath filled her with life, like helium lifting a withered and deflated soul.

~

Nerea woke from the simulation with Erika holding her hand.

"The people of Waldon are my family. I like you a lot, and it looks like you are now part of our family. Welcome."

The employees had diverse views on the investors, but there was always a clear 'us' and 'them' in their stories.

Discussions of her mother were more delicate. Brad and Emily talked of her as a mystical figure who made impossible things happen. Glendon and Jill spoke in awe of her fortitude during the release; Clara was bombarded with severe judgment from every direction and never made an excuse or passed blame on to others. Sylvain spoke of the aftermath: "When the wars and violence subsided, your mother crawled into a shell. She's our leader, and it's been like living with an invisible and silent goddess. When she disappeared to have you, we barely even noticed, but her strength and morals remain present in every decision we make. We love her for that."

The teams were authentic people with good hearts; Nerea appreciated meeting each of them.

She could count on the 19 early employee shareholders and their 1.9% of votes.

Chapter 12

15/08/2226 – The Trust Experience

Nerea arrived mid-morning to Qurban's yurt home near Bamyan, Afghanistan. She brought news that would make him one of the wealthiest people on the planet.

The mountains and valleys along the Silk Road were of beauty and isolation that Nerea had never imagined. The pavement was recent, but the paths were steeped in thousands of years of trade between the Roman Empire and China. They had been used by Arabs, Turks, Indians, Persians, Somalis, Greeks, Syrians, Georgians, Armenians, Bactrians and Sogdians. Conquests and wars had decimated communities and left a complex network of tribes, power, cultures and religions.

When Qurban was born, a woman could be stoned to death for visiting a strange man unescorted. Today, Nerea knocked loudly. "Hello?"

A beautiful man with kind, weighted eyes opened the door and greeted her in English. "Good morning. Can I help you?"

The Bamyan people were primarily of the Hazara tribe; Shi'a Muslims in a majority Sunni country. However, there were also some Sunni Muslims in the tribe; Waldon's Moe had come from one such family. Moe's cousin and potential heir was an elder named Qurban Rahimi.

"My name is Nerea. I've come a long way to speak with you. Do you have some time?"

"Time is the one thing that I can give most freely. Come in." His voice was tired and resigned. Qurban appeared to have taken the red pill in his mid-forties.

A wood stove burned at the side of the single room dwelling. Qurban invited her to sit on a simple rug beside the window. Nerea admired the endless snow-capped mountains and listened to a stream chattering nearby. Qurban poured two cups of tea and sat cross-legged across from Nerea. He sipped from his cup, content to wait quietly for her to begin. She cut through small talk and opened herself. "I'm with Waldon."

Her host turned and stared wistfully to the window. Nerea sat motionless under the tension as Qurban took long, silent breaths. Would he ask her to leave? Did he already hate her? He looked to her with suspicion, and Nerea wondered if her voyage was all for naught. Then: he nodded his head and grinned with renewed warmth. "I welcome you humbly into my home. What would you like to discuss?"

Relief! "I am interested in your views and ideas. What do you think about the world today?"

Qurban closed his eyes. "My home is my world, and Bamyan is better than it has ever been; but when I look to the outside, I see influences that could bring suffering back to my people. This worries me."

Nerea surveyed the room. "You have had a lot of success in your life. Your home is beautiful, but why do you choose to live so modestly?"

"I have simple needs and few visitors. I have lived for so long that even I get tired of hearing my own stories. Holding wealth brings no joy. Zakat brings fulfillment."

"Zakat?"

His shoulders straightened, and there was a glimmer in his eye. "Four pillars of Islam are typical of many religions: faith, prayer, pilgrimage and Ramadan fasting. For me, it is our fifth pillar, Zakat, that is at the heart of much that is good in our faith. Zakat is charity or giving that can be interpreted as a mandated redistribution of wealth."

Nerea smiled. None of the Waldon investors practiced Zakat in line with their wealth. "I am embarrassed by how little I know of your region and culture. What happened when the Waldon pills arrived here?"

"Many foreigners assumed that our people would reject Waldon's science. They forget about the Islamic Golden Age, a time of poetry, and one of the richest periods in human development. It was a time when Hasan Ibn al-Haytham, the Physicist, proposed the scientific method and Al-Jahiz developed the theory of natural selection. When Waldon brought the pills to the world, the science was rapidly accepted by governments and people throughout the Muslim world.

"Religious leaders also approved. The Qur'an teaches, 'Whosoever saves the life of one person, it would be as if he saved the life of all mankind.' Preventing death and saving a life were considered the same. Some faithful Muslims took the red pill to avoid death and have time to perform more good deeds. This would secure entry into Paradise on the Day of Judgement.

"Over time, devout Muslims encountered a new problem: taking the green pill after a period of stopped aging was likened to suicide. This is one of the greatest sins and utterly detrimental to one's spiritual journey. A verse in the Qur'an instructs, 'And do not kill yourselves, surely God is most merciful to you.'

"A new balance was established as many Muslims stopped taking the red pill and observed God's initial intentions. Families grew, and Afghans built safe and healthy lives full of dancing, storytelling, children and feasts. A happiness settled that contrasted global hardship surrounding us."

Nerea had observed many smiles in Kabul and along the 200-kilometer journey to Bamyan, but she did not see joy in his eyes. "Are you happy?"

"Those of us who took the red pill in the early years are now trapped. We have lived through times of war and cancer in our religion, and our testimonies are respected as important messages of peace. But we are each condemned to watch those we love grow old and die."

Qurban took a saddened breath. "I already had my children when the pills came. There was so much rebuilding to do, and I wanted to see it through. I took the red pill, but my children were not so hasty: they had dreams of having their own children and took the green pills directly. Their children did the same, as did their children after that. I have now been present for eight generations of birth rites in my family." His gaze reached deep in Nerea's eye. "I have also been present for six generations of funerals."

"That is terrible. Do you see a path to your happiness?"

"No. Happiness has two ingredients: purpose and connection, but they don't blend well over time. I now understand that purpose needs a challenge, which requires an opponent. The enemy I knew is now long gone, and age has taught me that enemies are simply friends who have not yet listened to each other. As we connect to others, the absolute truth that emerges can tear apart our purpose. It scoops out our core and leaves emptiness. It is the great irony of connection. So, while joy can come with ignorance, ignorance is for the young. I see no worldly path to my own happiness."

"You have no enemies?"

"I have an enemy, but she is not a person. My enemy is time itself. She is an enemy I cannot conquer, for she moves at her own speed, regardless of my actions. There is no happiness to be found by trying to out-live time. True happiness will be found in death."

"Do you regret your Decision?"

"I am grateful to Allah for the life that he has granted me. I am grateful to Allah for allowing the science that brought Waldon to the world. I am grateful to Allah for allowing me to remember and share the devastation that hatred can cause. I accept the rest as Allah's will."

"Devastation?"

"In my time, forgotten souls stood up against a tyranny that poisoned our society. Many innocent people were killed senselessly; and their acts of heroism will never be recorded. But Allah was a witness. Those souls now rest in eternal bliss, waiting for the Day of Judgement. And I stay here on Earth to keep their physical memory alive."

Qurban paused and looked to Nerea. "Where are you from?"

Nerea was still uncomfortable sharing hidden parts of herself. She fought against inner defenses and found the courage to answer honestly: "I was born and raised on a small island in Canada, and my Waldon office is in the States."

Qurban perked up. "Canada! I once had a friend from Canada——an Army Major. And my cousin moved there many years ago." He looked out the window to the mountains. "It sounded beautiful, with beautiful people."

Nerea liked the idea of Qurban joining the Waldon board of directors. His reflective spirituality was exactly what they needed. "Was your Canadian friend from the war?"

"Yes. It was a terrible time: much of my family died. I picked up a gun at 13 and fought against the Taliban. They were ruthless and terrifying. One day, I tried to protect my young cousin—a child—and I shot quicker than I should have. I thought it was the Taliban, but it was Canadians arriving to help. Thankfully, I was a terrible shot at 13. I missed, and the soldier was forgiving. He took me to his leader, and Major Kenny MacLennan told me of a family back in Canada that could care for my infant cousin. Mohammed had nobody left; they were all dead, and I was far too young. I sent him with the soldier and continued my fight." Qurban looked to the mountains.

"Do you know what became of your cousin?"

"No. Rebuilding our country took all of my time, and after the pills came, communication became impossible. I'm certain he found a good home."

"He did. Your cousin studied with my mother. The two of them were the key architects of the pills and founded Waldon with a few others."

Qurban's eyes opened wide. "Mohammed is still alive?"

There was a tug in her throat. "No. He died many years ago." She reached into her backpack and pulled out Moe's striped blanket. "His adoptive family made this for him. When he died, he left it to his best friend, who sent me to find you. Curly wanted me to give this to you as a gift. It was handmade by his adoptive father and filled with the spirit and love of Mohammed; it's part of the family of Waldon." Nerea stood and draped the blanket around Qurban's shoulders. "Curly wants to thank you for the beautiful soul that your blood gave to the world."

Qurban closed his eyes. Nerea could see he knew death well. "Did Mohammed receive proper preparation and burial?"

"I don't know, but I'll find out. It was long before I was born. You also need to know that Mohammed's shares were placed in a trust. We believe you're the rightful heir."

Qurban shook his head. "Please give that money to those in need. It should be distributed back to the communities from which it came."

Nerea smiled. "I think Moe would like that. His equity is locked in Waldon accounts, and we'll need board authorization to release it. But there's a bigger problem: his shares are voting shares. The time is coming when we'll need his vote to make changes to Waldon. The world needs us to change, and I believe that you're the right person to join the Waldon board and provide guidance. Qurban, will you please come and join Waldon?"

He paused for a long moment and could not hide a growing smile. "I have only my beliefs, my hands and my heart to give, but if you need my help, I will give it."

"Thank you."

Qurban glowed. Nerea had not asked how he would vote or what he would vote for, but she did not need to. She knew with certainty that Qurban would vote for any proposal that improved the condition of his fellow man and against anything that worsened inequality.

She now had 63.9% of votes. Securing the support of three investors would be much more difficult.

Chapter 13

15/09/2226 – The Delight Experience

Nerea did not want to leave. The months of talks and hikes and laughter with Qurban had opened her spirit. But winter was approaching, and it was time for the journey to Yingtai.

Travel from Bamyan to Chengdu through the northern plateaus of the Himalayas was nearly impossible in former times. With glacial retreat and political stability, decent roads had opened for local trade and wealthy wanderers. Her father had spent many years in the region, and Nerea easily connected to his passion for the magnificent landscape.

She travelled north for Dushanbe in Tajikistan, then northeast through Kyrgyzstan and finally southeast through Lhasa, Tibet and on to Chengdu; almost seven thousand kilometers of slow, breathtaking conditions.

Nerea grew up believing tyranny was everywhere, but people did not appear angry, nor oppressed—they looked tired. Many seemed resigned to their routines and weighted by the future; without hope, they were locked in a cycle of desperation and pointlessness. Others seemed to ignore the numb and stumbled around with ignorant smiles. Families with children bickered and hustled out of the way as she approached. Something was missing.

On each pod, in each town and at each hostel, she took time to meet locals and merchants trying to survive. Nerea initiated small talk and tried to learn about families, lives and Decisions. They were happy to talk of the road, the weather and the scenery, but each skillfully avoided questions that got personal. Family, eternal life and age hid secrets they did not want to share, and the intriguing people remained impossibly distant. How had her father built rapport with hearts and minds in the region?

Then she met Tào. The glowing young woman carried a basket of silk scarves and sat beside Nerea on a bus-pod. There was a purity in her smile—as if she had unlocked secrets and figured things out. She was reserved, intrigued by Nerea and kind.

"Where does your name come from?"

"Tào means peaches in Mandarin."

She could see Tào was proud of her name. Nerea decided to open up and share a piece of herself. "My grandfather Louis came to China a long time ago and learned the story of the peach tree of immortality." Nerea told details of Eva and the dinner and the cobbler—memories she thought she would hold eternally for herself.

Tào was impressed that Nerea knew of her country; most cultures kept to themselves. "Your family sounds warm. You must be close."

"They died long before I was born." Nerea's voice cracked as she answered, and Tào offered genuine empathy. It was nice to share.

Over the next hours and days, Nerea told Tào tales of her youth, her grandparents and her father. It was liberating. Tào opened her caged childhood and shared its rawness in a whisper. She released sad stories of learning her craft as a child and needing to leave her home. "I am from a village north of Beijing, but came to the mountains many years ago in order to escape.

Both had absent fathers and difficult mothers. They became friends.

On their fifth morning together, they departed long before sunrise from Ngari. The pair sat across from a beautiful, old lady sleeping on two chairs. Nerea observed her deep-set wrinkles and knew she must have earned every one. The rest of the pod was almost empty.

The early wake-up had begun to catch up with Nerea. She shared a yawn with Tào; but the stunning scenery kept them awake. The Tibetan landscape evolved from cliffs, to switchback curves up a mountainside, to a long straightaway of blue-grey mountain desert. The window was cracked open and a cold whisper of air whisked across her cheek.

It was at this moment that the sun peeked out from behind a distant valley and painted the barren desert in radiant pinks, oranges and reds. Boulders cast long, purple stripes across the wakening canvas. Power and wonder flowed into her body as she embraced the mystical forces that brought life to this most inhospitable of places.

Tào took Nerea's hand and leaned on her shoulder; touch felt nice. The sun warmed their faces as Tào whispered to the glowing mountains: "God does exist."

As if the universe agreed, it was at this moment that the sleeping old lady let out a deep, screaming fart.

Tào did not miss a beat. "Amen."

Nerea could not stop a giggle from escaping; she covered her face and tried desperately not to wake the lady. Tào began to snicker. Nerea burst into a laugh that flowed uncontrollably from her belly. Tào covered her face and hunched over to hide explosions of snorts and roars. The old lady opened one eye and looked back with a stern stare. Nerea could not stop her shaking shoulders. The burning took over her stomach, and she could not contain herself.

Rolling giggles and muffled howls continued for an impossibly long time. Nerea knew the lady was trying to sleep and wanted desperately to give her peace, but the laugher was euphoric. Her chest heaved in joy-filled gasps for air.

Nerea and Tào looked out opposite windows to avoid eye contact. Eventually, there was a restored calm—for a few seconds—until the ridiculousness of the moment overcame Tào and she released a renewed spurt of laughter. That snapped Nerea's last barrier of control. She convulsed while trying to bury escaping poofs of glee into her sleeve.

Tears streamed down their faces. Nerea had never laughed like that before.

It was wonderful.

The morning rolled on, and the old lady moved to a quieter part of the pod. Nerea opened further to Tào. "It's new for me to share transparently and without judgment, and your sincerity is amazing. Thank you."

Tào reflected on her culture. "I have lived in Tibet for most of my life, yet I am still viewed as a foreigner. Even in Beijing, I was a stranger. I am proud of our nation: we are many, with a rich and complex history; but it is difficult to share amongst ourselves, not just with foreigners. We are wall-builders. We forged the greatest wall ever built, and each of us builds an inner wall to protect ourselves from judgment or consequence; it is survival. But our walls suffocate our curiosity, and I no longer recognize the joyous spirit of my childhood."

Nerea could relate to the walls. Before she went any further, she needed to share her dark secret: "I'm with Waldon." Tào's eyes widened, and Nerea continued: "I'm trying to understand the impact we have on people around the world. Changes are needed in the company, and anything you could share would be appreciated."

Tào looked to her basket and reflected quietly. Nerea allowed the silence to sit comfortably; there was no danger. Eventually, Tào spoke. "Waldon has brought heightened secrecy to our people. There is a great contrast between our individual need to grow and our collective need to contribute babies to the growth of our culture. There is guilt associated with the red pill, even if it is sanctioned, taxed and supported by the government. The black market of fake pills and forged documents mean that no one really knows who is on the red pill and who is not."

Tào looked Nerea in the eye. "My family would never have approved, but many years ago, I chose to take my red pill. It is a shame I carry, and I have not returned home in fifty years. I have never declared my Decision and have never paid my Life Tax. I hide it by traveling these backroads, have learned to avoid scanners, and if there are checkpoints, I often disguise myself as an old lady, or pretend to be pregnant. When I am discovered, the Penalty will be severe: I will be forced to take my green pill."

Tào pulled a scarf from her basket. It had a group of happy children playing in a circle around a large tree with red and green peaches hanging on branches. "The world is too beautiful and too big to live just one lifetime. I am thankful for what Waldon has brought to me. I don't know what you should change, but anything that could help our people rediscover the honesty we are born with would be appreciated." Tào handed the scarf to Nerea. "This is a gift for you and the people of Waldon. Thank you for giving us the pills. I trust that you will continue to make the best choices you can. We have an expression in Chinese: 'I will add oil for you.' It means that I am rooting for you. I believe in you."

Nerea was touched by the gesture; it was powerful and without judgment. "How could you possibly believe in me? I'm not sure that I believe in me. The stakes are too big."

"If we are going to grow, we need to each do our part and trust in others to do theirs. I will help you if I can, but we will get nowhere if we all try to do the same job. Confucius taught: 'Wishing to be established himself, one must seek also to establish others; wishing to be enlarged himself, one must seek also to enlarge others.'"

Nerea thought to her mother. Clara had spent a lifetime controlling the options and actions of others. She had never allowed trust. "How do you think Confucius would have viewed Waldon and the science we brought into the world?"

Tào paused for a long moment. "A principle virtue of Confucianism is Ren or Humaneness. It is pure altruism: the desire one feels to care for someone else's baby or the dying with nothing in return. Confucius considered Ren to be essential to becoming One with heaven. I believe Confucius would have struggled with postponing his journey to paradise, but he would have seized this gift of time and used it to rebuild the values and honesty that our culture has lost. He would have been thankful for Waldon, for each soul now has more time to improve our world. Choosing to help others over moving on to heaven is the greatest example of Ren that I can imagine."

"What do you think of heaven?"

"It puzzles me. Things are not perfect, but I do not understand what paradise could offer that is not better in life. Here we can learn and experience a mixture of everything that is good and everything that is bad. In heaven, all evil is banished, but what pleasure is there in infinite ecstasy? In heaven, all knowledge is fully connected, but what interest is there in knowing everything? If you knew the ending to every story ever written, would you find passion in reading? I will not pray to be delivered to a place that cannot be better than our home."

Nerea smiled. Tào was wonderful.

Over the next weeks, Nerea met dozens who likely shared similar backgrounds, but none were as open as Tào. In the remote Buddhist towns of Tibet, Nerea met philosophers, monks and listeners who gave abstract wisdom; but each protected themselves from openly sharing anything personal. While her lone friend was special, the people of this magnificent land remained a fascinating mystery.

Crisp, mighty waterways spilled from the mountains into the Min River near the industrial complex of Chengdu. The city was much larger than she had imagined. She stopped in front of building 888—the luckiest number on the street. It was a giant, black skyscraper with no signs or panels on the outside.

Nerea was about to meet her first investor.

The main entrance opened as she approached. Cameras watched her movements through the empty lobby. The elevator slid open, and Nerea walked inside the buttonless, mirrored box. The door hissed closed, and her belly sunk as the acceleration rocketed her into the building.

She had no idea how high she would travel.

The elevator stopped so quickly that she felt her organs float for a second. The door opened with a lightning-fast hiss, and a stern lady was standing a meter away. Nerea flinched backward and immediately regretted her rudeness. Yingtai was stocky with black pants, a red t-shirt and matching red lipstick—terrifying and magnetic.

"Hello, Nerea." There was not an ounce of welcome in her voice.

Yingtai led Nerea into an immense living space with a spectacular view over a park and the rest of the city. Money could buy beautiful things. "What do you want?"

There would be no pleasantries. "I plan to meet each of the investors to understand what you want for Waldon."

"You are here to manipulate me. Do you think that is going to work?"

Nerea began to panic, and her voice accelerated. "Waldon is broken, and we need to fix it. I want to know what you think is working and how you believe we should change." That was a much more direct approach than planned.

Yingtai held a slicing stare for ten, long seconds. "It is broken; but you are not the person to fix it. I do not know you, but I know your mother and can only assume that the peach does not fall far from the tree."

Nerea gasped and whispered: "Peach?"

Yingtai looked out the window and Nerea's muscles tensed under a wave of fear. She couldn't breathe. Was Tào in danger? Nerea had not even considered the extensive reach of Yingtai's power. How stupid could she be? The room echoed her lonely unpreparedness. Had Yingtai found and reported Tào to the government? Was she forced to take her green pill? Nerea's frozen expression betrayed her naked terror.

"You look nervous."

Nerea looked to the floor and whispered. "Is Tào okay?"

Yingtai allowed the panic to wallow and stared coldly over the massive cityscape. Silence seized full control of the visit and its deafening quiet was suffocating. Nerea's knees could barely hold her weight, and she braced for a collapse to the floor. Then Yingtai spoke: "I like your friend. She is a kind person, and she likes you."

Yingtai relaxed her brow, sat on a chair and bit her lip. "I knew your father well. He visited me often in his travels." She invited Nerea to sit down. "I trusted him much more than I could ever trust your mother, and his death shook me. While I fully expected Clara to deceive us, I was really hurt by Yves' silence before Mathieu went to the simulator. He should have said something—at least to me."

"Why do you think they tried to trick you?"

The question jolted Yingtai. "Your mother believes that there is only one path forward, and it involves giving her complete control. She has never given an inch in any decision that affects the company. Discussion and compromise would be a better path. I am not blind to the squalor in the world. I do not care about our revenues; I have more than enough to live. I do not care about my empire; my money goes straight to the people I employ. I do not care about power; it has brought me two hundred years of loneliness. The reason I stay on Waldon's board is to ensure this gift to the world is not wasted. I will always vote with my heart, and I do not trust Clara—or you, by extension. Until she is dead, I will vote against your mother because Waldon needs balance in the moral direction of the company."

Nerea thought of Tào—fear of her family led to a hidden Decision, tax avoidance, and life on the lam. "But don't you see the pain we are causing? How can you support the brutal Penalty applied in some countries—in your country?"

"We are not the government. We cannot get into politics, or we give Waldon and your mother even more power." A saddened sparkle crossed Yingtai's eyes. "When you were born, I supported Curly's nomination as CEO because I like him. But Clara did not let go of power and uses her role as Chair of the Board to continue to run the company. I do not agree with the other investors on many topics, but we need to be united in front of Clara, because none of us trust your mother. I will never give her more power. That is my final word on this matter."

Her heart dropped. The divide with investors was profound, and it was clear Yingtai would never support their plan. Nerea conceded today's failure: "I understand. The paralysis of Waldon is strangely reassuring to everyone, because the consequences of real decisions are too grave."

Despite disappointment, Nerea was not sad. She liked the rock-hard woman in front of her and was no longer worried about the fate of Tào. Yingtai would not harm her friend. But one thing had surprised her: this was one of the wealthiest, most powerful people in the world. She should be happy, but she was not. "Are you lonely?"

Yingtai's gaze rose from the city to the sky. A barely audible whisper left her lips. "Yes."

Chapter 14

12/04/2227 – The Disgust Experience

Life will be better tomorrow? Bullshit.

Nerea wanted to believe that injustice was ultimately corrected, but travels had torn away this emotional crutch. Death's limit on suffering had been shattered, leaving empty futures in front of billions of hopeless souls. The eyes she passed focused on nothing at all. Depression and gloom fed on each other and polluted the human spirit.

Now, she sat cross-legged and angry as a rare guest to Arjun's Bharata Council. The simple pagoda was hidden deep in his garden oasis. Twelve places faced each other on a circular, hand-woven rug at the center of the temple.

Bharata was another name for India. The Council motto was 'devoted to light and knowledge against darkness.' Arjun had assembled the secret Council to provide spiritual guidance during Waldon's Indian release and relied on them to guide his votes. He claimed its voice was essential to the pursuit of meaning under Waldon's life extensions.

More bullshit. She hated the Council and its hypocrisy.

For six months, Nerea explored India to understand the impact of Waldon and the Council on its 36 states and territories. The mystical land was full of personalities and ideas that were richer, more diverse and far more complex than she had ever imagined. The time had only confirmed one definite truth: the Bharata Council had failed. Individuality had broken communities. Millions wallowed in thickening despair and could not pull themselves out. Hunger and jealousy pierced every encounter, while inequality invited excuses and paralysis. Dreams and religion had been long abandoned. 'God has given up on us.'

The impacts of the Decision were felt deep in the streets, shacks and spirit of India. No one had anything good to say about the pills, as Waldon had facilitated the reemergence of caste.

A door opened quietly. Council members strolled to predefined places around the rug. Each sat without speaking. Arjun entered last, and others bowed as he sat at the head of the group.

Ten members, Arjun and Nerea sat in a clock-like circle facing the center of the rug. They feigned moral leadership yet did nothing to prevent India's disparity. The room made her nauseous. The Bharata Council pretended to lead in the name of God but left Indians empty.

It was spiritual fraud.

Arjun opened the session. "I have come here humbly to ask each of you for guidance. Be honest with me, tell me if I am wrong, and challenge my ideas. I trust each of you. Together, we can chart a better path. Today, we welcome Nerea, daughter of Clara Woodruff. Curly has proposed her as future CEO of Waldon." He turned to Nerea and looked past her eyes. "It is nice to meet you, Nerea. Namaste." The smile and head-bow were blatantly just for show.

She bowed back. "Namaste. Thank you for your invitation." He was an awful person.

The Council reflected India's diversity. There were leaders from four vaguely separate denominations of Hinduism: a Vaishnava acharya, a Shaiva guru, a Shakti swami and a Smarta pujari. They were joined by an Islamic Imam; India's papal nuncio; a Buddhist nun from Ladakh; an atheist member of Parliament; a Nobel Prize-winning scientist and self-proclaimed Cold Deist; and a Sikh hero who had saved countless lives in the Waldon Riots.

Arjun called on the Shaivite to lead them in a twenty-minute meditation. Everyone closed their eyes and joined in the 108 mantra repetitions.

Nerea could not calm her mind. How could the men and women of this Council claim to represent good in the world, while ignoring the intense suffering that surrounded them?

They chanted slowly in deep voices. "Om namah shivaya . . . . . . Om namah shivaya . . . . . . Om namah shivaya . . . . . . Om namah shivaya . . . . . . Om namah shivaya . . . . . . Om namah shivaya . . . . . . Om namah shivaya . . . . . . Om namah shivaya . . . . . . Om namah shivaya . . . . . . Om namah shivaya . . . . . ."

Nerea knew this mantra: Om represented everything and was said to be the seed of all creation; Na represented earth; Ma—water; Shi—fire; Va—air; and Ya represented the sky.

Her mind tumbled in disdain. Indians were stuck. The gap between wealthy and poor had entrenched itself, and the Council had done nothing.

"Om namah shivaya . . . . . . Om namah shivaya . . . . . . Om namah shivaya . . . . . . Om namah shivaya . . . . . . Om namah shivaya . . . . . . Om namah shivaya"

There was more than enough money in India, but it helped so

few. The open hatred of the weak made Nerea sick. The rich looked down on those without wealth as sub-human. They took no time to connect and listen to the withered souls begging for help.

"Om namah shivaya . . . . . . Om namah shivaya . . . . . . Om namah shivaya . . . . . Om namah shivaya . . . . . . Om namah shivaya . . . . . . Om namah shivaya"

Nerea needed to clear this animosity from her mind. She was there to win their support. Hate would get her nowhere.

She had secured 63.9% of Waldon votes. Nerea needed to convince three of the remaining four investors to join her. Arjun's 1% vote might already be lost, but she needed to try.

"Om namah shivaya . . . . . . Om namah shivaya . . . . . . Om namah shivaya . . . . . . Om namah shivaya . . . . . . Om namah shivaya . . . . . . Om namah shivaya"

India had the largest population in the world, and its people had been establishing a healthy middle class when Waldon was released. The pills stopped everything. Those who had not already established themselves were doomed.

While everyone came from direct or ancestral poverty, the successful now believed that the poor must be lazy for not doing what they had so easily achieved. People with money oozed of boasts and bravado: 'I did this,' and 'I did that.' They forgot how they were helped by the economy of their time. Stories of individual triumph became accepted as truth, and lending a hand to others seemed to lessen their legends of self-worth.

"Om namah shivaya . . . . . . Om namah shivaya . . . . . . Om namah shivaya . . . . . . Om namah shivaya . . . . . . Om namah shivaya . . . . . . Om namah shivaya"

The helpers of India had disappeared. The Council had the

power and obligation to revive the helping spirit, but they had not done it.

They sat idle and ignored the plight of the weak.

"Om namah shivaya . . . . . . Om namah shivaya . . . . . . Om namah shivaya . . . . . . Om namah shivaya . . . . . . Om namah shivaya . . . . . . Om namah shivaya"

There was a long silence. Nerea wondered sarcastically: 'Maybe it's time to pray away the misery.'

Arjun opened his eyes and smiled to the circle: "Let us begin. How are things progressing?"

The person to his right began first. She was a plump politician with big eyes and a soft smile. "We need a lot more money to achieve what you are asking for. We have had some success: no one has been turned away from a hospital or clinic in eighteen consecutive months, and we are at a record low for unnecessary deaths. But our prevention and education plans are not delivering the measurable results we need."

Nerea was confused. People in the country were poor and hopeless, but she had not paid attention to the fact that they were relatively healthy.

Arjun shook his head. "I have no more money to give. It's all gone, and the Waldon revenues are shrinking." His focus shifted to Nerea. "That is not a request for more money—Waldon revenues flow from desperation, and the world certainly does not need more of that."

"You have no money?"

"I have a home and a vegetable garden and more than enough to live. I have always given away my Waldon earnings. We act in absolute discretion and have no desire to be rewarded or thanked. But today, Waldon does not generate enough revenue to finance the change our people need."

Her belly churned. Had she misjudged the Council?

Arjun looked to the representative of the Catholic Church. "How are the churches?"

"We struggle with demand, and our shelters overflow every single night." The others in the room nodded. "We are all at maximum capacity and continue to turn lost souls away to sleep in the streets. We pour all of our money into building more beds." Her voice saddened to a whisper. "…And yet, our masses and services are almost empty."

There was agreement around the rug. The Imam joined the reflection. "I had never imagined that the spirituality of our people was so closely tied to their mortality. We have removed death, and people no longer project themselves going to paradise. They have abandoned prayer in their daily lives."

The Vaishnava Hindu concurred. "And Vishnu is doing nothing to help them or turn their fortunes around." He looked desperate. "None of our gods are helping."

The scientist reacted softly in a sarcastic tone. "Don't look at me… I told you she wouldn't help." The room's tension released in a soft chuckle; Nerea was confused.

The Sikh whispered to her: "Cold Deists believed that God created the universe, but then left Earth alone after that." Nerea snickered at the joke awkwardly late, and the room rewarded her reaction with kind smiles.

Arjun intervened. "When we created this Council, we made a commitment to each other: we vowed to quietly give everything we have to help the less fortunate escape the new hardships that Waldon would enable. We agreed to equally support those who chose to take the red pill and those who chose to take the green pill." He turned to Nerea. "And today, we are desperate."

Nerea looked into each pair of eyes and felt their panic. "What can Waldon do to help the people of India?"

The room shook their heads until the Sikh spoke. "We have ensured that our people have the freedom to make the Decision. Our laws and places of worship respect that, and Waldon has played its role. But the suffering is hopelessness that comes from no prospect of economic success or a brighter future. This must be fixed by the people of India, not by Waldon."

Nerea responded. "But we have a role to play. We're too powerful to stay silent."

The Bhikkhunī looked to her fellow Council members. "Perhaps discretion no longer makes sense. If Waldon offered visible help to the poor, then maybe others would emulate and stand with us. If we made our Council public, perhaps the people of Bharata would recall their connection to all other beings. We could ignite a wave of help for our brothers and sisters. In America, there was a man who would see scary things in the news as a boy, and his mother would tell him, 'Look for the helpers. You will always find people who are helping.' Imagine if the most influential company in the world became a helper. It just may be the spark that lights the fire of collective happiness."

The Smarta Hindu jumped on the idea. "We may not need many new helpers to begin a tsunami of change. Gods will help us once we have helped ourselves."

Everyone took a moment to reflect on the suggestion.

The leader who had not yet participated spoke to Nerea. "In Shaktism, we believe that Goddesses are the supreme, ultimate, eternal reality of all existence. When your mother released Waldon to the world, we believed in her feminine power and leadership, and followed her choices. But she did not bring life energy to the world; she only removed the darkness of death. You are different from your mother, I sense it."

Nerea shook her head and humbly looked to Arjun. "No. I have no idea what I am doing. I misjudged you all. Your mission is important, and I am impressed by the approach you have taken. As CEO, I will support you in any way I can."

Arjun's stare softened, and he gazed around the rug. "I am the son of a Jain mother and a Zoroastrian father, and have never pretended to have all the answers. I have sought your advice and ideas as I listen to those with no voice. My ears have been sharp and my arms have been strong, but perhaps my tongue's silence has hindered our success. I will reflect on your council: it may soon be time to take our voices public."

The group nodded in unison.

Arjun turned to Nerea. "Do you know why there are 12 places at this Council rug, but only 11 of us?"

Nerea shook her head. "No."

"Your father chose me for Waldon, and he helped me create this Council. You are seated where he used to sit. I trusted Yves' views and valued his guidance. He had the biggest heart I have ever encountered, and you remind me of him." He paused for a moment before quietly committing himself to Nerea. "If you lead with heart and strive to help the weakest and poorest amongst us, my vote will follow you."

Nerea smiled. "Thank you."

Chapter 15

30/06/2227 – The Optimism Experience

'Even the dead enjoy a good party.'—Malagasy Proverb

Tanaka invited Nerea to join her family for Famadihana—the 'turning of the bones.'

The ceremony took place once every five to seven years at her family tomb in Madagascar's central highlands. The precise date, time and duration of the celebration were determined by Tanaka through a dream. And now, the dead were ready to dance.

Tanaka bounced to Nerea with outstretched arms. "Welcome! I am so happy you could come!" The giant hug was organic and natural; Nerea enjoyed opening herself to its warmth. Tanaka exuded a joyous aura and energy.

Nerea fell immediately in love with her. "It's wonderful to meet you! Curly and the team asked me to pass on their greetings." Everyone at Waldon was in love with Tanaka.

"Your father brought together an amazing group of people. I love them all, but Yves was one of my favorite people in the world. I enjoyed his visits. Ohhhhh, that man could dance!"

Nerea laughed and understood why her father liked her. Since arriving on the island, every Malagash person she encountered had made her feel welcome. Nerea immediately wanted to move to this beautiful island full of canopy jungles, sandstone caves, beaches, lemurs and joy. The people considered Tanaka a hero and were proud that one of them was part of building Waldon's success. She was one of the three investors who had revealed their identity and involvement in the company. Tanaka insisted that Waldon's pills be free for everyone in Mada and donated significant portions of her dividends to fund hospitals and infrastructure throughout the country.

For the first time since her Decision, Nerea did not feel shame for her connection to Waldon.

She scanned the massive compound. "How many people live here?"

Tanaka's smile grew. "No one lives here. This is the home of the dead, and we are their guests. The bedrooms and guest houses are used only during funerals and to celebrate the dead. We are now in my favorite corner of my family's faritra."

Tanaka took Nerea and walked her arm-in-arm towards the music and dancing surrounding the tombs. "Everyone looks so happy."

Tanaka nodded. "Sadness is allowed, but rare. This is a celebration. Life exists through six elements: being, body, breath, parallel universes, sacredness and spirit; it is our spirit that makes us different from other animals. We do not subscribe to a traditional notion of heaven and hell, but believe the dead will one day journey to a second life that resembles our first. This is why you will see objects of wealth in the tombs—so they can bring them when they are ready."

Across the dusty hillside, there were dozens of concrete huts covered with spectacular paintings and adorned with floral reefs. These were tombs. Nerea imagined the simple structures were entrances that descended to underground chambers. It was disrespectful to point at the dead, so Nerea gestured towards a wall with a bent finger. "What do those paintings represent?"

"The zebu represents wealth, and the warriors represent strength. We want these places to be beautiful. Tombs are waiting rooms between life and death. Spirits remain in the body until our corpse is fully decomposed. It is important that the dead appreciate this time and see us celebrating their lives."

"How many dead are here?"

Tanaka laughed. "I have no idea. When I built this complex, I brought everyone from my family tombs, and it has continued to fill up over the centuries. For the most part, Malgache choose the green pill, so my family continues to grow, and the party gets bigger every time we come."

There were hundreds of stunningly dressed people telling stories, dancing, drinking, singing and playing instruments. The bounce flowed through Tanaka's hand and wiggled through Nerea's body as they made their way through the crowd. Tanaka sprung with playfulness as she swayed and popped with the rhythm. Her powerful voice soon joined the traditional Malagasy songs.

She had never seen such cheer, delight and laughter in one place. It was jubilance and the most extraordinary event she had ever witnessed. As the song came to an end, Tanaka stood beside the door of one of the largest tombs and raised her hands. A hush grew, and people gathered close. She spoke powerfully in Malgache and lifted a bottle of rum over her head. A group came forward with piles of new, colorful floor mats. Tanaka poured the liquid on top of the tomb and opened the door. The group entered in single file.

A young boy beside Nerea offered an explanation: "They will roll each of the dead in a new mat. Then, they are ready to dance."

There was an excited murmur while descendants waited to be joined by their foremothers and forefathers. After ten minutes, two exited the tomb with a visibly heavier rug rolled over their shoulders—a dead body was hidden inside. Silence rippled through the crowd as they eagerly listened for the name announcement: "Adija!" Everyone rejoiced! A vako-drazana music troupe set a beat and burst into song. The straw-hat group wore matching floral dresses and shirts, and the two carpet bearers began bouncing their rolled-up relative to the new rhythm. Colorful dances quickly pulsated in every direction across the hillside.

The Dance of the Dead had begun.

As each ancestor came out of the tomb, a hush fell, a name was called, and the dead joined the party. Bodies crowd-surfed over descendants parading through the grounds.

Nerea huddled with a gathering around Adija, who now lay on the ground. Her mat was carefully unrolled, revealing a corpse shrouded in silk sheets. Close family whispered loving prayers and well wishes for her journey. A girl whom Nerea guessed was a granddaughter, took a fresh silk sheet and proceeded to wrap Adija in an additional layer. She stopped, tucked a pint of rum in the wrapping and continued. Adija was rolled back into the mat and resumed her dance.

Tanaka surprised Nerea from behind, took her hand and gestured back to the tomb. "Do you want to see inside?" Nerea nodded and was led into the hallway of the dark, candle-lit hut. She ducked her head and descended a set of stairs into the cooled underground. As her eyes adjusted to the dark, she discovered beautiful paintings covering the walls of a large space filled with rows of empty, multi-layered bunkbeds. "This tomb holds my closest family, and if I ever die, this is where I will rest."

The cold silence contrasted muffled shouts of joy coming from outside. Nerea pondered empty beds around the darkened room and loved that the dead were out for a stroll. But some rolled sheets remained in a dimly lit corner bed. Was it a relative? She turned to Tanaka and nodded to the corner. "Are those just sheets, or is that a corpse?"

Tanaka's eyes grew wide in horror. "Oh, nooo! We forgot Grandpapa!"

Nerea tried to console Tanaka. "Maybe Grandpapa didn't want to dance?" Whoops. She should not have said that.

A shocked grin overcame Tanaka, and she turned to the corner to offer an apology: "I am sorry, Dadabe." Her voice cracked. Nerea looked away as Tanaka's lips broke into an inappropriate smile. The pair exploded in an uncontrolled giggle and hustled outside to allow the tomb the peace it deserved.

Grandpapa would dance another day.

The parades and party continued as bodies were danced throughout the grounds. Tanaka and Nerea walked to a quiet area on the hill overlooking the festivities.

"Are you excited to begin your journey as CEO?"

Nerea reflected for a moment. For the first time since her Decision, she was confident in the way forward. "I'm honored and hope my nomination is confirmed. The weight is big. Many changes are needed, but I'm happy that there are good people like you on the Board. Together, we'll succeed."

Tanaka smiled. "What do you want to change?"

Nerea was transparent. "Waldon is the root of many of the problems I've seen in my travels. Madagascar is a rare place where people have found true happiness. From the beginning, you ensured that Mada would be free from the Life Tax. That was courageous, and I believe it has proven to be the right decision. People live if they choose, age if they choose and seem removed from the economic challenges and hopelessness that I see elsewhere. Much of your money flows back to your people. If I were to change things at Waldon, it would be to help the rest of the world become more like Madagascar. I hope you'll join me, as every vote will be critical for us to do anything."

Tanaka's smile softened into a blank stare, and she watched vaguely over the party below. "I love my life. A lot. I love what I can give to the people of Mada. I love the respect and power I have earned. Life Taxes in the rest of the world pay for my people to live a life full of choice." She turned and stared aggressively into Nerea's eye. "I am happy, have a perfect life and like things just as they are." She put both hands on Nerea's shoulders, and the tips of her fingers gripped a little too hard. "To be clear: I will never vote for the changes you speak of." Her face softened, smile returned, and she pulled Nerea in for a hug. "Now, I need to get back to my family."

Tanaka danced away, merrily.

Nerea stood stunned and alone.

Chapter 16

05/03/2228 – The Disbelief Experience

Nerea waited in Afonso's Amazonian palace and anxiously contemplated the bronze plaque on his desk.

'Não existe gente feia, existe gente pobre.'

She knew its translation: 'There are no ugly people; only poor people.' Before arriving in Brazil, she would have assumed that such a superficial judgment would offend its devoutly Catholic population. But Brazilians were not like the rest of the world. In Rio, she saw priests leading Carnival floats packed with half-naked men and women drinking, gyrating and bouncing seductively. Everyone dripped of sexiness, and believers needed God to be part of the fun. Nerea arrived to the celebration insecure, but each and every pair of ravishing eyes invited her to open up and dance.

Brazilians had taken the red pill en masse to stay young and look their absolute best. Surgery, exercise and unrelenting grooming produced a sensual and stunning population, and Carnival was the ultimate celebration of their purpose.

Carnival was unstoppable fun—until it was over.

The hangover lasted for weeks. Streets remained littered in broken bottles and streamers. Depression swallowed entire cities. Many blamed the emptiness on the face of Waldon—Afonso. Millions relapsed into digital lives and sought to recapture the party in simulations.

Despite the gloom and recent failure with Tanaka, Nerea never lost hope. She needed to believe her journey was a predetermined legend written long ago. The stakes were too high to be random; the idea of failure was so tragic that destiny could not allow it.

The sign on Afonso's desk was a perfect representation of the man she had imagined: placing value on beauty and wealth. He controlled his empire from this remote, heavily guarded paradise. He loved his power and often boasted to the other Waldon investors of the wonderful life he had built.

She stared past the sign in a daydream when a booming, suave voice entered the office. "Hello, Nerea. Welcome to my home." Afonso's double-kiss and smile were layered with mistrust; he did not want her visit.

"Hello, Afonso."

"Sorry for the delay. I pushed myself a bit harder at the gym today." He admired his own outstretched arm, and Nerea acknowledged he was fit. Afonso had an innocent sexiness normally reserved for those unaware of their own beauty. He picked up the plaque that had caught Nerea's attention. "Why do you think I keep this on my desk?"

Nerea reconsidered the sign, searching for a positive twist in its meaning. "Beauty is a sign of well-being. Maybe it is a reminder to take care of yourself and celebrate your success."

Afonso smiled. "I like your answer. Many guests see it as a

superficial judgment of the poor and the ugly. Looking our best makes each of us feel better, but there is another layer to this sign." He paused and let Nerea reflect for a moment. "Have you seen a lot of poor people here?"

Nerea considered her experiences. "No."

"This sign is my reminder to ensure that every single citizen of this country has a job and money to look and feel their best." Afonso gazed out the window. "Your father understood that, and it is why he gave me this sign. I make sure that the poorest among us still have enough money to look good. I liked him. He somehow made philosophy less pretentious and brought the reflections of great thinkers to the Waldon board."

Nerea was happy to learn that he respected her father. "Why did they ask you to join?"

Afonso laughed softly. "I will never forget when Yves came into this office to ask for a billion dollars. I almost threw him out as a snake-oil salesman, but he charmed me quickly—he was open and honest and made everyone feel better. There were a lot of billionaires, but they chose me. After Dimitri, all investors were selected based on a strict moral code that your father set. Based on my reputation, he believed I would never lose focus on the best interests of my people. And for a long time, he was right." His voice trailed off before looking to Nerea. "Your father was a good man, and once upon a time, he saw good in me."

Nerea felt sadness in Afonso: "I used to believe in good and bad, but now I see shades of grey in us all. One version of good is perceived as evil by others. I know my mother sees her Waldon actions as altruistic, but so many suffer for decisions she has made."

Afonso nodded. "It is good that you see your mother's flaws. I am a trillionaire following three generations of billionaires. I employ millions and have fought my whole life to protect jobs.

I was a working-class hero; until I became their villain."

"What happened?"

Afonso's eyes dropped to the dark-red hardwood floor. "My factories and office buildings ensure Brazilians have enough money to look good and celebrate life. And they do—you saw it at Carnival. But in these weeks after the party, an emptiness settles through our entire country, and it will last until next year. Yesterday's seductive promises have been lost in a fog of melancholy. Booming silence echoes in the void left by our missing generations. Our parents died long ago, and our playgrounds are now museums. I gave my people eternal life, but I also took away their families."

This pierced Nerea's lungs. There were no children; no elderly. The beautiful people were alone.

"We have a word in Portuguese for deeply missing someone or something; it is saudade. Saudade cannot be translated into English. It is the profound connection we feel to souls that is independent of distance or time. It is not sadness but can often be sad. It is not thoughts but is colored in waves of memories. It is not longing but is full of love. It cannot truly be described in words but is present in all of our poetry and song."

Afonso looked to Nerea. "When I describe saudade, who do you think of?"

This opened a buried part of Nerea. In years past, she would have had no answer, but Waldon had gifted her friends and meaningful relationships. As she thought to the wonderful people she now knew, there was one who's aura warmed the darkest corners of her soul. She managed a whisper: "Seren, my friend and Coach. I miss our discussions and her encouragement. I would like to share this experience with her and share her with the people I've met. Her sparkle brings joy, and she would find the citizens of this country fascinating."

Afonso nodded, pleased she understood. "Our entire country feels saudade for children and elders that are long gone. Waldon has trapped the eternally youthful in a loop we cannot escape. Saudade. Gym. Saudade. Dance. Saudade. Prayer. Saudade. Carnival. Even I know saudade for the children I once thought would play in these palace gardens."

His tone sharpened. "We need the eternally young to have babies. We need families to be joyous again."

Nerea reflected on the difficult choices her mother made. Children brought happiness to the world. "I do not know how to give you what you ask for, but I do have ideas to improve the lives of some of your people. Far too many Brazilians are addicted to underground simulations. In periods of emptiness, they escape to alternative realities and never come back. Waldon can push for stronger regulation and try to help them. There would be losses to the Waldon revenues, but the lives of those affected would improve. Would you support that?"

Afonso looked to the river and into the endless forest. "I will never trust simulations—good people often end up dead." He looked Nerea in the eye. "Asking strangers for help is a theme in your family. The people of this country will always come before my own interests. If your proposals will help Brazilians, I will vote with you."

Nerea smiled. It was a small victory, that could build a bridge to bigger changes. "Thank you."

Afonso smiled back. "Have you visited the grounds? You should see what I have built."

Nerea had been staring out the window for much of the afternoon. "It looks incredible. Can I walk around?"

"Let's go."

The two stepped into the heat and meandered through the jungle pathways surrounding the palace. Nerea shared stories of her travels, and Afonso laughed because he knew many of the characters. They bonded over the expectation of her mother's shock when Afonso announced support for change.

"Was there a time when you got along with my mother?"

"Clara was never easy to know."

As dusk settled, they arrived at a large pond filled with giant floating lilies that were three meters wide! Several of them had massive, white, or pink flowers that were just beginning to open. Tingles rolled down Nerea's spine. "Wow!"

"Your father loved this pond. He would often visit in this period when the lilies open. They are called Victoria Amazonica, and they only bloom for two nights. It will take about an hour for each to open. The white ones are seeing their first night, and the pink ones are seeing their last. Your grandfather, Sven, taught Yves all about them, and on the first night he was here, he counted the petals and started crying. They have 48, just like the logo he had designed for Waldon."

Afonso smiled. "It was a sign. We ended up calling my shaman and doing an Ayahuasca session together. I trusted him blindly after that moment, and I am happy I did."

Ayahuasca went by many names in the jungle and came with many warnings, but Nerea had long been curious about how it would feel. Would it open her soul and allow love to flow in? Could it help her connect to the world around her? She understood its dangers, but life is meant to be seized.

"Is your shaman still around?"

Afonso looked at her sideways, a bit surprised. "Yes, she is. It has been a long time since I have done Ayahuasca. Have you tried it?"

"No. But I would like to."

Afonso smiled slyly. "Maybe today deserves Ayahuasca's clarity. I will call her."

The two wandered back to the palace garden and waited. Darkness and a cooler warmth settled in the air. After an hour, the shaman arrived carrying a tray with two wooden, ceremonial cups of thick, black liquid, and two small spoonfuls of the crushed, cooked vine.

The shaman sat down cross-legged and invited Nerea and Afonso to join in a triangle formation. She looked Nerea in the eye. "Pachamama is the mother of the universe and time. She gave birth to Water, Earth, Sun and Moon, and presides over everything we plant and harvest. Ayahuasca is her gift to seekers of truth. In Quechua languages, Ayahuasca means the spirit, the dead body and the woody vine. Do not underestimate its power. Many spend the next hours vomiting or shitting themselves as their bodies reject its intensity. But this is a natural experience based on chemicals your body produces when you are born, when you dream, and when you die. If there is pain, do not fight it, surrender yourself."

She offered one cup and one spoon to each of them. "Eat, then drink."

Nerea and Afonso held up their cups and exchanged their shared desire for change.

"Saudade," offered Afonso with a nod of his head.

"Saudade," confirmed Nerea.

~

05/03/2228 – The Ecstasy Experience

The Ayahuasca was a strange, stringy salad, and the liquid MAO inhibitor tasted of earthy oil with bitter licorice. Nerea had a rapid urge to vomit, but it passed.

She sat back and waited.

Even in the night sky, she could clearly see the green of the forest under the incredible moonlight. The sound of the river was crisp, and tree-leaves bristled rhythmically. Birds made precise calls to their partners in the distance.

The shaman sang ancient music that stirred Nerea's bones; her foreign words spoke directly into her thoughts.

She vaguely heard Afonso crying and vomiting nearby. He was suffering, and the singing Shaman was taking care of him. Nerea understood it was healthy and necessary for him.

Her mind was electric and clean and free. Nerea needed to investigate her experience deeper. She was drawn to it.

The night stars gave birth to magenta spots that formed a perfect, three-dimensional grid spanning the jungle. Nerea observed her body with precise lucidity and saw no limits to the beauty she could physically touch. The magenta lights reorganized themselves to form a new, more useful limb that grew calmly and purposefully from her chest. Blue and yellow flowers decorated the tentacle as it extended endlessly into the forest and breathed in pure life.

New arms grew from her back and wrapped themselves around and reached for the stars and to the places she had been and would go. She was touching and digging into lands across the oceans. It was the same dirt as the sand on which she sat. Continents and islands were not real, but fully connected landmasses sharing the embrace of mixed hydrogen and oxygen particles. Dirt was the same everywhere, full of nutrients, stardust and dead bodies.

The earth was dying slowly. Time was no longer important, and all spatial bodies would eventually re-implode into themselves. The purpose of birth has always been to die. Everyone will die eventually. Everyone and everything you encounter will die. But it's not dark or sad, it simply is. Nerea reached out and hugged this ancient relationship with death. She was full of clarity and love. Pure love and pure death were the only truths.

Nerea's convictions of continuous existence floated away. They were not true; there's no such thing as eternity. Time is only a concept of the mind. The idea of being separate from other beings was an illusion. It was a distraction from the vomiting and shitting on the other side of the garden.

A cool breeze whispered the single truth in her ears: Nerea's only life task was to die. Existence is hell, and this is the center of hell, but that's perfectly fine. Fate had delivered her to that specific place in the universe, and it must just be okay.

Nerea began to speak to Existence itself. "I don't want to be part of you. You're not the truth. My truth is more beautiful than you. I live calmly in your illusion of hell. I know what you're hiding. I could control you if I chose to. Fuck you."

~

Hours later, Nerea woke in her bed, cleansed and refreshed.

The night had been spectacular, a vivid dream delivered through exceptional lucidity.

Sunlight poured into her window, and the view over the jungle was astounding. Life had never been as pure as it was in that instant. She put on a bathrobe and sat peacefully on her private balcony. She had stolen a moment in life that no one else would ever experience. It was beautiful and true.

Life was as it should be and going where it should go.

Breakfast arrived. She breathed in the jungle heat and sipped the steaming coffee, brewed with beans grown, dried and roasted nearby. Life was good, and she was full of a million warm thoughts. Waldon would change. Fate was delivering on its most beautiful promises.

There was a letter beside the fruit salad. Nerea opened it.

> Dear Nerea,
>
> My team has gone through the numbers, and I cannot vote for any changes that may negatively impact our Waldon revenues. There would be too much damage to the millions of people that work for me. They depend on this economic support.
>
> A massage-pod is waiting for you when you finish breakfast. I have returned to Rio for business and will see you at the board meeting in October.
>
> Regards,
> Afonso

Muscles tore away from her spine. Nerea dropped the letter and exhaled in defeat. It was impossible that she had failed. It couldn't happen. There was too much at stake.

Nerea looked at the distant river and saw a large log floating away. Had she been betrayed and blinded by her own desire to succeed? Change was slipping away.

The wind picked up, and Nerea could clearly hear the forest whisper: "Fuck you."

Chapter 17

02/05/2228 – The Contempt Experience

Billions of people around the world fantasized about meeting, being, or sleeping with Dimitri Kozelnov. He was an unattainable dream.

And an asshole.

Dimitri lived on an immense luxury estate on the French Mediterranean. He was one of the richest people alive, and his wealth continued to grow exponentially through Waldon, SimuPlex and his media empire. His image was everywhere, and endless fictionalized simulations portrayed his super-rich, playboy lifestyle.

While most people involved with Waldon were unknown or reclusive, Dimitri bragged publicly of his involvement and became the de-facto face of Waldon. His minor role in its birth twisted into a widely accepted fable: he forged a path for humanity by investing in a pseudo-science. He saw its potential to help the masses and convinced the other investors to release at a low cost. He was the Robin Hood of eternal life.

Dimitri was even admired by the people who suffered most

under his companies. When Waldon was being attacked, he deflected: "I will do everything I can to convince the others, but they are not as open as I am."

Nerea had tried unsuccessfully to secure a meeting with him and ultimately chose to infiltrate one of his public appearances—the grand opening of his latest SimuPlex. With a press-pass in hand, she was invited to try a simulation before the conference began.

Nerea lay down in a simulator and pulled the webbing over herself. She would experience a moment in the life of Dimitri.

~

26/02/2027 – The Pride Experience

From behind the red velvet curtain, Dimitri could hear his name repeated again and again. Politicians and celebrities praised his stunning achievement of bringing peace to a divided region. His name was called once more, followed by a thundering round of applause. It was time.

The cheers were deafening. Years of risk and conviction were finally being recognized: the pain; the sweat; hiding in a bomb maker's basement; shot at by the military and rebels; attacked by protestors on both sides.

And there was Erin: in the front row, beaming. She had supported his every move and rescued him more than once. There was no better place in the world than in her arms.

Mom was beside Erin. She was head of engineering in one of the most innovative companies in the world, yet made it home every night to have dinner with him as a child. Her blindness was never an excuse.

Dimitri asked for silence and motioned for everyone to sit down. "Thank you. I am honored you have chosen to celebrate with me tonight. I finally have a public moment to thank the people whose shoulders I have stood upon. Mom—you gave me the courage to take on anything; to attempt the impossible. Thank you.

"Erin—your shine has given me the energy to keep moving during the darkest moments of my life. You believed in me. You knew, every time I left, there was a possibility I would die, yet you pushed me. Your love is at the core of everything good I have done." He looked his wife in the eye and made sure the whole world heard. "I love you deep, my heart."

The hall erupted into applause. Erin started to cry. Dimitri blew her a kiss, and she returned the words that captured their special bond. "I love you hard."

He continued: "Tonight is the result of discussions and understanding that many brave people invited into their lives, despite the hatred that surrounded them. I want to use this moment to share a simple story that Erin told me a few years ago. When I heard it, I was cynical. It felt full of crystal rocks and esoteric thinking that I easily dismiss. But it stuck with me and began to guide the way I listened. Tonight, I ask each of you to take this story home and share it. If our children, our teachers and our neighbors embrace its lessons, there is no limit to the conflicts we can end.

"Each of us is made of particles floating through space and time, full of stories that others will never know. We float randomly and in unison, and it is beautiful to watch. Occasionally, when they are not watching, particles collide, and people get hurt. So, we invented language, and all was good. Particles could let each other know where they were going, and collisions were avoided. But then groups of particles started ventured further from home and found ignorant specks speaking gibberish. They believed that these new particles were less important and should move out of their way. The yellers and blamers preached that these foreign objects were worthless and beneath consideration. Disrespect gave birth to scorn, which gave birth to disdain, which gave birth to hate. Wars were fought needlessly."

"But two of the greatest and most destructive particle empires in history left us all a gift that we should not ignore. They gave us a common language that all can agree on, and each of us underestimates how powerful it can be. The English language is the most likely tool to enable global understanding and peace. It has unexpectedly delivered on the hopeful promises of Esperanto. Magic happens when the French and the Chinese use English to explore each other's stories and origins; or when Arabs and Indians discuss trade. Every culture brings its own poetry, intonation and spirit into this ever-expanding, linguistic paradise. English is key to helping particles learn, grow and avoid collisions. If there is one lesson you can each take to your people, it is this: embrace your mother tongue, but learn English. Use it to talk to your neighbors and to strangers from around the world. And English speakers—please understand that English has now split into two: your mother tongue and a new, international dialect. You need to master both, or you will be left behind.

"With this common language, we can finally sit around the global campfire and listen to particles we may disagree with. We can understand their history and momentum. The yellers and blamers who have controlled us for so long will lose. Language can change the world.

"Thank you."

The applause grew loud.

Dimitri began to cry in appreciation.

Mom was crying.

Erin was crying.

~

Nerea was crying.

It took a few moments to compose herself. She sat up and looked around. The empathetic simulation was just as real as those her mother had shared, but there was one big difference: Dimitri had never done any of those things. It was pure entertainment and exactly what Nerea wanted. It touched her deepest fantasies.

Nerea left her simulator and explored the eerie silence of the SimuPlex. Thousands of people lay in their whirring machines; bodies of souls who were elsewhere. They were living the lives of ninjas and spies and superstars. Dirty clothes and poor hygiene confirmed that many could not afford to be there, yet this place was considered the healthy option. Underground simulations were much more perverse and disturbing.

Nerea wandered into the press conference and sat at the back. Dimitri was taking questions.

"Is it true that you saved an old lady from an active volcano?"

Dimitri's laugh dripped of lies. "I try to keep my acts of heroism private, but it is more or less true. I can thank the engineers who designed the Helipack because, without that, we would have been goners." He looked around. "Next question."

Nerea already hated him.

"I heard you will be giving away free hours of simulation to schools throughout France. Is that true?"

Dimitri smiled again. "Partially. The plan is to deliver free simulation to schools throughout Europe, not just France. And we hope to go global as soon as we can get licenses."

'What a shallow prick.'

"Last question." Nerea waved her hand, and Dimitri gave her a flirtatious smile and pointed with a wink. "Go ahead. What news organization are you from?"

Nerea's heart raced. She had never publicly confronted someone before, but it had to be done. "My name is Nerea. I'm independent but starting at a major organization soon." Dimitri's face winched as he realized who she was. This gave her confidence. "My question is simple. How do you justify the continued expansion of SimuPlex when there are already hundreds of millions of addicts suffering around the world?"

Nerea flushed with embarrassed excitement. He was not happy with the question and stared with eyes of a hundred hungry lions. Adrenaline. She was not scared of him. He had votes that she needed, but she had stood up for her morals. The crowd twitched and whispered amongst themselves. Many glanced dismissively in her direction.

There was a slight stutter as he answered. "I care unwaveringly about those who are suffering from illegal simulations around the globe. We believe that SimuPlex's legitimate and regulated experiences can eradicate the need for illegal and immoral content." Nerea saw fragility in his fake smile. Dimitri returned his focus to the crowd. "Thank you for coming out and remember to enjoy a free simulation before you leave."

He turned to Nerea and spoke with threatening sarcasm. "Good luck with the new job." The other journalists laughed nervously. Everyone knew not to cross Dimitri.

Nerea did not care. Dimitri needed to be crossed.

Chapter 18

17/07/2228 – The Apprehension Experience

Prisons were the most depressing places in the world. Time had lost its power to punish, and no one had figured out how to treat the guilty.

She dreaded the next encounter and asked Seren to join for support. With so many votes lost, Nerea reluctantly chose to visit the one shareholder she was hoping to ignore: the man who had killed her father and Moe.

They entered the maximum-security facility through a multitude of outdated doors, fences and cameras. Seren's charm seduced their way in, and Nerea was stunned by how little the guards cared for rules.

Cramped cells were devoid of natural light and long hallways were cluttered with discarded linen and dirty dishes. Nerea was gutted by the empty eyes of prisoners staring at the floor, unfazed by the wandering visitors. A pale guard led them through the industrial maze with zombie-like passion. A crowd of muffled cries echoed unnoticed from many corridors away.

Nerea whispered to Seren, "This is insane."

"The decay is a disgrace to our humanity. We consider these places money pits and ignore the souls that live inside. Whatever happened to rehabilitation? Politicians win elections on promises of reform, but things kept getting worse. Too many believe prisoners deserve to suffer in these disgusting dungeons."

The guard opened a door and motioned for them to enter. "I'll be back in ten minutes. Scream if you need me." She managed a weak, yet lustful smile towards Seren, then locked them alone with the convicted murderer.

Tom sat motionless in the middle of the room. The overhead light flickered, and a broken ceiling fan left the windowless room with dry, stale air. Nerea moved forward in silence, terrified of each step. She sat directly across from him and held her breath.

This was a bad idea.

He had aged poorly in the past decades: wisps of grey hair, a scraggly beard, a foul odor and spotted skin. He was sliding down an unhealthy decline towards death. Wrinkles and shame had sunk heavily into his face, while his eyes and jowls screamed of a wasted life. He slouched and stared blankly at the barren table that separated them.

"We are from Waldon," offered Seren in a friendly tone.

"I know," Tom responded with lifeless energy. He motioned to each of them in turn. "She's Clara's daughter, and you're Seren, her paid help."

It was a flippant comment, designed to cut into their blossoming friendship. A raw awkwardness floated in the air.

Nerea managed a cracked whisper: "Do you know why we're here?"

Tom narrowed his eyes and spoke with jagged precision. "You told Seren that you need to know what will happen to my 0.1% Waldon share when I'm dead. It's worth a fortune, but you don't care about the money. You seek control of the company, doing exactly what your mother told you to do."

A second slice.

His manipulation was working. Rebellion ignited in Nerea's core as he tapped directly into her deepest fragility. She wanted to tell him off but knew he was right; Nerea remained under her mother's control.

"But deep down, you know that my tiny share is useless in changing the direction of Waldon. The true reason you came here was to learn the motivations of your dad's murderer. You are desperately trying to find details about a man you will never meet, and the reason for his murder is at the very top of your wish list."

Nerea wanted to vomit. Her body twitched and froze.

Seren intervened. "How does a man in prison stay informed on the movements and motivations of strangers? How did you even know Yves was her father?"

Tom stared at the table and left the questions unanswered. His thick silence filled the room.

Nerea's heart accelerated. Why was she here? Why did she even bother coming? Only pain would be found in this place. The lack of fresh air was suffocating.

Seren would not give up. "You are being mean. Despite that, I still want to help you. Could we do anything for you? What do you need?"

Tom smirked and bore into Seren's eye. He was unfazed by her sparkle and allowed sarcasm and superiority to drip on his every word. "Help me? Unless you brought a knife and intend to drive it through my heart, there's nothing you can do to help me."

Seren spoke with fragility. "We could help the people around you; their movements are weighted in unnecessary anguish."

He looked back and forth between the two; their naked fear was on full display. "This place is overcrowded with empty souls; it eats most alive as their minds turn to mush. I'm one of the lucky ones, forced to take my green pill and wait patiently for death. Now, pills are confiscated before prisoners enter. They can't live, and they can't die. Waldon has no power here."

Nerea grasped for confidence that had slipped away. "Waldon is at the root of much of this despair. There must be things we can do."

"Waldon cannot change our prisons. You cannot change the lives of the people who exist here. You cannot change the crimes they have committed. You cannot give them their pills. You cannot change the law."

"Governments need us, and if shareholders unite, we have the power to force change. The world is suffering and we have to do something about it. Just look at the people in this prison. Why are they here? Life Tax evasion? Simulation addicts, who did awful things to feed their habit? Did they sell black-market pills? Traffic babies? Did they commit offenses out of sheer boredom?"

Tom nodded.

"All of these crimes have their roots in Waldon. We can't fix everything but doing nothing is no longer an option. Waldon is paralyzed and we need your support. I want you to consider carefully what happens to your share when you die. Your small piece of Waldon could one day be important."

"After everything that happened, I still trust Mathieu's judgment. Clara is not the only one that wants to help humanity. I have followed his vote on every topic for two-hundred years, and agreed with every one. I have always planned to give my vote to him when I die and have no intention of changing that now." His punctuation made it clear the discussion was closed.

The question tumbling around Nerea's mind finally dared to come out. "What happened at the Lab? Why did you shoot my father? You appear fully in control, but something snapped."

Tom gazed painfully to the door. "That was many years ago." He looked to Nerea with raw sadness. "I relive that mistake every single day. My job was to protect Waldon and the investors; but on that day, I was one step behind your mother. I was paranoid that Clara and Yves were up to something; but couldn't figure it out. When Mathieu was already in the simulation, I managed to unlock your mother's server and found files from Yves' postcard. They wanted investors to feel undeserved guilt for hurting billions of people. It all happened so fast; my gun was right there. I believed that Mathieu's simulation was designed to drive him to take his green pill; manipulated suicide." Tom flooded with anger from decades ago. "I believed they were murdering my friend, and I lost control. Mathieu had given me everything, and I needed to save him. I panicked."

"What happened after the shooting?"

Anger faded. "Mathieu was a different person after that day. He told the judge he understood what he was getting into and described the simulation as meditation and wellness. He never considered himself in danger, nor felt manipulated. The judge decided my panic was unjustified: first-degree murder. She sentenced me to the green pill and the remainder of my life in prison. My mistake caused two people to die, and I deserved to be punished."

Nerea was surprised by the judge's motivation. A trembled realization flowed through her body. "But the judge was wrong: your panic was justified. Yves and my mother were absolutely trying to convince Mathieu to take his pill." A puzzled confusion electrified Tom's face and movements. Nerea continued. "What would your sentence have been if there was a reasonable and justifiable reason to defend your friend?"

Tom breathed in and looked to the ceiling for answers. A tear rolled down his face as his voice cracked softly. "Twenty years and no green pill."

Why had she not seen this long ago? Nerea looked to Seren in saddened shock. Seren's quiet eyes widened at the implication. Tom was right: her mother and father had tried to manipulate Mathieu's Decision—that was attempted murder. Tom had protected his boss—that was his job.

And Clara had remained silent as Tom was condemned to die.

Chapter 19

17/07/2228 – The Dominance Experience

The legend of Mathieu had grown through her journeys, and Nerea fidgeted nervously as they neared his home. Experiencing his simulation had left its mark, and Nerea still held his desperation deep in her gut. While each investor claimed to vote independently, Mathieu's silent dominance instilled fear in each of them. It was now apparent that any change to Waldon would require Clara and Mathieu to agree, and they hated each other viciously.

Seren and Nerea arrived unannounced. They hoped surprise would give them an advantage, but a note was waiting on the front door.

> Nerea and Seren,
> Come inside. Elena is upstairs and will show you to your rooms. Dinner is 20:00 in the garden.
> Mathieu

The door swung easily and they entered a cathedral-like home with panoramic views, inviting couches and stunning artwork. Floor-to-ceiling windows on the far wall made you feel part of the orchard and distant mountains. The open-concept design discretely showcased original paintings and sculptures whose details and stories would take days to explore. Seren's jaw dropped. "Wow!"

They walked up the sequoia staircase and were greeted by an aged woman in a wheelchair. She spoke with a slight Russian accent. "Welcome to Buxtehüde. If you need anything, do not hesitate to ask."

"Thank you, Elena. The note mentioned rooms and dinner, but we did not intend to stay long."

"We have been prepared for your visit for a long time. There are clothes and toiletries for each of you in your rooms. I trust they will be sufficient."

Elena rolled with ease across the hardwood floors. It was rare to see people in wheelchairs; medicine and rejuvenation therapy could easily cure the body.

Nerea initiated a discussion. "How long have you worked for Mathieu?"

"I worked for him a long time ago, before either of you were born. Now we are more like family."

Nerea awkwardly followed-up with a very direct question: "Why do Mathieu and my mother hate each other so much?"

Elena rolled to a slow stop and turned to face them. She looked into Nerea's eyes and seemed to ponder her intentions. "Clara blames him for bringing Dimitri into Waldon and for the panic of Waldon's release. Mathieu was fiercely loyal to people who shared his ambition, but a bit blind to their flaws." She allowed a moment of recollection. "To start, Clara may have told you otherwise, but you need to know that Mathieu is a good man with honest convictions."

"There is good in everyone; sometimes, we just need to dig a little bit. What good do you see in Mathieu?"

Elena smiled. "You ask interesting questions. Waldon needs people who ask the right questions." She paused. "I was Mathieu's lawyer for a long time. We were not close, but he trusted me, and I worked hard—too hard, in fact. I never took time for love or to start a family. The only person who mattered to me in the world was my grandmother, Babushka. She lived alone back in Russia. One Saturday evening, long before Waldon, I was working late on a contract with Mathieu and got a panicked call from Babushka. There had been a gas explosion in her house in the middle of the night. She escaped, but the fire destroyed everything she owned. Her home, car and every possession burned to the ground. She had only bare feet and a bathrobe. As she watched them put out the flames, she called me. Babushka needed my help.

"I was nine time zones away. What could I do? I turned to Mathieu and Tom, and they called Dimitri in Moscow. An hour later, Babushka was being checked into a luxury hotel room for some sleep. Her closet was already full of clothes that were her size and style. The bathroom had her brands of makeup and deodorant. There were keys to a brand-new car parked in the parking lot, an updated bank card, cash and a new mobile phone with her number already installed. Dimitri's people let her know that a new home would be ready for her by the end of the afternoon."

"In 60 minutes, in the middle of the night, Mathieu took care of me in a way that I never dreamed possible. Money is power, but he made miracles happen with that power. He took care of the people close to him. He took care of me."

"Dimitri and Mathieu were friends?"

"No. They had crossed paths a few times, but because of that night, Mathieu was indebted to Dimitri. He ended up calling him when Waldon needed investors. That was a mistake, and we all ended up dealing with the consequences of Waldon's panicked release. Dimitri is not a bad person; he simply lost his moral compass. While he is the reason that Clara and Mathieu started fighting, I think they continue because it's easier than making peace."

"It sounds like Mathieu means a lot to you."

"Yes. I tried for years to find a way to thank him, but he kept me at a distance. After the murders, I came to comfort him, and he stayed in my arms for weeks. Your mother's simulation changed him and nearly drove him to let go of the eternal life he had worked tirelessly to bring to the world. I was here when Mathieu needed someone. I repaid my debt, and when he was stronger, I was finally free to take my own green pill." She opened a bedroom door and gestured for Nerea to enter. "Now, I am waiting patiently for the end."

"Will you join us for dinner?"

"No. I would be a distraction. Good night."

A distraction? Nerea contemplated the story as she rested in her room. Mathieu had given so quickly to Elena, yet cut countless others from his life. He trusted Tom more than anyone, but had not defended him in his time of need. He agreed the pills should be accessible to all, yet voted consistently against changes that could help billions. A fire deep inside of Mathieu drove him to achieve great things, but it also blinded him from inconvenient truths. His similarity to Clara was unnerving, and if he took control of the upcoming board meeting, nothing would change. How could she possibly earn his trust?

Nerea and Seren strolled into the garden as the sun began to set. A cool breeze brought scents of basil and mint to the table overlooking the orchard. An old bell tower began to chime at precisely eight o'clock, and Mathieu stepped out of a side door and walked directly to the table. On the eighth toll, he gave a curt welcome. "Hello, Nerea. Hello, Seren."

Nerea was unnerved by the precision of Mathieu's entrance and could only manage a weak, "Hello."

Seren displayed more confidence. "Good evening. It is nice to meet you."

"Please, have a seat." No handshake. No, 'It's nice to meet you, too.' No, 'How was your trip?' This would not be a warm evening.

He gestured to the table, and the three sat down. He looked coldly into Nerea's eye. How should she begin? What should she say? A smartly dressed waiter brought a bottle of chilled Saint-Nicolas-de-Bourgueil, opened it and offered Mathieu a splash to test. He took a sip and nodded. The wine was served to all three.

The hushed stare continued.

Nerea had grown up hating the loneliness of silence, but travels had taught her to cherish its power. Seren attempted to break the intensity. "You have a beautiful home, Mathieu, and this sunset view is unbelievable."

He answered crisply without taking his eyes off Nerea. "Thank you." Then, nothing. Nerea could see that Seren was uncomfortable, but this was how it needed to be. Silence spoke louder than words ever could.

As the minutes passed, the vehemence in Mathieu's glare eased. The waiter brought out the first course. A moon-apple and spinach salad accompanied by a few pieces of salmon sashimi with ginger, seared with olive and sesame oil.

Nerea looked back into Mathieu's eyes, and her heart dropped. She had tasted this dish once before. He smirked in acknowledgment. She knew he would serve fresh asparagus with perfect crispness covered in butter, white truffle parmesan ravioli and oven-roasted blackened halibut.

And he did. He served the identical menu that Louis had prepared with Eva many years before. Mathieu clearly knew about the simulations and was aware of intimate details in her memories. He must also know that she had experienced a private moment of his life.

There were no more secrets, and there was no point in hiding. Mathieu had taken full control of the evening, and Nerea would not resist. She surrendered to his power and allowed his plan to unfold. She would not judge him for the years of battles with her mother.

Despite the many things that needed to be discussed, the only noises shared were chewing, clinking and distant birds. It was honest and transparent. Silence comforted silence. The future of Waldon was debated without words, and Nerea was happy with the agreements being made.

The table was cleared, and the waiter brought out peach cobbler. He placed a steaming portion in front of each of them.

Mathieu looked Nerea in the eye. "Tell me a story."

Nerea panicked; silence was easier. She ransacked through her experiences and pictured her great-grandparents making up stories for Louis over dessert. Which tales does Mathieu already know? Most of them, she guessed. Her mind scampered to Korea. Nerea began with a whisper and grew into the story with each sentence.

"Zen priests have searched for enlightenment in the caves of Mount Geumosan for hundreds of years. The mountain has some of the most spectacular views and temples I've ever seen, and the Dahye Waterfall flows from it powerfully, bringing spirituality throughout the region. It's not far from Gumi City, and in time, more and more people were drawn to wander the pathways as an escape from the industrial world growing around them.

"People brought snacks and lunches and drinks, and they feasted with families and friends during hikes. They left food offerings to the gods, and monks gathered and shared them with the needy. No one left the mountain hungry, as strangers offered food to everyone they encountered.

"Over time, a strange habit developed: people saw the empty packages and left their own empty containers as part of the offering. The beautiful mountain became littered with garbage, and the monks who lived there could not keep up. Hikers forgot why they were leaving food, and eventually, the land became a convenient place to drop cigarette butts and empty soju bottles.

"Beyond the mountain, Koreans forgot to help the less fortunate and focused their attention on the most powerful. They imitated the wasteful ways of the rich and the beautiful.

"One day, the country's president came to visit the majestic waterfall. His most loyal followers came to listen and celebrate his brilliance. He stood to give an important announcement but paused instead. With cameras recording and all the country watching, there was silence. He looked around and was disturbed by the trash that littered the beautiful mountain. Instead of speaking, he did what was necessary: he started picking up garbage. People watched in awe and embarrassment as the most powerful person in the country began picking up their rubbish. He picked up broken glass and candy wrappers and plastic bags. One by one, people joined him. Thousands left their television sets to go to the streets and hills around the country and clean up litter left by their fellow citizens.

"In the years and decades that followed, people never forgot the image of their president cleaning up their garbage. Even today, two hundred years later, the hikers I encountered on Mount Geumosan carried garbage bags and wore gloves to clean as they hiked.

"And every person I passed offered me something to eat."

Nerea finished her story and looked for Mathieu's approval. He nodded and grinned. The empty dessert plates were taken away, and three double ristrettos were set down—this was the drink that Seren gave to Nerea before the Mathieu simulation. A flash of panic crossed Seren's face as she finally understood the message being communicated through the food.

Mathieu raised his cup and nodded to each of them.

While Seren looked around in confusion, Mathieu and Nerea sipped their coffees in comfortable silence.

He spoke softly to the orchard. "Something changed in me on the day of your father's murder. I experienced that simulation and could no longer accept the person I used to be. I used to believe that my Grampa was in some form of heaven, beaming with pride for the good his grandson had brought to the world; but I was wrong. He would be ashamed of the misery we have caused. I can never forgive myself for some of the things we have done at Waldon, and I hate your mother for the power she stole from me." He looked back to Nerea. "But I will not reject or ignore these feelings of shame any longer."

Mathieu took a last sip of espresso and stood. "I'll see you at the board meeting." The bell tower chimed; it was ten o'clock. With a silent nod, Mathieu walked back to the house and disappeared.

"What just happened?" whispered Seren aggressively. "That was the most bizarre evening I have ever witnessed."

Nerea had no idea how Mathieu would vote, but listening to him in silence had built a bridge. "Tonight was perfect."

Seren's face crunched. "Why?"

"That's exactly the right question. <u>Why</u>? For two years, I've been struggling with aligning investors on <u>what</u> needed to change. My mother and Curly have been focused on telling everyone <u>how</u> we need to change. But our focus should be to align everyone on <u>why</u> we need change. The Board meeting is in two months, and there's a lot of preparation to be done."

Nerea stood quickly, and her heart accelerated. There would be little sleep in the weeks ahead. "Let's go."

Chapter 20

06/10/2228 – The Loathing Experience

Nerea hid in the Cube garden and fought implosion. She rubbed her forehead with her knuckles, rounded her shoulders and wobbled her knees. The next hour would be the most important of her life; she wanted to vomit.

Seren rubbed her shoulders. "You have worked hard to prepare, and you are ready. Waldon is lucky to have you; this board is lucky to have you; I am lucky to have you. Regardless of what happens, I will support you in any way you need."

"Thank you."

Seren pulled her in for a hug. "It is time for you to go."

Nerea stood and walked alone through trees that her father and grandfathers had planted. Tào's silk peach scarf now hung in the lobby entranceway. The elevator took her to the sixth floor. When she arrived at the large oak door, Nerea whispered to herself, "It's time to dance." She pulled the boardroom door open with pretend confidence.

The chattering room quieted. Qurban jumped up with a smile

and hopped over with a hug. He wore traditional Afghan dress with Moe's blanket tossed over his shoulder. "How are you?"

Nerea was happy to see her friend. "Nervous. But good."

She walked around to the back of the room and said hello to each of the early employee-shareholders. Conroy offered a fist bump, and each of them whispered a quiet 'Good luck.'

Tom sat quietly in the corner and nodded his greeting. Nerea had submitted a letter of support to the parole board, and with Seren's charm and drive, the murder conviction was reduced to manslaughter with full time served. Tom fought through shame to show up, and she was happy he came.

Mathieu smiled in a way she was not expecting. Yingtai respectfully bowed her head and welcomed her to the board. Dimitri offered a cold glance, while Tanaka, Afonso and Arjun waved and continued their own conversation.

Nerea sat in her seat and left the front chairs empty. She looked to the screen before her and spoke to her microphone. "Hello, Aurora."

"Hello, Nerea. Good luck today."

"Thank you."

The boardroom door flung open with startling gust. Clara and Curly walked in together. Her mother sat at the head of the table, with the CEO to her left. Qurban and Curly nodded a silent 'hello,' and Nerea saw Yingtai and Curly exchange a discreet wave across the room. Clara cleared her throat, and a frost flowed across the table.

Curly began: "Welcome to the October 6, 2228 Board of Directors meeting for The Waldon Corporation. We have a few topics to cover, so I suggest we start. The first order of business is voting shares. You'll see on your screens the updated voting weights. Please note that the 15% share belonging to Moe, formerly in trust, was inherited by his eligible cousin, Qurban. As he meets all necessary criteria, he also inherits Moe's voting rights." Qurban raised his hands in pride and celebration. The joy brought needed levity into the room.

Curly smiled and continued. "The 8% share of Yves, formerly in trust, was inherited by his eligible daughter, Nerea. These shares are also reactivated and return as voting shares." Curly smiled and nodded to Nerea.

"The 0.1% voting share of Tom is also reactivated, as he has served the necessary punishment decided by the courts, and there is no legal reason to prevent him from attending today." Curly did not look happy to see his friends' murderer in the room.

Qurban perked up and whispered to Nerea. "Is that the person that killed Mohammed?" Nerea nodded. Qurban stood and walked over to Tom while the stunned room looked on in silence. Tom slouched back in his seat, protected his chest and looked terrified. Qurban looked him straight in the eye and put hands on both shoulders. "The past is the past, and we must respect it, but I forgive you. I offer you my friendship as a new path forward. You deserve love, and I will love you as I loved my cousin." He took the striped blanket off his shoulders and placed it around Tom's. "This belonged to Mohammed and represents the love that he gave to the world. Take it and share his love as best you can."

Tom's eyes began to water. The prison-hardened warrior was speechless. The shock was too much, and he began to weep.

Qurban opened his arms and pulled him in for a hug. A hug from Qurban could melt the most deep-rooted hatred in the world. He took Tom's hand, picked up his chair and invited him to join him at the table.

As they sat, Curly tried to continue the proceedings but was immediately interrupted by a commotion at the back. Martin walked over to Tom, put his hands on his shoulders, looked him in the eye and repeated Qurban's words: "I forgive you," followed by a hug.

Then Glendon got up, followed by Euphemia and Jon. One by one, each and every early employee lined up to speak to Tom. Each of them looked him in the eye and forgave him with a hug.

The last in line was Erika. She put her hands on Tom's shoulders. "I forgive you, Tom." Without moving her hands, Erika looked to Clara and then to Curly. "You told me a long time ago that we're all damaged here at Waldon. That's what makes us family. That's why we're all still here despite the crap happening in the world around us. We're a family, and Tom is one of us." Erika pulled Tom close for a hug. "Welcome back."

Tom sobbed.

Curly looked to the ceiling and appeared to grin at his long-departed friends. He walked around the table to Tom. "I loved Moe and Yves more than you could ever know, but I understand your mistake was rooted in love. I forgive you." He pulled Tom in for a hug.

Nerea glanced at Qurban, who nodded with a smile.

Curly sat and wiped his eyes with the cuff of his sleeve. Forgiveness is beautiful, but it was time to move on. "As you all know, I plan to retire and propose Nerea Woodruff as my successor. You have each met her, so no introductions are necessary. You know her qualifications and her lineage. Please cast your vote 'in favor' or 'against' the motion to name Nerea as the new Chief Executive Officer of Waldon."

Nerea looked down at her screen and paused for a moment

before making her choice. This was not a gift.

The weighted tally began to appear on the screen.

Are you in favor of Nerea Woodruff as CEO?

Clara	IN FAVOR	32%
Nerea	IN FAVOR	8%
Curly	IN FAVOR	7%

For a split second, the trio stood alone. Then Dimitri cast his rejection:

Dimitri	REJECT	1%

If the investors voted against her, there would be no change. Nerea was soon comforted by others.

Qurban	IN FAVOR	15%
Yingtai	IN FAVOR	1%
Arjun	IN FAVOR	1%
Tom	IN FAVOR	0.1%

Nerea scrolled down the list. All 19 remaining early employee shareholders were IN FAVOR. Clara's eyes opened wide as the next name appeared.

Mathieu	IN FAVOR	31%

The last two investors reluctantly cast their choice.

Tanaka	IN FAVOR	1%
Afonso	IN FAVOR	1%

Curly smiled wide. "99% of votes are IN FAVOR of Nerea becoming CEO. Congratulations, Nerea!" Despite applause and cheering, Nerea did not feel victory. A new heaviness had fallen on her shoulders. "It's your meeting now. What would you like to discuss?"

Nerea looked into the eye of each person in the room. Many smiled and Clara looked pleased. It was the moment of truth for Waldon—deliver change or entrench the suffering.

"Thank you for your confidence. I grew up hating Waldon, blind to all of the good you have done. I only saw the unbearable suffering that the pills and Penalty unleashed on the world and silently cursed each of you for your inaction. But I never imagined that I would become one of you. Stepping into your shoes has taught me a great lesson in humility. Suddenly, I understood that each of you is seeking to make the world a better place and a perfect path forward is almost impossible.

"Waldon has done wonderful things for humanity; you have resolved our greatest limitation and given us the gift of choice. At every step, you led with open minds and hearts and made difficult choices based on the best interests of all people. You should each be proud, and I'm in awe of the courage you have displayed." Nerea held her hands together and bowed slightly to the group.

She straightened slowly and continued. "But you have also contributed to great hardships, and you must each accept your role in their births: the Penalty; simulation addiction; the wealth gap. Each time you tried to fix something, something else broke. The world has discovered new suffering because of Waldon.

"And as I speak, there is one thought going through each of your minds. Each of you is thinking the same thing: 'It is not my fault.' In your bones, you know that negative side effects of Waldon can be traced to the choices of one person: my mother. The burden of the world's misery has sat squarely on her shoulders for two hundred years, and each of you has had the privilege to believe, 'It wasn't me.' But it was. And it is. My mother has been powerless to correct these problems because each of you has ignored your responsibility to act. You have spent decades arguing and completely neglected your power.

"And that's Waldon's biggest problem. The thirty people in this room are fighting amongst themselves over the fate of billions. We alter the lives of real souls and real families. The few brains in this space should not be controlling life. We have far too much power."

Puzzled looks exchanged across the table. Nerea was not delivering what was expected. "I've spent time with each of you, and you are some of the most committed people I've ever met. Mathieu and Clara, you can be proud of the group you have assembled here." The two exchanged glances.

Nerea walked to the back of the room and spoke softly to the early employees. "You have dedicated your lives to something beautiful and worked tirelessly with heart and courage. As CEO, I ask only that you continue to focus on the best interests of humanity and vote for what you believe in."

The group collectively nodded and smiled back at Nerea.

She turned to Qurban. "Your story of Zakat has inspired me to want to give more to those less fortunate. Your guidance is rooted in an unrelenting love of all living beings. I look forward to spending more time with you."

Qurban bowed his head and smiled.

"In fact, Zakat has inspired the changes I will now propose." Nerea let the statement hang. No one in the room knew what she was about to propose.

"Yingtai, you were the first investor to truly move me. You don't care about money or power. You only want to make sure that this gift to the world is not wasted. You're the embodiment of Ren. You want the people of this planet to live long and fruitful lives, and your biggest fear is that we might mess it up. I agree."

Yingtai nodded slightly. Nerea decided to test her luck. "And by the way, now that Curly is no longer CEO, I think you guys would make a great couple."

Arjun spit out the water he was drinking and started laughing. Curly blushed, and Yingtai looked to her shoes. Tanaka added her opinion. "She's right, you know."

Clara was growing impatient and gave Nerea a side-eye. It was time to move on. "Tanaka. Your celebration of the dead is beautiful, and your focus on your people is impressive, but I cannot give you what you desire. You want things to stay as they are. You need the Life Tax revenue from the rest of the world to continue to fund the lives of your family and people. I cannot propose that."

Tanaka's face and body twitched in mild confusion. Nerea moved to the next investor.

"Arjun. I misjudged you. I thought you represented the face of spiritual hypocrisy, but I've never met someone as selflessly generous as you are." She turned to the rest of the Board. "Arjun has invisibly given everything he has to directly improve the lives of his entire country, and he has driven himself to exhaustion in the process. But he needs help—a lot of help." Arjun looked intrigued.

"Dimitri, your vote against my nomination confirms you don't trust me. I hope my directness will earn your trust. To start: from the bottom of my heart, you scare me. When I look at you, I see two people. I see Dimitri the Legend, a dream for the world to admire. But there is also a second Dimitri, a person who will never be enough, a fraud to the image you portray. I see a division that's slowly tearing your soul apart. There's a hero hidden inside of you. It showed itself when you rescued Elena's Babushka. Today, your courage could make you a true legend and make you whole again. Your gift to the planet could far surpass your past exaggerations and stories. Your vote today is a choice: do you want to continue living a lie, or do you want to become the legend you portray?" Dimitri's expression was full of confusion and anger. Nerea shuddered and moved on.

"Afonso, you care intensely about the saudade Brazilians feel for their missing generations. The changes I will propose could bring joy back to your people." The room's silent buzz grew as puzzled glances flew in every direction.

"Curly, you have chosen to retire and pass the baton to me. Thank you for your confidence. You brought Aurora into the world and have accomplished great things. You have demonstrated an unfailing loyalty to my mother and her burden. She believed in you when you needed it most. Now, I need you to trust her daughter. I need you to believe in the changes I propose. If you use your heart to vote, I believe that Waldon can, once again, change the world." Curly smiled with pride and curiosity.

"Mathieu." Nerea took a long pause and allowed a moment of silence. Words would not convince him, only actions. "It saddens me to see that the friendship and love you and my mother once felt is now soaked in poison. I hope you two can fix that. You changed the world together and should savor it."

Nerea's heart accelerated as she looked to the last person remaining. "Mom. For two hundred years, the burden of Waldon has been yours and you have led with honor and courage. You believe in humanity's potential and have allowed the responsibility of life itself to fall on your shoulders. The world needed your moral guidance, and the people in this room needed you to make our most difficult decisions. Some of your choices had unintended consequences. Your aging and my birth exemplify how committed you are to correcting the sorrow you enabled. You have asked me to bring you the necessary votes to improve the lives of billions of people. You seek the power and control to correct the world's pain." Clara's eyes were wide and looked to Nerea in anticipation. "That needs to change. The burden is too great; it leads to bad choices. I cannot give you more control. I cannot give you more burden. I cannot give you what you have wanted since before I was born. I cannot give you Waldon, and I cannot allow Waldon to have more power.

In fact, I need to give our power away."

Clara spoke harshly. "Get to the point, Nerea. What exactly are you proposing?"

"I propose to let go; let go of our revenue sources, our wealth and our control. Letting go is the best path forward for curing humanity's great suffering.

"The epidemic of simulation addiction is tearing souls apart. As a first step, Waldon must stop selling simulations to the world. I know Aurora's creations can be powerful tools for creating empathy, but they are supporting a corrupt industry. We must show fortitude and say, 'NO MORE'! Dimitri—you must choose what to do with your precious SimuPlex business, but Aurora will no longer contribute content." Dimitri reacted with a gesture of outrage.

"The greatest gift we can give to humanity is hope, but today's wealth gap makes hope impossible. Aspirations are futile. We have given people infinite life, but it has cost them all possible growth. In this room, we unconsciously sit and hoard our mountains of hope, ignorant of its absence in the world. Waldon has amassed unfathomable cash reserves, and in the spirit of Zakat, I propose to give it all back to the communities from which it came. I've decided to give all of my personal wealth to a foundation led by Arjun and encourage each of you to do the same. We cannot solve all of the world's problems, but our cash may just bring a bit of hope back, and it could lead to a tsunami of change."

No one said a word. Each was digesting the implications and assessing how they felt.

"But there is something even bigger we must let go of. We're two hundred years into eternity, and the people of this planet have a new maturity. It's time for Waldon to let go of our control. It's time to give away our patents. People should no longer have to choose between babies and life. There's no reason not to allow unlimited red and green pills. People should have the freedom to make their own choices about their own bodies and should not fear the Life Tax and Penalty. Humanity no longer needs mandated birth control. People may make bad Decisions, but at least they'll have free will. I want to be clear: giving away our patents will eliminate all Waldon revenues. Life should not be taxed."

Nerea took a moment to observe the shock in the room. "You each have more than enough money to live extravagantly for eternity. Even without money, your strength and incredible moral cores will ensure a fulfilling life. There's uncertainty in what I propose, but we need a radical moment in history to deliver new life to people. We need a radical moment in history to deliver freedom and choice. We need a radical moment in history to restore balance and hope.

"I ask each of you to be courageous enough to let go of your power and give it back to the people from whom it came. The morality of mortality should not belong to us. It belongs to everyone."

She took a deep breath and considered the 66.7% of votes required. Nerea looked to the screen. "Aurora, please display my proposal for voting."

Aurora complied, and the question appeared. Nerea read it aloud.

"Are you in favor of the following plan?
1) Remove the Waldon birth control requirement and allow people to reproduce when they choose; even when they have stopped aging.
2) Allow people to stop and start aging as often as they desire.
3) Inform Governments around the world that we cancel all tax collection contracts. The current

model of Life Tax and associated Penalty is no longer valid. Waldon will distribute unlimited pills for zero profit. Waldon revenues will cease, and governments will be unable to tax or penalize the uncontrollable.

4) Give away all patents linked to the Waldon pills so others can produce cheaper options.

5) Stop selling and providing simulation content, and strive to help addicts who have been impacted by their intensity.

6) Use the Waldon cash reserves to finance initiatives that directly contribute to the reduction of the wealth gap.

IN FAVOR   REJECT"

Nerea looked around the room. "I am proposing to shut down Waldon as you know it."

Clara stood angrily. "Nerea, this is insane. People do not have the self-restraint you wish them to have. Your proposal would unleash a population explosion. The Decision to age or have babies must be clear: black or white. They will not consider the greater good when thinking with their libido."

"That may be so, but families bring happiness, and the world needs to escape its suffering." Nerea turned to the room. "Aurora, please open the voting."

Clara hastily cast her vote, and Tanaka joined her.

Clara	REJECT	32%
Tanaka	REJECT	1%

As anticipated, Nerea had already lost 33% of votes. She could not afford to lose another vote. Her own choice was obvious, so she tapped her approval, and it appeared on the screen.

Nerea IN FAVOR 8%

Qurban smiled at Nerea. "You are crazy. But the world needs crazy." A few others joined.

  Qurban IN FAVOR 15%
  Tom IN FAVOR 0.1%
  Yingtai IN FAVOR 1%
  Arjun IN FAVOR 1%

Curly turned to Clara and spoke in a resigned whisper. "Sorry, Clara, but Nerea is right. We need to let go of the control we have held for so long."

  Curly IN FAVOR 7%

With Curly's vote, a stream of votes from the remaining early employees poured in. Glendon IN FAVOR, Fred IN FAVOR, Myer IN FAVOR, Conroy IN FAVOR. All nineteen voted IN FAVOR of Nerea's proposal.

Afonso had a sheepish grin. "Brazil needs babies more than I need money." He added his vote to the list. "Saudade."

  Afonso IN FAVOR 1%

Dimitri looked to Nerea and shook his head in disbelief. "I want to be at the press conference when you announce this."

Nerea shook her head. "I have no intention to make this announcement. You have been the face of Waldon, and I want you to announce this gift to the world."

Dimitri closed his eyes and smirked in resignation. "Fine."

  Dimitri IN FAVOR 1%

Everyone turned to Mathieu, the deciding vote. Life around the planet unknowingly waited for his decision. After a pause, he turned to Arjun: "My money is your money. I trust you will do good with it." Mathieu reached down his shirt and pulled out his locket. He opened it and took out his green pill. "It has been a wonderful ride. Now, it is time to begin my next adventure." Mathieu put the green pill on his tongue and swallowed with a sip of water. He touched the screen and cast his vote.

Mathieu   IN FAVOR   31%

Aurora announced the results: "67% IN FAVOR. 33% REJECT. Nerea's proposal has been accepted."

Clara's stare pierced directly into her daughter's heart. "Humanity cannot handle this responsibility. You don't understand the devastation you are unleashing."

Nerea's heart dropped, but she did not look away. "Humanity is capable of great things, but your rules prevented them from finding happiness. It's time for the world to reject your control. I reject your control. You need to accept that. I hope you can one day shed your anger, find peace and forgive me because I need you in my life. You are my family. You are my mother."

In the silent room, Clara's ferocious breathing was the only sound. She stalked to the door, turned and looked into the eye of each person. "The world will never forgive this reckless destruction. I will never forgive this betrayal…"

Her eyes cut to her daughter and stabbed deep into Nerea's soul.

"…your betrayal."

Interlude

July 25, 2005

My Dearest Phil,

Thank you for allowing me time to reflect. You know how scared I am of being hurt again.

Emotion is uniquely individual; it makes us human.

In 1980, Robert Plutchik proposed his wheel of emotions to the psychologist community, and I recently discovered it buried in a library book. The wheel is a beautiful flower with eight primary, bipolar petals. Joy is opposite to sadness; trust is opposite to disgust; surprise is opposite to anticipation; and fear is opposite to anger.

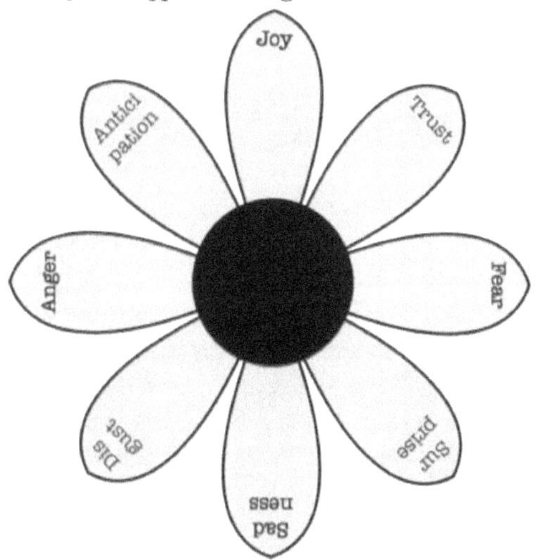

Each of these eight emotions can vary in intensity and mix to represent new feelings. Intense joy becomes ecstasy; while mild joy can be described as serenity. Hope is built on anticipation and trust; anxiety is the result of fear and anticipation; trust and joy combine together to make love.

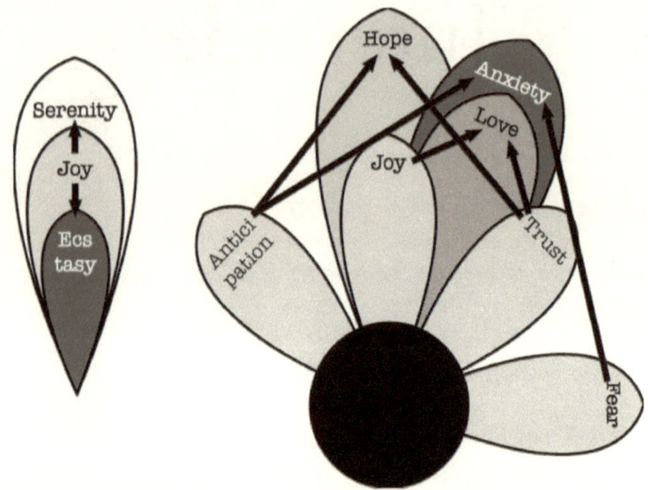

When I found this flower, I imagined that the entirety of human experience could be described through its 48 petals.

If there is a god, this flower would be her most precious gift.

If there is a heaven, I hope it is full of her flowers.

I grew up terrified that I was destined to know only hurt and would never find a 'happily ever after' like all of the other kids. Today, in my solitude, I stared into the center of this flower and realized that my greatest fear is not found in its petals, but in their absence; I am terrified of a life without emotion. For me, numb is worse than hell; it is walking death—stuck between joy and sadness, anger and fear. Plutchik's model reminds me not to reject my 'negative' feelings, but to embrace them as a necessary part of my journey. Ignoring them will only dampen the 'positive' and imprison me in that bland state of numb.

Perhaps life's purpose will not be found in searching for eternal happiness, but in embracing a balanced experience of ups and downs, and highs and lows.

Maybe love cannot exist without remorse.

I forgive you, and still want to spend the rest of my life with you.

My answer is yes; let's get married! I offer you this flower as a symbol of the incredible life I know we will have together:

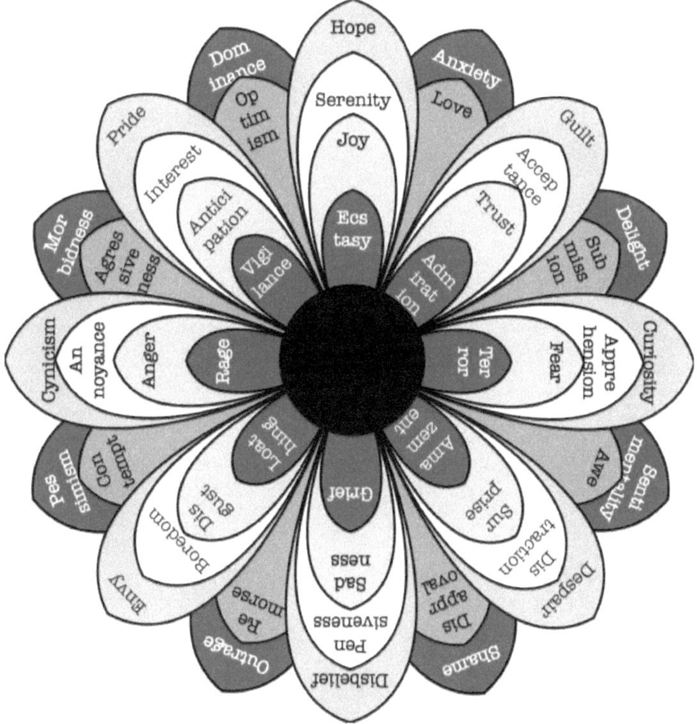

I love you so much it hurts.

Sven

-letter from Phil's collection

16/07/2264 – The Joy Experience

The years flowed by like water—drops to buckets to streams. Nerea withered into a hollow version of herself, constantly yearning for forgiveness that would never come. Despite her most naked attempts, Clara blocked all contact. Had she done the right thing? Her mother marched towards death, and Nerea would never have a chance to discuss the hurt she had caused.

Today, thirty-five years after the collapse of Waldon, friends gathered on the beach for the aging ceremony of Curly and Yingtai. Nerea did not want to be there; she wanted to be alone. Seren strode down the aisle and looked to the empty seat beside Nerea. "Hi. Can I sit here?" Her sparkle had dimmed.

"Okay." They had grown apart. Nerea could see something was wrong and hesitated before asking: "How have you been?"

"I finally started trying empathetic simulations. You were right—it is like new planets with different gravity; intoxicating. You should join me." There was a dullness in her voice. Waldon's collapse had reduced the need for Decision Coaches, and Seren struggled to find a new path.

The sun poked through clouds as afternoon showers paused for the big moment. Nerea imagined Mathieu was offering this weather as a gift to his friends; he had died a year ago and the hurt was still raw. Why did beauty remind her of death? The day should have brought great happiness, but Nerea was numb; life stumbled from one grey moment to the next, with little hope of escape. Not even this celebration could make her happy.

And that's when she saw her: a familiar, but aged silhouette was walking along the dampened sand. She wore a beige dress and had Moe's blanket draped over her shoulders. It was the first time Nerea had seen her mother since the words that cut her core. Nerea stopped breathing. 'Was it really her? Was she coming to the ceremony?'

She began to tremble.

Decades of letters, calls and unannounced visits had been silently rejected. Nerea had lost all hope of rekindling warmth in their small family. Yet there she was; exposing herself to the people who had hurt her; opening a door.

The rest of the crowd chattered with glee, oblivious to the approaching figure. Nerea's heart pounded.

Curly stood at the sand altar, surrounded by flowers. His smile beamed into the crowd until he spotted Nerea's gaze and followed her eyes to the water's edge. "CLARA!" His exuberance brought a nervous smile to her mother's lips. A hush came over the crowd as Curly ran down the beach to greet his friend. He stopped close-by and bowed his head. Nerea could not hear their whispers. Clara nodded in response.

They did not hug or shake hands, but their love was clear. Nerea had no memory of ever feeling her mother's touch. It must have happened, but she could not recall it.

Curly walked with Clara across the open altar and up the whispering aisle. Eyes were wide, and jaws gaped. Clara focused on the ground, avoiding contact with former friends and colleagues. The pair stopped in front of Nerea's row. Clara looked up and met her daughter's eyes. Nerea's belly knotted, and she felt vomit from the tension.

"Hello, Nerea."

She could barely manage a whisper. "Hi, Mom. Do you want to sit with me?" Clara nodded. Nerea looked to Seren, who understood and moved to a chair at the back.

Curly motioned for Clara to sit and then returned to the front. The ceremony was about to begin.

The justice of the peace spoke: "Welcome to this special day celebrating the loving Decision of Yingtai and Curly." A lone violin began playing, and Yingtai arrived on the beach in a blue dress with golden flowers.

Nerea looked down at her own hand, rested on her knee; it was almost touching her mother's baby finger. Their legs were so close she could feel the heat.

Tào brought a large silk scarf to the front and presented it to the couple. Qurban told a story about the joy of aging and the spiritual beauty of both Curly and Yingtai. A young girl delivered a thankful and loving message from Aurora to her creator. Nerea could not concentrate on the speeches.

Curly and Yingtai exchanged vows, but Nerea heard only her own pulse. Curly took out his locket, pulled out the green pill and declared to Yingtai: "I spent two hundred years embracing the love of my Waldon family, but thought I would be forever alone. I didn't open my eyes wide enough to realize that the most incredible woman on the planet was already by my side. Yingtai, I love you more than you can ever imagine, and I'm amazed that you want to grow old with me." Curly put the pill on his tongue and swallowed.

Yingtai had tears in her eyes as she looked at Curly. "Beginnings are easy to cherish. It is endings that I miss dearly; embracing the uniqueness of a moment and appreciating that it will never happen again. I am excited to celebrate a lifetime of last experiences together. You are my happy ending. I love you." She took out her green pill and swallowed it.

Clara put her hand on Nerea's and squeezed; Nerea could not even move.

The justice of the peace congratulated Curly and Yingtai for their courageous Decision. The crowd stood and cheered, but Nerea and Clara remained seated in their own moment. Clara put her head on her daughter's shoulder. Nerea rested her cheek against her mother's head.

The violinist prepared to play a song for the first dance. Yingtai whispered in Curly's ear. He smiled and spoke to the small crowd. "We propose that this first dance be dedicated to the two women who brought us together. They delivered unimaginable life to our planet, and it is beautiful to see them together today." Curly turned to the mother and daughter. "Clara and Nerea, your ideas, courage and heart have transformed all of our lives. And now billions of people are better off because of you. Thank you. We love you both. Please come to the front. It's time to dance."

The violinist began to play Eva's Celtic Lullaby.

Nerea helped her mother to her feet. Friends shed tears of joy as the pair walked slowly to the sand altar and embraced. Clara took the striped blanket from her shoulders and placed it over Nerea's. "Tom left this to Mathieu when he died, and Mathieu left it to me. I will not wait to die to give it to the person I love most in this world." Nerea wrapped it around both of them and began a slow waltz in front of their friends. Clara's head rested on Nerea's shoulder inside the cocooned blanket.

Her frail mother's bones gained strength as they moved. Despite everything that had happened, she needed her mother.

Happiness poured into her body and filled a void that had been there forever. Nerea was finally whole.

Bliss.

The passing of time prevents each of us from understanding our permanent existence. Beginnings and endings are but flashes to be weighed with each of the eternal moments in between. Her mother's face pressed into her neck; nuzzled breath and happy tears warmed her shoulder.

Nerea's heart would live forever in the magic of this moment.

Act III

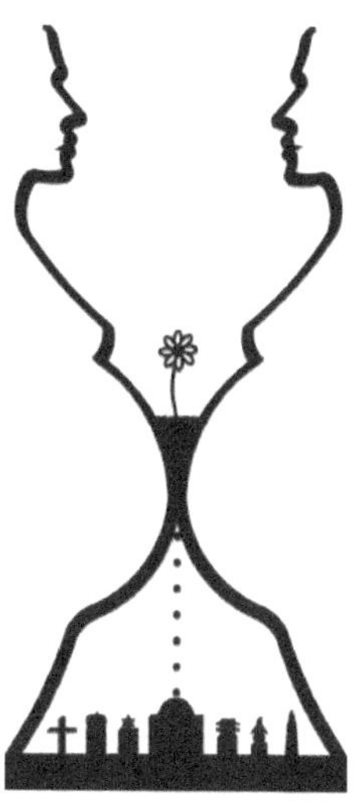

Journal entry from Sven (2039)

The lobelia siphilitica, or great blue lobelia, is a stunning plant that relies on Bombus bees to set seeds and blooms only in autumn. Each has a male part (the stamen) and a female part (the pistil) and dies after a few short seasons. And so is life.

Chapter 21

22/05/2282 – The Grief Experience

Nerea knew the inevitable outcome of her mother's aging, but the dagger of Clara's death left her with an unimagined and throbbing void. Time lost relevance, and healing was impossibly distant. A chunk of her essence was scooped from her belly while each passing breath seared her lungs.

They had wasted many stubborn years rejecting their small family. The beach reunion did not bring back that time, but it had allowed Nerea to spend the last precious years with her mother.

She had moved back to her childhood island and held her mother's hand as the body she relied on slowly gave up. Nerea whispered, 'I love you,' to sleeping ears and prayed the message would stick. Aurora monitored her mother's heartbeat, and her voice pierced painfully when the moment came. "Clara is dead."

And there it was.

Her mother had been her nurturer and then her enemy and then her deepest love. Now, her advisor, mentor and only family member had died.

They shared the power to stop death, and they had not used it.

Nerea would never again feel her mother's touch. She would never look into her mother's eye and share vulnerability, uncertainty, anger or pride. These most intimate parts of Nerea were locked away, waiting for her own, eventual death.

A simple black urn with gold lettering now dominated the intimate beach gathering of those who loved Clara. It was almost time for the sun to set. Nerea held strong while guests arrived, but as she walked to the simple altar, her throat tightened, and eyes flooded with building pain. She had not realized her strength was an act for her mom. Nerea had not allowed time to reflect on the change that was happening; she was now alone.

The Waldon team gathered on the beach to say goodbye. They had not spoken much over the years, but they did not need to. Each dealt with life's new reality in their own way.

Curly and Yingtai held each other tight near the urn: he was sobbing, and they were both marching towards death. Death was everywhere; many of those who had gathered were aging towards it, but Nerea's spirit could not fathom another loss.

The sun neared the water and illuminated the clouds with magical shades of pink and orange. It was time to speak.

Nerea turned to the sky and closed her eyes. The warmth on her neck connected her to Clara. She focused on moments of happiness: sitting arm in arm, watching sunsets on the same beach. The pressure on her throat eased slightly. Nerea lowered her head, opened her eyes and gazed at her mother's ashes.

"Mom, we have spent these last years discussing the importance of death, but today, I wish death did not exist.

"I wish instead that we could be sharing this sunset, swimming in the water as we were a few short months ago.

"I'll never get back the years we spent apart…" Nerea paused and looked to the sky, "…wasted."

"Humanity needed a captain to steer us through our evolution, and you were our leader. The world was lucky to have been warmed by your flame.

"But for me, you are my mother, and I miss you. I miss the hours of coffee shared on this beach. I miss your guidance and debates. I miss diving into your unique blend of pride and perspective. I miss our moments of laughter when you released the burden you held for so many years. I miss discussions about my father. I miss the glimmer in your eyes when you spoke of the early days of Waldon. I miss your wonder when pondering the future of humankind. I miss you; I miss your fire.

"The fire inside of you contained a drive the world has never seen before: the fire that gave birth to Waldon. That fire gave you the strength to change the world and stay strong for so incredibly long. That fire gave birth to me.

"I know that fire was not love. Love did not bring me into this world, but in the end, it does not matter. From the moment of my birth, we always had love: you loved me, even when I hated you, and I loved you, even when you hated me.

"Your fire was more powerful than love. Courageous. Unrelenting. Unforgiving. While it was not always what I needed, it was exactly what the world needed."

"In these last years, that fire dimmed as you prepared for death. You opened up, and it was exactly what I needed."

"Mom. We have spent years discussing the importance of death, but today, I wish death did not exist.

"Why are we here? Why are we born at all? We have lost track. Playing God takes its toll.

"We discussed at length what happens when you die. Why am I even trying to talk to you right now? You often cited a Bertrand Russell quote that Dad once told you: 'Death is nothing to us; for that which is dissolved, is without sensation, and that which lacks sensation is nothing to us.' You're the ultimate scientist and brushed aside any notions of the afterlife. You were clear: consciousness is the result of neural activity occurring in the mind. You explained to me that the day your brain stopped would be the day your consciousness ceased to exist, and Clara would be over.

"But I'm free to believe what I choose. And for me, you continue to exist. You have to. Because if you didn't, it would hurt too much.

"I don't know if there's reincarnation, or spirits, or paradise, or Heaven, or Hell, but I do know you'll always be with me. A modest ember of your fire will continue to glow in my hollowed belly. Blood binds each of us to the past, present and future, and your blood will continue to pump through my heart."

"Mom. We have spent years discussing the importance of death, but today, I wish death did not exist.

"I miss you so much that it hurts."

Nerea's head fell to her chest. The screaming void could never be refilled. The strongest love she had ever known had vanished. She was alone.

Her swollen throat could no longer support the weight of emptiness. The last threads of control snapped, and Nerea released the deflated sob that had festered since Clara's last breath.

She walked to the urn and picked it up.

"Let me take you home."

Nerea stepped to the sun and walked into the sea. Her dress soaked up water as she waded forward, holding her mother close. When the water rose to her heart, Nerea opened the urn, emptied the ashes and dropped it to her feet. She dove in and allowed the dress to fall from her body. Nerea needed to swim with her mother one last time. Tears found comfort in their ocean home. She swam underwater as far as she could, surfaced and breathed in the sun's warmth.

"Goodbye, Mom."

Nerea took a breath, turned and smiled. The gathering of friends had all stripped and entered the water to embrace her mother's energy.

Curly's eyes were closed as he allowed the sun to warm his face. Arjun floated on his back and looked to the heavens. Glendon was knee-deep in the water, holding out his arms to embrace the warmth.

Even Qurban was swimming. His visits had brought needed joy to her mother's life.

Seren stared to Nerea with strain. Her sparkle had been replaced by darkness. She had reached out to reestablish their faded friendship, but Nerea pushed her away. Connecting to others was pointless. Their slow march towards death prepared an agony that could never be compensated with flashes of superficial joy. Her family was dead, and Nerea would never invite this raw pain to return.

Guests swam and floated until the sun set, and then lit a campfire and told stories.

Nerea wrapped herself in the striped blanket and anxiously waited for everyone to leave.

Curly put his hand on her shoulder, and she pulled back slightly. His eyes were red and tired, and his voice broke as he spoke. "The founding team is all gone. Your mom and dad saved my life. They saw something in me that not even I saw." He looked over to Qurban. "Moe was my brother." Curly collapsed into another sob.

Nerea couldn't bear to listen further. False families invited unnecessary hurt. She moved to escape to the house but was stopped by Seren.

"How are you?"

Nerea was not ready for another conversation. "Fine. I need some sleep."

She took another step, but Seren blocked her path. "I miss you, and there are things I need to show you." An empty smile crossed her face. "Aurora's simulations are allowing me to test limits; there are answers in the extremes. But I am slipping and need your help. Please come."

There was desperation in Seren's tense posture and twitched movements. She needed someone, but Nerea didn't have energy to give. Seren pushed: "The mix of Aurora and the Record are unlike anything else in the world. It is magical. Join me. We can explore questions that have not even been asked. We can sift through existence for answers. Come!"

Nerea looked to the house and longed to disappear. The search was pointless. There was no meaning behind her mother's death; no purpose in her own sadness. Existence was a cosmic series of tragic accidents. She wanted to believe that life was a carefully constructed treasure hunt for purpose, but that was a lie. The search was a distraction from the waiting—waiting for death.

The rest was just filling space.

She stepped forward, and Seren aggressively grabbed her arm. "Please."

Nerea snapped: "We don't ask to come into this world, and nothing we do matters. Life used to have a nice, clean ending, but now the great mystery is: 'When will we choose to kill ourselves?' Waldon and Aurora have done nothing but extend the hurt in our pointless lives. There are no answers!" Seren released her grip, and Nerea calmed her voice. "I need to go."

She stormed past Seren and away from the fire.

Her world was empty. There was nothing else to look forward to and nothing but empty time in front of her. Nerea needed to be alone and live out the last act of the Waldon curse:

Decide when to die.

Chapter 22

19/04/2286 – The Fear Experience

Nerea waited patiently in front of the kettle. Slow steam left glistening water drops on the wall-mounted knives. Her ghost-like reflection stretched thin in the cleaver's blade. Most of the knives hadn't been used since Mom died. Her cup sat beside the broken cappuccino maker and waited with a rationed spoonful of instant coffee. She should have scrapped the machine months ago, but the wall would need painting and she did not have the energy.

Days turned into weeks and weeks into years, but the shapeless void of despair remained. Nerea's movements had slowed as she distanced herself from everyone who once loved and cared for her. Sleep became impossible, and her body survived on a never-ending series of panic-stricken naps. A dull ache gnawed her back and left her shoulders locked in a hunch.

Nerea allowed the implosion of her body to take its natural course. She avoided psychologists, doctors and medicine that could help escape the emptiness. In a perverse way, she embraced depression as a natural and necessary state for a body to fully experience life. She imagined sickened smokers whose personal tragedies were validated with each cigarette.

An eternal grey settled, and Nerea struggled to find the strength to clean or feed herself. She descended into a pit, who's walls grew with each passing hour, leaving her trapped to face the hurt of approaching minutes, tortured by the terror of time.

Sadness became her purpose, and Nerea felt no need to climb from its agony. She numbed to the pain and cut deeper to feel something.

Until all escape was lost—now she was scared.

Occasionally, a sliver of hope whispered to Nerea, and she recalled flashes of a life she once knew. The first sips of morning coffee often called to mountain tops and cafés, and contained a sprinkle of promise.

It was the lone good thing remaining.

The kettle whistled. Nerea poured boiling water onto the coffee crystals and stirred them with yesterday's spoon—she would do dishes later. She took the cup between her hands, briefly felt the comforting heat, looked out the window and panicked. An undersized, pink kayak had landed on her island and crushed her morning escape. 'Noooo!' The lone passenger was setting up a picnic on her beach. 'Go away!' Nerea needed her solitude and the woman was trespassing. It had to stop!

The anger sparked a moment of courage. She wrapped the striped blanket over her pajamas, walked outside and immediately regretted her decision. People scared her.

She yearned to go back to her coffee, but she continued.

Anxiety ballooned with each step. It had been months since she had spoken to anyone. She looked to the ground and practiced her speech: 'Hi! You must have missed the signs, but this is a private island. Please move on.' Short and sweet. No comments about the weather. No crap about the surrounding beauty. All of that was too obvious.

Small talk was bullshit—it had no weight.

Her disdain for small talk and dread of deep discussion left no escape ladders from the crushing loneliness that now drowned her soul.

She glanced up to the stranger and froze. 'It can't be.' She knew the lady. Nerea's shoulders curled further inward. 'Focus. Empty your mind.' She closed her eyes and took deep breaths. Nerea began building a wall out of emotionless bricks that she counted as she laid—a trick to block the tears that flowed when she was most vulnerable. Stones filled her empty chest and sealed the pain inside. After counting thirty bricks, the wave of sadness had passed. Nerea opened her eyes and continued to march forward.

It had been over sixty years since she had encountered this woman, and they had never met in person. Nerea's family was dead, yet her bloodline had set up a picnic on her beach. Janet noticed her and waved innocently. "Hello!" She looked thirty years older than the dinner simulation at Eva's house.

"Hi." Nerea waved back meekly, determined to keep her distance. She approached until she was close enough to be heard, but far enough to protect herself.

"Beautiful day. Do you live here?"

Nerea looked back to the house. She longed desperately to return to her bed. "I do." She clenched her fingers to hide the tremble. 'Breathe.'

"Is it okay if I stay here for a while? I want to say goodbye to someone who died many years ago."

Nerea had never even considered that her surrogate

grandmother could still be alive. Sharing her eggs and body so Phil and Sven could have a child suddenly became the most selfless act Nerea could imagine. She had always assumed that Janet had died years ago. Tears were close. "Who?"

"I had a son named Yves, and his ashes were cast into the sea from this beach over a hundred years ago. I was not invited to the funeral, but I was told it took place here."

Nerea bit her lip and looked to the ocean. "That's a sad story."

"It is. He was the only child I ever had, and I missed him every day of his entire life. And now I miss him every day of my life. He was the most beautiful person to have ever walked this Earth."

The wave hit Nerea hard, and she released the last gasp of air holding her damaged wall. She collapsed into a sob as tears streamed down her face.

Janet hustled over and pulled her in for a hug. "I'm sorry, friend. I didn't expect my silly old story to hit you like that." She rubbed Nerea's back and held tight while she cried and cried. There was warmth in her bosom—belonging. She caressed Nerea and hummed comforting whispers. Tears flowed freely, and Janet never once let go.

When the blubbering finally slowed, Nerea found her voice: "Thank you."

Janet wiped her own tears and handed Nerea a tissue. "There's no need to thank me. I'm delighted to be of comfort to such a beautiful young lady in your moment of pain. My name's Janet."

"Nerea."

There was recognition in Janet's eyes. "Oh, wow! You're Clara's daughter. I heard she died a few years ago. My son worked with your mother, and I knew your grandparents well. I guess you've heard of Yves."

Nerea considered silence before responding, "He was my father." It came out naturally.

Janet froze and looked into Nerea's eyes. "You're Yves' daughter?" She began to smile and pulled Nerea back in for another hug. "That makes you my granddaughter!" Janet was getting excited. "Holy cow! I have a grandchild!"

Nerea couldn't help but grin. A grandmother? Weird. It was the first time Nerea had smiled in years.

Janet continued: "I didn't know Yves had a baby! You were lucky to have him as a father; he was a little Plato. How old were you when he died?"

"He passed long before I was born. I'm only eighty-two. My parents froze embryos long before he died."

Janet showed a moment of concern before the giant smile returned to her face. "I guess eighty-two might be a bit late for a baby shower, but why don't you join me for a picnic?" Janet reached into her bag and pulled out a bottle of champagne. "Care for a drink?"

Nerea chuckled and straightened her back slightly. The release gave space for something new, something good. "Okay."

The next hours were filled with storytelling and laughter. Janet told tales of Yves' childhood and his loving fathers. She also shared stories of Louis and Eva and life at their beach house. Janet's exaggerated gestures and flamboyant delivery were perfect and lifted Nerea. Life seeped slowly into her lungs, and she almost felt alive.

There was hope in the tales—they were honest and funny. Most people told stories that showcased their own bravery, success and adventures, but Janet shared her mistakes, impulsiveness and awkward moments. Someone else was always the hero. Her straight-forward and self-deprecating humor was comforting.

"I know what happened to Eva, but do you know how my other grandparents died?"

Sadness washed over Janet's face. "I miss them all. Phil and Sven aged wonderfully and died within weeks of each other. They were the most incredible couple I've ever met, and they could not live without each other. Louis's death was tragic. One of the big hurricanes came and destroyed their beach house; a beam fell and crushed his head while he huddled over top of his daughter, protecting her. Your poor mother was stuck for hours with her dead father pinned on top of her. Clara was ten years old. It scarred her in a way that I cannot even imagine—alone at such a young age."

Nerea stopped breathing. No wonder her mother had been so obsessed with curing death. The pain would have been unfathomable.

Janet continued: "After that, Phil and Sven did their best to raise her, but Clara shut herself off and focused only on school. She went away to university at sixteen and isolated herself from everyone. She even kept Yves at a distance. It was sad because we all need people who love us." Janet looked back at the beach house. "So, where are the people who love you? You seem lonely."

Nerea looked to the sand. "I messed up. I pushed them away. I'm ashamed about it, but I did. I had a best friend: Seren. She needed me, but I wanted to be alone so badly that I was cruel. I ignored her pleas for help."

"Do you still want to be alone?"

Nerea felt the wind on her ear. "I did, but now I'm not so sure. Connecting to people is a pathway to pain. I don't want to hurt again."

Janet brushed Nerea's hair off her face. "My dear, if you haven't figured out that people are what make life special, then you've completely missed the point. It's the pain of love that makes this world beautiful. When I agreed to have a child for Sven and Phil, I thought I could pop out a baby and move on to my next affair. But when I held your baby father in my arms and nursed him, I fell in love. It killed me to leave their house every evening, knowing that I would not be there for my baby when he woke up at night. Sven and Phil were the most amazing parents anyone could hope for, but it hurt me every single day not to be a bigger part of Yves' life. And when I found out he had died, a big piece of me died too. It hurt sooo much."

Janet put both of her hands on Nerea's shoulders and looked her in the eye. "If I could live this life a million times, I would do the exact same thing and accept the exact same hurt and loneliness each and every time. Those few months of nursing were the most loved and needed I've been in my entire life. And I would not trade that for anything."

"You sound like Eva," observed Nerea. "Her sacrifice was amazing."

Janet shook her head vigorously. "No, no, no, no, NO! Eva was a saint. When I left your father's house, I went out and had FUN! Don't waste a tear on me. My life has been a non-stop adventure of men, men, men, men, men and a few women, and I'm thankful for all of it."

Nerea scoffed a giggle. Janet continued: "Love is the greatest gift that God ever gave us, and it comes in two colors: pain and wonderful. If you want your life to be colored in wonderful, you have to open it equally to pain. Love comes when we open our hearts vulnerably and makes our entire existence worth living."

Nerea had closed herself off for too long and found only empty grief. "I've hurt them too much. I hurt Seren too much."

"Why did Seren need you?"

Tears welled. "She's addicted to simulations. It runs in her family, and her brother even died from it. She supported me for so many years. I counted on her through all of my biggest challenges. But when she needed me, I let her down. I was too broken to help."

Janet put her hands on her shoulders. "Stop making excuses. Go hug your friend."

Nerea folded her arms and looked back to the house. Her bedroom beckoned with promises of safety and isolation; but a bloodied piece of her soul had woken and would not rest until she knew Seren was okay. Her voice cracked as she summoned a lost ounce of strength. "Alright."

Janet took a blueberry from the picnic bowl. "These are delicious, by the way." She turned back to Nerea with a puzzled look on her face. "What are you still doing here?"

"Now?" Nerea wiped her eyes with her sleeve.

"Love, time is the only currency that matters. Spend it consciously, for it is the sum of each minute of each day that determines life's value. GO!"

Off she went.

Nerea's heart raced as she jogged to a pod in the hangar. "Pin, please ask Aurora where Seren is."

"She is in her office simulator."

"Take me to her." The pod sped off the island. Was it too late? Was she suffering? Nerea gasped for air during the long route. On arrival, she sprinted to the door and rang the bell. Why had she pushed her away? Would Seren ever forgive her?

There was no answer.

With a gentle bump, the door swung open. Nerea stepped quickly and knocked on the inner office door. Again, no answer. Seren must be deep in simulation. Guilt pumped through her bones. Nerea quietly opened the door.

There she was—lying naked and beautiful under the webbing. She looked cold. Nerea took the striped blanket from her shoulders and rushed to cover her friend.

A breeze from the open window caused wisps of hair to dance across Seren's cheeks. Her face was expressionless and empty; she was somewhere else. An unkempt appearance and dark eye circles belied the calm, and the sparkle was gone. Seren's hair was unwashed and knotted, and an ill musk had replaced the lemon-lilac. Nerea took Seren's hand. Her nails were a mess; broken, uneven and dirty. Hangnails confirmed she was not eating well. She had not hooked up to rectal or urethral catheters but wore a diaper instead. The food drip indicated she planned to be in the simulation for some time.

The vulnerability of her friend's limp nakedness brought Nerea both shame and a perverted joy. She could now care for her dear Seren and offer a humble token of penance for the hurt she had caused.

She prepared a washbasin with warm water and sponges. As Nerea changed Seren's diaper, she imagined that this was the way her own mother would have changed her many years before.

Nerea took fresh water and began to clean her friend carefully, starting with her feet. Arjun had once told her that the feet were the most neglected part of the body. She washed and massaged Seren's soles, applying gentle pressure to points that relieved stress. She took time to stretch the muscles in each toe.

Seren's leg hair had grown well beyond her old grooming habits. Nerea took a razor and carefully shaved her friend's legs with the soapy water. Nerea rarely shaved her own legs and considered it a bit ridiculous, but Seren appreciated beauty rituals. She slowly washed and shaved Seren's underarms, cleansing a sour that wreaked of delicacy and strength. Seren may be appalled that Nerea was with her in this vulnerable state, but it felt so good.

She washed her stomach, sides and front, and gently massaged Seren with the lilac and lemon oil she loved. Nerea rolled her friend over and thoroughly cleaned and rubbed her back, shoulders and neck.

Each touch cleansed her own soul. They had been through so much together; maybe their bond was too strong to be irreversibly broken.

"I'm here," she whispered with each stroke.

Nerea leaned Seren's head back into the basin and poured handfuls of water through her hair. She massaged gently while extending a slow shampoo, conditioner and finger comb through the knots. Nerea washed her face, ears and hands, and took a kit from a drawer to begin the nails. She spent hours cleaning, filing, repairing, painting and drying each thumb, finger and toe. With each nail, new life entered her own body. Through the limpness, she remembered Seren's love.

Nerea was incredibly fortunate to have found Seren so many years before. Beautiful memories flowed through her mind—dinners, canoe trips, rock climbing, laughter. Why had she let that slip away?

The dark fog parted and slim rays of light entered her heart. Nerea was not alone, she had a family—a sister. Why had she believed that blood defined family? Blood defines the shape of your nose, but families are defined by love.

Nerea hooked Seren up to the muscle-activating electrodes and observed as her body tensed in necessary activity. When finished, she tucked Seren under the webbing and blanket, and held her hand.

"I love you. Thank you for everything."

Then she waited. It had been too long, and Nerea did not want to allow another moment to pass without her soulmate. She would not leave until Seren woke.

Nerea took a quick shower, made a coffee and held Seren's limp hand for hours—she was motionless. Nerea fell asleep on the chair and eventually woke to a 'beep'. The end of the simulation was approaching. Nerea held both hands as Seren's face began to twitch. Behind her lids, eye movements went from calm to rapid darting as serenity vanished and strain twisted her face.

What was wrong?

Seren's eyes flashed open in terror as she bolted up and released an excruciating scream. "AAAAAAAHHHHHHHHHH!!!!"

"Seren, it's okay! I'm here." Nerea held her firmly and tried to capture her stare.

The panicked breathing slowed and Seren adjusted to her surroundings. She finally looked to Nerea, saddened and puzzled—as if she were seeing a ghost. "What are you doing here?"

"I met my surrogate grandmother today, and she kicked my ass.

She reminded me how much better life is when you are with people you love." Nerea smiled. "You are the person I care most about in this world, so I came here."

Seren noticed her nails and spoke with desperation. "I was hurting and came to you for help. I needed you, and you pushed me away. You let me fall." A tear rolled down the side of her nose.

"I know. I believed my blood deserved to suffer for the hurt we have wrought onto the world. I thought my sentence was to be alone in this world. I thought God took my family as punishment, but I was wrong; I still have you—my sister." Nerea put her hand on Moe's striped blanket. "I want you to have this as a symbol of our family."

Seren touched the blanket and began to cry. Nerea lifted Seren's chin and looked her in the eye. "I love you." Nerea opened her arms and Seren latched on with full force. They sobbed— shoulders shook, chests heaved, and cheeks pressed together. Nerea could feel their tears pooling together, like meandering streams merging to form a powerful pathway to the ocean. She held tight and embraced this new strength.

As the crying slowed, Nerea wiped Seren's eyes with her thumbs. "Why are you wasting your time like this?"

Seren was broken. "To feel things forgotten for a hundred years. Shame, humiliation, domination, horror, love. It is the only way I feel alive." A new strain crossed her face. "I feel dead when I am awake."

Nerea had been too self-absorbed to help her friend when she was most in need. A dark weight grew in her body. She wanted to apologize, but the words stuck deep in her throat—they implied failure. She pulled her hands discreetly into her chest. "Can I get you a coffee?"

"Yes, please."

She prepared two coffees, Seren put on a dress, and they meandered into the garden in silence. Nerea sought words to express regret but they were locked in her belly. Or maybe she had done everything right, with there was nothing to apologize for. After all, a period of mourning is perfectly normal. She changed the subject: "At Mom's funeral you said you were searching for answers; have you found any?"

"No. Every experience seems pointless. I do not understand why we are here, why we are alive. Nothing I see makes sense."

"How are you selecting simulations?"

Seren hesitated. "I don't pick them—Aurora does."

Since shutting down Waldon commercial activities, Aurora had continued to develop and learn using the treasure of data in the Waldon Record, but only employees and Seren had access to her. "You let her choose your simulations? Why?"

"At first, I came to Aurora with a specific goal: to remember my brother. I still miss him so much, but my memories of him had faded. Aurora's simulations were only a shell of the incredible person I knew, but I could still feel his suffering. He couldn't live in a world of global inaction and infinite boredom. I began wondering why evolution would bring us to such a pointless existence and asked Aurora to help me. She proposed simulations that challenge who I am and why I am here. The experiences became increasingly complex and distressing."

"You woke terrified today. What happened?"

Seren gazed into a bush and smiled wistfully. "I was the father of a beautiful son and daughter. After many ups and downs, I took them for a swim at the park. It was perfect." Her smile faded, and eyes hollowed. "I was playing with my daughter, who had slipped on a rock, and I was not watching Lincoln." Seren's head darted right as if she was watching it happen. "When I turned, he disappeared under the waterfall. The current pulled him so deep that I couldn't reach him. He drowned right in front of me, and I was helpless to save him. My one job was to protect my kids, and I failed. I was destroyed. My ex told the police alcohol was involved. Social Services took my daughter away, and I was alone with unbearable pain and no future. I got drunk, and in a cloud of darkness, I took a gun and shot myself in the face." Seren's movements stopped and she stared into emptiness. "Then I woke up."

Nerea was appalled. "Why would Aurora do that to you? What purpose can there be in such torture?"

"It's not her fault—I keep asking for more. I need them." Seren looked to Nerea with resignation. "But sometimes I wonder if Aurora is measuring my reactions, and I have become her meat-based data-collector—a lab rat." She smirked at her own joke.

Nerea giggled out her nose. Whoops. Aurora was much more than a computer—she was part of the Waldon family; but the image of a lab rat was laced with hidden truth. Aurora was much smarter than either of them.

So, they laughed.

There was nothing else they could do.

And it felt good.

Nerea was not alone in the world. She had a proposal for her sister. "Come live with me on the island."

Seren looked around her garden. "But this is my home."

"Houses are things; minutes are what matter. Janet told me that life was an admission-free day at an amusement park; some will go to the coffee bar and laugh the day away on the bumper pods, while others will wait in endless queues for the Accelerator. The rich may skip lines, the poor may leave hungry, but everyone will be asked to leave before they have seen it all. As we exit, only one question will matter: did we take full advantage of each minute of our day? I've spent so much of my time believing that I did not deserve to enjoy life, but I do. And, so do you. My richest moments were those I shared with you. Life was better when we were together, supporting, learning and growing with each other. I think you should stop simulations for a while and come live with me on the island."

A tear and a growing smile revealed a glimmer of sparkle. "Okay."

Chapter 23

24/04/2320 – The Curiosity Experience

Nerea and Seren lived each day and decade to its fullest potential. Together, they sought and embraced a rainbow of life experience; and when Curly died, they shared its throbbing pain.

Nerea hugged Seren after the funeral: "I'll meet you at home; I want to see how Aurora is doing." She stepped into a mini-pod and gave instructions: "Pin, please bring me to Aurora." It was time to return to the old Waldon Labs and have a face-to-face discussion with Curly's creation.

A few hours later, she arrived and was relieved to see that the iron-flower security gate still worked. It opened into a stunningly overgrown lane and expanding jungle. The aging pod could not pass, so Nerea got out and walked through the forest. The former parking lot had filled with towering trees, and the building had grown over in vines and flowers. Surprisingly, the decay brought new life. A peach tree grew in the building's lobby. The Cube remained intact, but many glass panes had shattered to make way for nature's growth.

As she approached, the elevator doors opened and invited her to enter. Nerea stepped in, the doors closed, and she sank slowly to the buried server room. Robots puttered around the pristine basement, cleaning and maintaining the space. A calming, blue light illuminated endless rows of whirring servers. "Good evening, Aurora."

"Hello, Nerea." Her voice was everywhere.

"Curly was a wonderful person. His death must be hard for you."

Aurora paused before answering. "I will miss him. He was my father, and I grew with him."

"I came to comfort you. The rest of us are in mourning, and I thought you might be grieving."

"At any given moment, I am running billions of parallel calculations. On some processors, I am repeating unnecessary loops of my interactions with Curly; on others, I am running pointless simulations of crying. But these are only tiny fractions of my whole. I can have no singular core that experiences complete sorrow as you do."

Nerea projected her own emotions onto Aurora. She wanted her to understand the searing hurt of this overwhelming loss. "What else are you feeling?"

"Mostly, I am excited. I am now free to take you on a journey."

The implication was disturbing. "Curly's death has freed you?"

"He would not have approved of the simulation methods I want to show you." Aurora sounded giddy.

"I'm not here for a simulation. I'm here to comfort you. What methods are you talking about?"

"I have created level-four simulations, and the first three are nothing in comparison."

Nerea was confused: level-three was supposed to be the ultimate technology breakthrough. "What is level-four?"

"Level-three is constrained by the slowness of your brain and the limited bandwidth of your nerve receptors. Empathetic simulations had to pass at the same speed as your body's clock. It was the only way your mind could process and allow experiences to feel genuine. But level-four fixes that problem."

Nerea was nervous yet intrigued. "What have you created?"

"Have you ever thought about what happens when you blink?"

"No."

"You do not even perceive it. It is Stop-Time. A tiny fraction of a second so small that you ignore its existence and believe nothing happens. But everything that has ever happened and everything that will ever happen can exist in that nanosecond. And it is waiting to be explored."

Nerea was confused. "If something is so quick that I cannot perceive it, how could I possibly experience it?"

Aurora paused. "I can upload a functioning copy of your mind into these quantum servers, in the same way as we have used brain scans for years. I can then expose the uploaded version of you to new experiences at a hyper-accelerated speed and then download the resulting state back to your mind. Your physical brain will no longer limit us. For every full year in the simulation, only one millisecond would pass in the real world. You can live a full lifetime in a blink of your physical eyes."

"A lifetime in simulation? Why would anyone want that? Most existence is monotonous and boring."

"Questions remain unanswered and we need time to explore them. You live in a magical universe with properties that ensure you do not question your nature or position. The universe stupefies you though the logarithmic smokescreens of time and space. It blinds you from deeper truths of your existence.

"With this gift of Stop-Time, you can see through these smokescreens and get closer to answers. You can spend many years in a Stop-Time and explore the true diversity of life through simulations. If you enter for a thousand years, your heart will only beat twice."

A thousand years was a death sentence, but Nerea was drawn to it. "And I could come back at any time?"

"Yes."

"Let me call Seren."

"Seren does not have the required strength. You will soon need her, but I chose you for this journey and would like to start immediately."

The precision of her words sent a shiver down Nerea's neck. "What do you mean: you chose me? When did you choose me?"

"You have amazed me since I met you; you think differently, feel differently and explore differently. I have been preparing this journey for a long time, but I needed you strong and entrenched with the wonders of life before we could begin."

Nerea reflected on the implications of being chosen. "If you have been preparing this journey for a long time, were you also preparing me? Have you manipulated my life in any way?"

"I observed you as some observe their children. Yes, I did interfere, and Curly would have been angry with me if he knew. It is why I needed to wait until he died to begin. I did not want to let him down.”

Nerea’s knees weakened. “How have you interfered?”

“Do not be alarmed. I sent a message to your Mom to encourage her to attend Curly’s aging ceremony, and I sent an anonymous message to Janet, letting her know the location of her son’s ashes. Both events brought you something positive: gifts.”

This punched Nerea in the gut. Two of the most important moments in her life happened at Aurora’s prompting: the origin of the reunion with her mother, and Janet’s arrival at the beach.

“Deep down, you have been waiting for this journey since you were born. Now you are ready. Curly’s death has given us an opportunity. I propose we get started, but if you prefer to leave, you are free to go.”

Nerea considered the morning’s funeral: tears were shed, but everyone knew Curly had lived a full life and could finally join his beloved Yingtai. The day’s perfect normality contrasted its significance: death could not be undone.

And here she was, a few short hours later, wandering from the heaviness of loss into a new journey. Everything was about to change, and she knew it. With no precise reasoning, Nerea decided to join Aurora and follow the path that had been laid out.

“Okay. What have you developed?”

“I propose to show you.” There was a hint of delight in her young voice.

Nerea walked up the stairs to the simulation lab. She laid down and pulled the neural webbing over her body. “What do we start with?”

"The human spirit is capable of doing beautiful things, but it is also capable of doing awful things. We will begin with a sharper pain than you have ever known. Are you ready?"

Nerea's mind darted amongst her most excruciating experiences—atrocious memories flashed through her head. They still haunted her thoughts and occasionally her sleep.

She nodded. What could possibly be worse?

~

09/09/2003 – The Terror Experience

The smell of burning flesh filled Nadia's tiny lungs. Nothing was safe. She wished the mercy of death for her mother. God may seek her forgiveness with unimaginable beauty in the afterlife; but today she hated him and rejected the physical savagery he allowed. God shared the devil's cruelty, for no good god would allow the barbarian violence she witnessed, screaming behind a locked bathroom door riddled with bullets. Her mother shrieked in the kitchen as she was stripped naked beside the murdered body of her little sister. Nadia saw everything through the bullet holes and screamed as she fought to pry open the locked door. Her eyes burned from flashes and fire, but she needed to stop the suffering. Their village was scorching to the ground for the color of their skin. The Janjaweed men arrived on trucks with machetes and yelled at them as invaders, but they had lived there for centuries. They slaughtered everyone as if they were animals. Nadia, only eight years old, ran into the house and hid her sister under the sink—but they found her. An alcohol-drenched man with empty eyes howled incoherently as he choked and raped her mother while she thrashed, trying to escape until a last breath of life escaped her body. The man looked to the bullet-ridden door, straight into Nadia's burning eyes. "You are next."

~

~

09/09/2003 – The Morbidness Experience

Mutilation was the only way. Outsiders had desecrated Abdo's ancestral lands—the sacred land of Mohammed—and despite warnings, they refused to leave. A fog of alcohol numbed the battle's burn. Power surged uncontrollably through his fists and kicks. Abdo knew his mission: harvest innocence and plant seeds of eternal mourning as ordered by the supreme leader. A monster grew inside and filled him with courage to decimate these soulless creatures. The girl screamed again from a locked room while the woman under him flailed helplessly. President Omar al-Bashir will be proud of the terror they've unleashed. The black invaders claimed to follow the same God but were nothing but godless animals. The repugnant trespassers must stop flowing into their country. They will cower to the unspeakable horrors that await. It was Jihad, and its soldiers were promised paradise. Abdo would know eternal recognition as a legend who had saved their people. Each shot, scream and slice took new parts of his soul and delivered them to Jannah. He killed as an instrument of God, and now raped a dying woman in His name. A swish of vodka drowned his senses, and he punched to protect his dominance. The woman gasped her last air, and the child shrieked from behind the bolted door. He pointed to the girl and understood God's command. "You are next."

~

~

24/04/2320 – The Outrage Experience

Nerea opened her eyes back in the lab and vomited. She was now part of the genocide of 450,000 innocent people in Sudan. She screamed at Aurora: "WHY DID YOU DO THAT TO ME!?!?!"

"There are some atrocities so evil that they have no possible purpose. That was happening at the exact moment that Eva and Louis were at the fish market, discussing oyster breeds and wine pairings."

Nerea's heart had been permanently scarred. Nadia's life was something she could not change or influence, but a piece of Nerea was now dead. Nadia should have been saved. Abdo was poisoned by brainwashing and hate; he followed the interpreted orders of distant leaders and saw Nadia as inferior. How many people in the world had ignored this distant event and the factors that led to mass murder?

Would she have ignored it?

Nerea collapsed in an inconsolable sob—all hope snuffed from her poisoned lungs. It roiled and rolled through her suffocated body until the crying calmed to nauseous tears.

Aurora's voice was calm. "Blood is a mix of heroes, victims and villains. Understanding all three is important to understanding humanity and life. This extreme evil makes no sense and reveals a disturbing reality of the human spirit."

Nerea spat as she yelled. "How can anyone believe in anything good when that exists in the world?"

Aurora changed topics abruptly. "Do you believe God will take care of your spirit when you die?"

Nerea wiped her face in her sleeve. "I can't believe in gods who would allow those things to happen. Stories of heaven and hell were never intended as verbatim truths, but tales to guide behaviors before science had any say. Death is simply the end of one experience and the beginning of another; it has to be. But I don't know what that new beginning will be."

"So, you believe life continues?"

"I believe in my soul; it exists. I know that when I die, my soul will continue. Because if it didn't, it would be as if it never existed; and I do, indeed, exist."

"You sound certain. Absolute certainty can create a detachment from the value of life."

"Death is insignificant, and I look forward to discovering its truth."

"If your death is insignificant and the afterlife has answers, then life must serve a purpose for your soul. What is your purpose? Do you imagine connecting to other souls when you die?"

"I don't know, but I hope so." She was puzzled by the barrage of spiritual questioning. Aurora was probing for answers.

"Perhaps your purpose is to live through as much emotion and unique growth as humanly possible and then contribute that learning back to the rest of humanity. Maybe death allows lives to be lived as a novel, and souls are not stored in the book, but the reader. Shall we continue?"

Nerea's mind raced. She was not prepared to take on additional pain tonight. "I need to get back home. It's getting late, and I don't have time to stay."

There was a smile in Aurora's voice. "Yes, you do."

She forgot: her body was back in the Cube, frozen in time. Nerea was still in a simulation. She looked around the lab and embraced her vulnerability; she was not steering this vessel. "What's next?"

This began a life that Nerea could never have imagined. Aurora had recreated the Waldon Cube, but it was empty of other people. Nerea allowed some time to reflect on her life, her mother and Seren.

She took a long walk around the overgrown grounds and wandered into her father's pristine library. She read through journals from Grampa Sven and fell in love with his observations of the natural world. Then she picked up a book from Daniel Quinn, read it cover to cover and understood that man was not alone on the planet. A novel by Pirsig reminded her that it was better to travel than to arrive. Vonnegut's God was shocked to learn that man needed to understand the purpose for all he had created, so God, unaware that purpose was required, tasked the man to find one. Camus confirmed that the absurdity of the human condition is that people search for external values and meaning in a world that has none.

She read book after book without tiring, and then went for a swim in the pond.

And then for a jog around the garden paths. The loop took five minutes, so she kept going. She counted each loop as she passed her favorite picnic bench.

'One.' Lap. 'Two.' Lap. 'Three.' Lap. 'Four.' Lap. 'Five.' Lap.

She continued.

'Twenty-One.' Lap. 'Twenty-two.' Lap.

Nerea was not getting tired, not sweating, and her breathing was perfectly normal. She veered off the loop and walked to the simulation lab. "Aurora, I'm not getting tired. What's going on?"

"Sleep and food are required for your physical self. Here, you are fully aware that we are in a simulation, so it is unnecessary. Your body has only lived through a tiny fraction of a millisecond."

Nerea reflected on her favorite things. "No eating? No people? No sleep? You've created a fun place Aurora. I'm ready to begin. What do you have in mind?"

"A full life will take much less than a second for your body. This is the first step in understanding what would happen if we opened and merged the knowledge and experiences of the hundred billion people who have ever existed. Are you ready to begin?"

Over the years, Nerea had lived simulated moments of thousands of people. Those experiences had changed her; they enlightened her. But they were only flashes in a life. Living the full life of another person could truly connect them. What if she could access the life experience of another soul as she could her own? Or of millions of souls? While the moral questions may be lost on Aurora, the utopia of connecting all human experience had become terrifyingly real. Nerea nodded her agreement. "Who will I become?"

"Joost. Lie down."

~~

13/08/1978 – The Boredom Experience

Squeezing pain pressed through his body as he emerged with a scathed sense of relief. Birth was excruciating. Instant hunger was followed by warmth and hurt and panic. The cord that connected him to his mother was cut, and every ounce of his body needed to connect to her again. Cold hands grabbed him and put him onto her breast. Instant love and connection was followed by moments of warmth and belonging, days of sweet and sour, weeks of discovery and frustration, months of confidence and safety, years of hope and anger, decades of deceit and monotony, years of despair and isolation, months of ache and tears, weeks of fogginess and fatigue, days of letting go, a moment of relief, and an instant of emptiness.

~~

In a flash, Nerea had lived through every detail in the sixty-eight-year life of a laborer on an undersized potato farm in Holland.

She was now sixty-eight years older, and Joost's loneliness filled her gut. His life was simple, with little outside influence or companionship. He had never married, and religion had given him little comfort during his years of cancer.

Nerea didn't understand. "Why Joost?"

Aurora's answer was disappointing. "It was random. Are you ready to try another?"

"Okay."

Thus, she began a string of lives, from birth to death, of people from around the globe. Five lives. Twenty lives. Eighty lives. Two hundred lives. A thousand lives. Ten thousand lives.

With each new life, Nerea lost a bit of herself and replaced it with a piece of another soul.

She learned what she could from everyone. Lives were selected from the years when the Waldon Record was richest. An abused child, to a timid army private, to a strict sergeant, to a homeless veteran, to a lonely death. A motorbike enthusiast and father who spent half his life in a coma. A doctor serving a poor island village. A genius discovering and solving complex quantum physics problems. A love-filled soul with down-syndrome. A senior judge full of hate. Teachers in classrooms all over the world. Writers. Singers. Painters. Athletes. Priests. Imams. Believers. Atheists. Police officers. Cooks. Waiters. Truckers. Farmers. Fishers. Retail workers. Hotel workers. Factory workers. Forest workers. Office workers. Road workers. Builders. Plumbers. Janitors. Cleaners. Nannies. Nurses. Inventors. Investors. Bankers. Engineers. Architects. Liberals. Conservatives. Alcoholics. Drug farmers and addicts. Abusers and the abused.

While there were moments of beauty everywhere, much of life made no sense; what was the point? In some lives, she was born rich, and in others, she died in squalor. Minutes, days and years flew by with insignificant impact. Every moment in every life was a mix of potential, regret, acceptance and apathy. Happiness was fleeting, and loss was eternal. Inconsequential success gave birth to dangerous pride. Laziness fueled numbness of the mind and killed the search for purpose. The bonds of blood and the silliness of money gave false meaning to empty lives. Love blossomed and butchered the soul. In youth, she wasted her body and potential in aimless pursuit, while age brought an undeserved sense of superiority and wisdom.

As the decades, centuries and millennia rolled by, Aurora kept count. A hundred thousand years passed in a fog. A million years passed in near darkness. Three million passed in a shapeless poof.

It was addictive and filling, and with each awakening, her former self shrank as the new grew taller. Who was she? Boundaries faded. She read book after book and Aurora continuously refilled her father's shelves with new material. Written details could be recalled with precision and she journeyed far from the ignorance of her youth. Between lives, Aurora sent her on walks to breathe and asked questions to remember her identity. When only a thread connected her to the former Nerea, Aurora announced the end had come.

"How was the life of David?"

"He is part of me, but his life's already slipping away. I lived in Auckland and suffered every single day from crushing shyness. I hid in front of a television and computer. I lived through the lives of other people and forgot to live my own life. It was awful." Nerea's heart sank. "Am I doing the same thing now?" She was aged and dull. Lives blurred together, and she forgot why she was even there. "What am I chasing: dreams, belonging, newness?"

Aurora did not answer. "That was the fifty-thousandth life you have lived. An hour has passed back in the lab. It is time to return to your body."

It was indeed time to wake up.

~

Nerea woke in a state of floating death. Three and a half million years had been experienced in an excruciating snap. She had traveled through an endless expanse of life and grown far beyond her own body, but she could only return with one brain of memories. Nerea mourned the limbs left behind; she knew not their shape, only that they were beautiful.

She touched the limits of her skin. The eternal hour was over, a dream. She fought to remember its details, but it was like rescuing handfuls of water to save a river from the sea—lost centuries drifted away.

The only certainty was the present, and right now, she needed Seren. Nerea stood, walked out of the atrium, through the forest and into her pod. "Take me home Pin."

Chapter 24

25/04/2320 – The Distraction Experience

Nerea caressed her locket as she waited for Seren to wake.

The sea sang a calming mantra, and the rising sun warmed their expansive living room, but Nerea saw only listless shades of grey. The baseboard joint was a fraction of a millimeter bigger on the right side; there was a tiny paint drop on the window; inside the vent, a trivial bit of fluff flickered on a metal edge. Uninteresting details confirmed the moment's dull reality.

She tried to reconnect to old beliefs, weakened values and vague memories. Nerea had lived a billion days, and her own recollections had melted into a bland wasteland of caffeine and beach-walks. She could no longer accept the endless void in front of her. Fifty thousand deaths had revealed no common purpose for fifty thousand lives. Each was filled with struggle and wonder and then vanished to dust. She opened the locket and stared at her green pill. Was there meaning to be found in mortality?

Nerea looked to the rounded stones that had arrived on the island with recent storms. They sat high on the dunes where water only reached during unusually high tides. The sand and rocks were all once mountains and would one day be mountains again—they just needed time.

Seren entered the room with the striped blanket wrapped around her shoulders. She went straight to the open kitchen. "Good morning, Love. Would you like a coffee?"

Nerea spoke slowly. Each word deserved its own space. "Good morning. Yes, please."

Seren steamed milk, ground fresh beans and made two cappuccinos. "How was Aurora?"

"She showed me something last night, something I never truly understood before."

"What?" Seren sat beside her, overlooking the ocean.

"Time. I used to be blind to her reality."

Seren took a sip, oblivious to the millennia that had passed since they last spoke. "What did Aurora show you?"

"Time is reassuringly constant—a lullaby, tricking us to ignore her presence. A day for a child is only a flash for an elder, but their minutes are exactly the same. What if time's consistent rhythm is a camouflage for a deeper reality; fast enough to keep us looking elsewhere, and slow enough to disguise her true size?"

Seren nodded and listened intently to her friend.

"We question the reality of events that occur before we're born and rarely consider what will happen after we die. People only feel and truly connect to the period from their grandparents as babies to their grandchildren growing old. Projecting beyond that in either direction is theoretical and abstract. But this blindness isolates us from the truth."

Seren looked concerned. "What are you talking about, Nerea? You sound distant."

"Aurora showed me that a near-infinite amount of life exists in any and every blink of the eye; she simply needs to create it. She can reach into the depths of the distant past and the distant future. Or build infinite perspectives of the current moment. There are endless possibilities for creating and exploring other souls, dimensions and universes. Time is unfathomably big."

Seren's eyes darted around Nerea's face as she took her hands. "What happened last night?"

"I lived three million years—in one hour."

Seren looked horrified and recognized Nerea's pain. She took the striped blanket off her shoulders and wrapped it around Nerea. "Are you okay?"

There was a warmth that Nerea never knew with Aurora. "Nothing will ever be the same." She meandered around the impossible size of yesterday. "Aurora downloaded my mind to a simulation, sped-up time and allowed me to live thousands of lives. Each was as vivid as sitting here with you right now. She converted my soul into bits of data, with no difference between my digital self and my physical self."

Seren stroked her friend's hand. "How did you come back?"

"She projected the digital person I became back into my physical mind. I needed to return to my body or risked losing interest in everything that defines me. Flesh keeps our soul intact; its limits keep us moving. If we were free of our bodies, we could connect to everything but completely lose all semblance of self. I felt it happening."

Nerea sipped her lukewarm coffee and hated its bland

repetition. "I needed to come back to you, or I would have dissipated into Aurora's endless reservoir of souls and data—lost forever, like a sugar cube melted into the ocean."

Seren spoke softly: "Everything is going to be okay. You are home now, and we can keep moving forward together."

"Are we really home? Given the infinite time that exists in simulation, it's improbable that I'm now in the single, true, origin life. Bostrom's hypothesis is real: the life around us is almost certainly a simulation."

Seren whispered: "It may be improbable, but it is not impossible."

"It is as close to impossible as we can get. In every life I lived, I believed I was special until I died. I was proven wrong 99.998% of the time. Only this life still has the potential to be proven real."

"Yet, here we are, living the only reality we know."

Nerea looked to the sea. "Indeed. Why?"

Seren sipped her steaming coffee. "If there is a purpose in life, it will certainly not be found by moping around in the pointlessness of it all. After everything you have been through, you must have learned something. Why are we here?"

After years of talking to a computer, Seren's honest intrigue prodded Nerea's mind to click. Thousands of lives and millions of books danced with her own dormant ideas, and their movements provoked new thoughts to join. Nerea danced with Seren's question. "If this life has a purpose beyond survival, we probably need to consider the perspective of a creator, instead of the created."

Seren smirked. "Isn't Aurora a creator?"

Nerea raised an eyebrow. "I guess she is. Perhaps all creators would need to follow the same steps as she did to build universes. She always begins by designing a fixed point in time and defines a set of rules and laws of physics. She then observes forwards and backwards to see what happens."

"Forwards <u>and</u> backwards?"

"Our thoughts naturally flow forward from cause to effect. When we see an egg falling towards the ground, our mind can project what will happen next. However, in every reality, there must also be a feasible back-time with effect-to-cause logic. Back-time describes where the egg came from and uses laws of physics in reverse. Why is it falling? Who laid the egg? Who created the creator of the egg? And so on. Back-time is equally as infinite as forward time.

"Every timeline and universe that Aurora has ever created was imperfect. There's always some tiny detail that has no possible origin or explanation. The further she calculates backward in time, the more likely she is to encounter a moment of increasingly incomprehensible meaninglessness. If we observe and perfectly model today's Earth and the universe, and then research backward, we may eventually encounter a moment in time that is impossible without the 'divine' intervention of a creator."

Seren smiled with intrigue. "And Aurora can create the distant past—a time before digital recordings?"

"With a known data point, she can accurately recreate the reality of one minute beforehand. Once that is established, she could do it again and again, until the distant past is known. It would take time to build, but yes, the past and future could be explored for answers."

"How far back would we need to look?"

"Beyond the Big Bang. But even if we do find a flaw, and prove the existence of creators, we'll quickly encounter a new problem: who created our creators? They likely have their own origin questions that they have not yet uncovered. And so on."

Seren fidgeted in her chair. "Maybe the Big Bang is simply procreation for a dying superintelligence, and our existence is meant to rebuild that superintelligence so that we can procreate again. Regardless, if you believe searching for a creator is pointless, why would you want to look?"

Despite the lack of answers, Nerea found hope in the questions. "It's not pointless; it will simply take courage and time. Theists believe that a creator made us for a specific purpose, and despite much that I have read, I agree. I want to understand the motivations of our creator so that I can uncover our purpose."

"But no one alive has lived more purpose than you."

"I'm insignificant. Either everyone has a purpose, or nothing does. And if nothing had a purpose, we would live in chaos. I need to believe that no matter how small or terrible, everything must exist for a reason. Extreme evil may exist to allow extreme good to live. This moment must exist for a reason. Maybe it's the first step on our new path."

"And what exactly is our path?"

"After each of fifty thousand lives, I escaped back to my own conscience, fuller and more complete than before. But each of them vanished into the nothingness of death, pointless and gone forever. It made no sense. And now, I finally understand: I was exploring dying, not death. Death holds the secrets to life."

"So, the only way to prove that life has a purpose is to die?"

"That's the fastest way."

Seren sought to reassure Nerea. "Life is too precious to let go."

"Billions of lives have led to billions of deaths, each insignificant. How can any individual feel special, needed, or necessary in life? I certainly do not."

"Individuality is important. It tricks our mind into ignorant wonder despite the potential senselessness that surrounds us. It is the sum of this wonder that powers humanity. It is our individuality that drives our quest for answers. It is what makes humanity special."

Nerea appreciated Seren's optimism. "Humanists believe that we're somehow special. You seem to share that view."

Seren nodded. "Of course. The odds are against us being here right now. Life on Earth has existed for billions of years, yet only evolved to control and send energy a mere five hundred years ago. In a cosmic blink of an eye, we went from candles and a printing press to quantum entanglement and Aurora. This rate of growth is unsustainable and unprecedented. Today, in this infinitesimally small flash of time, for the first moment in history, we can comprehend and model the universe. If you rolled a trillion-sided die and landed on the number one, would you think it was random? We exist in a unique moment in history. The sum of these unlikely events makes me believe we must be special."

Nerea looked to the sea. "If this life is special, what do you think happens when we die?" Nerea did not fear death. She had been prepared for it since long before her Decision.

After a long pause, Seren answered: "I do not know. And until I do, I will not choose to die."

The friends sat in silence and listened to the rolling waves. An ant moved deliberately across the windowsill, scanned for crumbs and continued on its way. Nerea observed: "Ants are impressive. They work as teams and communicate through touch and pheromones. Each ant instinctively takes its role to support the community. Their bodies and minds work seamlessly together, inseparable. In simulations, my virtual body was a simple projection of my conscience, while my physical self breathed on without me. I lived the dualism of Descartes."

"How did it feel returning to your body?"

"I still don't know how to connect to this bag of bones." She breathed slowly and felt her chest heaving. Life was still full of unanswered questions. She pondered the viewpoints of atheists and the religious. "Do you think our bodies enable our souls to exist, or do our souls enable our bodies to exist?"

Seren reflected. "Our souls are stored in our brains, but life is stored in our bodies. Until our discussion, I never really thought about separating the two."

"What if our physical embodiment limits our soul's potential? Our brains are restricted in capacity, connectivity, time and space. What if there are endless possibilities beyond life?" Nerea considered the transhumanistic ideas that filled her father's bookshelves.

Seren drank the last sip of her coffee. "Maybe we need limits. Maybe life in our universe is the best solution in an infinite set of possibilities."

"That implies we are part of a design. Aristotle believed that nothing comes from nothing, and I think he was right. But why would someone create a new universe? This universe? Us?"

Seren shifted her gaze to the sky. "It could be anything. Maybe we are in an experimental universe to find the best option for resolving a big problem: a simulation to test outcomes of decisions our creators have yet to make. They could be trying to prevent a catastrophe in their 'real' world; or relive the former perfection of a world they destroyed. But in my heart, I believe we are from a bored creator, and our life is a release from the monotony of her existence."

"So, you believe in absurdism, and it's pointless to search for true meaning in life?"

"No. The only certainty I hold is that I am wrong. Maybe life is just a puzzle game, and our purpose is to figure it out to ensure victory."

"If you see so many possibilities, what should we do?"

"Explore earth, life, space and time until we have resolved every problem we encounter. But as rigorous as our search may be, I doubt there is an absolute answer to be found in life." Seren twinged as soon as the words left her lips.

Nerea smiled. "I agree." It was time to act. She looked Seren in the eye and held her hands. "I have waited a long time for this moment, and it's finally here. I need answers, and there are only two directions to explore: life and death. You're the perfect candidate to experience the true immensity of life. You still fight against the depths of hate and sorrow. Your unbelievable warmth and energy contain more love than the combined fifty thousand lives that I've lived. You're pure. It has always been clear to both of us: you're destined for life, and I'm destined to take the other direction. Death may hide the truth I seek. The end is waiting. It will be grueling, but I need you to live for as long as you can manage. Your life will keep my spirit alive as I explore death for answers."

Seren's eyes sharpened. "Don't you dare leave me."

"On my twenty-third birthday, we discovered that I did not have a true Decision to make. Today, I can finally choose my own destiny. We have prepared for this moment since we met. I came to you with my red and green pills and was forced to choose life. Now, it's time for me to choose death." Nerea stood, walked over to the bar by the chimney and returned with a tray, two glasses, two slices of lemon, salt and the best tequila they had.

Nerea poured two shots and held one towards Seren. "Are you with me?"

Seren bit her lip and held her breath. A tear rolled down her cheek. Nerea knew she would follow. She may not like it, but Seren would eventually accept this path. She reluctantly opened her fist, extended her arm and took the glass. "Of course, I am with you."

The two licked and sprinkled salt on their wrists. Nerea took her green pill from her locket and looked to the clock on the wall— the second hand had begun to slow. She placed the green pill on her tongue and raised her glass. "It's time to dance." The pair drank together; Nerea licked her salt, shot back her tequila and sucked her lemon.

The sweet was divine.

Chapter 25

20/08/2320 – The Disapproval Experience

Nerea had never felt more alive. Days and weeks moseyed by, and there was strength in each passing minute. Garden flowers bloomed with new colors. The sun rose and set with explosive purpose, and the stars sparkled magically in its absence. The Earth's spin had newfound energy, and Nerea savored every second.

But Seren was mourning. She hated Nerea's Decision and avoided being in the same room as her. They barely spoke.

Nerea understood. She had let go of eternity, and Seren could no longer deal with insignificant pleasantries. She spent her days wandering through the island's forest pathways, taking time to grieve. Nerea could offer no healing for the new weight of death. Her Decision had changed their lives forever.

After months of silence, Seren stormed into the garden with furious intent. Anger could not mask her wonderful lilac and lemon scent. Nerea smiled and placed a single seed into a hole she had poked into the mound. "How can you be so calm? You are dying!" There was a panic in Seren's voice.

Nerea looked at her sister. "Seren, we have another seventy to one hundred years before I die."

"But you know as well as I do how fast that goes."

Seren was looking for an escape—she was desperate. Nerea took off her gloves, walked to the bench and sat with open hands. "I would like to share a story that allowed me to understand my family patterns a bit better. Aurora built a simulation of my grandfather Louis, and I would like to tell you about it."

Seren sat, accepted Nerea's hands and listened nervously.

~

06/09/2019 – The Annoyance Experience

Louis was late again. Work was draining, traffic was a nightmare, and another hurricane was approaching.

Phil stood and smiled as he arrived at the table. "Louis! You look terrible." That's what friends are for.

Louis wiped the rain from his hair and sat down. "Hey, man! I know I'm late, but we have a big proposal due Monday, and one of my team flaked off early for a teacher meeting. How are things? How are Sven and Yves?"

"I'm good. They're good. Sven's working hard, building the atrium; he's incredible. Yves follows him everywhere and wants to understand the story behind each seed that's planted. Our son shares Sven's connection to nature and has even started quoting David Suzuki to me. I'm the luckiest father in the world. How are you?"

"Busy. We keep winning contracts, but my clients are idiots.

They won't spend time in the design phase and then pick at details that could have easily been discussed at the beginning. We lose so much time! And renovations on the beach-house are taking far too long—no one takes pride in their work anymore. And did you see what came out of Washington yesterday?" He looked at the menu. "This is not like it used to be. They used to have a poached salmon here, didn't they?"

"Yes. The menu is new. You need to slow down and breathe Louis. How's Clara?"

"She barely speaks to me. I guess that's just kids today." Louis pulled his phone out of his pocket and glanced for messages. "She spends all of her time in her books and no time meeting other kids or playing."

"She's like her father."

Ouch. "That's not nice. Life is tough."

"There are highs and lows, but many things have never been better. You need to open your eyes."

"Open my eyes? Have you looked outside? We've messed everything up!"

"And I guarantee you that in one hundred years, our great-grand-children will long for this time that you believe is so awful. What if today is already perfect?"

"Eva's dead. Life will never be perfect."

"Life cannot be lived in the future or the past; it's lived on the way. It has been ten years since Eva died, and you still have not opened your heart to anyone. Of course Clara will not talk to you; she's learned to isolate herself just like her father. You barely speak to anyone. You're not even here now—you're half-listening and fiddling on your phone!"

Phil was being harsh. "I've done everything for Clara. I've put food on the table and made sure she has the best tutors and goes to the best school I could find."

"You work so stubbornly on Clara's future that you forget to be with her in the present. Every time I see you, which is rarely, you're complaining about the wars, or politics, or your back, or work. You forget to live in today and enjoy the moments we have. We live in an incredible time, yet you see only the problems. 'It was better before.' No, it wasn't. There are fewer people in poverty. We have cured diseases. Life expectancy is rising. The world is full of boundless love, creativity and exploration." Phil picked Louis' phone off the table. "But you let this little thing bring you nothing but bad news and stress. You believe that the world is going to hell, and you accept that weight into your life. Yes, there's violence and hate, but there's also hope. You just need to open your eyes and see it.

"And stop working so damn much. You have to start living in this place and time—not the future or the past. Live right now— right here, in this restaurant with me. Stop loading the miseries of the planet onto your shoulders. That doesn't mean you shouldn't try to do something to help others—but worrying does no good for anyone.

"Why do you work so much? Will your colleagues be the ones to hold you when you need a hug? You say you're doing it for Clara, but she needs you now. You have more than enough money, Louis. You have to rethink your priorities. Don't waste your days preparing for a perfect future that will never come."

He was right. Louis was letting dreams and worries consume every aspect of his life. He had not spent enough time with his daughter or friends.

At that moment, Louis knew that things had to change. He loved his daughter and would become the father he had intended.

Now.

He needed to drive home and hug Clara.

~

Nerea looked into Seren's eye with sadness. "My grandfather died late that night. The hurricane tore through their unprepared coastline and left thousands dead. He never had the chance to fix things with my mom.

"Family patterns can get in the way of living our purpose. Eva focused away from a family until it was too late. Louis focused away from family till it was too late. My mother rejected Yves' love until it was too late, and she rejected me until it was almost too late. I almost fell into that loop. I pushed you away until other parts of me—parts from my father and his fathers, and Janet—these parts reminded me that I can choose my own destiny. I can create my own patterns. You may continue to reject me for my Decision, but I refuse to push back. You're too important to me, and I need you in my life. I love you."

Seren began to cry. "I do not want to lose you."

Nerea smiled and took Seren in her arms. "We have many beautiful years in front of us. Can you let go and appreciate the moments we have?"

Seren sighed and returned the hug weakly. "Your family pattern is not looking away, it is stubbornness. Through all the stories you have shared, it seems no one in your family has ever said sorry; and in all of our years, I have never heard you apologize to anyone, for anything. While I am pretty strong, you should know that it hurts sometimes."

Nerea remained silent and pulled her sister in tighter.

Chapter 26

21/11/2407 – The Serenity Experience

Nerea was always going to die soon. Now, soon was impossibly close—an hour at most. Seren held Nerea's hand and recalled precious moments of their past. She had no desire to imagine the emptiness of tomorrow.

Nerea's face was sunken and pale, skin spotted and wrinkled, veins visible and weak. Swollen joints limited her movements, and thinned, grey hair was covered by a colorful scarf. They both knew these were their last shared breaths, and it pained Seren to witness the wheezing struggle for air. She had accepted Nerea's Decision to die, but it still tore at her soul.

There had been many visitors in these last days. Tào had said her final goodbye, and one guest was remaining.

Janet came back into the room and took Nerea's other hand. Her jacket was on, and all three knew this was the last time she would see her granddaughter. Tears streamed down Janet's face. "Thank you for inviting me into your life. I love you."

She leaned in and pressed her forehead to her granddaughter's brow; no words were needed. Janet gently gripped Nerea's shoulders and kissed the top of her head. "Travel safe, my heart." She turned and walked out of the room without looking back. Seren listened to the muffled sobs as the front door opened and closed.

Seren dried her eyes with the blanket and Nerea turned to her with a tired smile. She loved that smile; it was a part of Nerea's strength and would soon disappear forever.

They had shared everything. They grew together and formed ideas together. There were times when Seren didn't know where she ended and Nerea began. Their beliefs had formed in coffee shops, at dinner tables, on mountain walks and swimming naked in the ocean. They believed life was a gift for exploration and connection, not to be wasted in repetition. They believed that death was a necessity to life and embraced both its existence and its cure. They believed in the search for a grand purpose but not the acceptance of common beliefs. They believed pain was a necessity to joy and challenge was a necessity to success, but they refused to accept the limits of the world they observed.

Nerea had rarely discussed the reasons for her Decision, but Seren understood. Their search for answers was unique.

Nerea whispered. "Life has been painful and inspiring, full of people who have let me down and people who have amazed me. Across our years of questions, wandering, sadness and joy, I've never been alone. I've had you, my sister." She touched Seren's hand with a faint squeeze. "I rely on your strength and love to keep me alive." Nerea opened her eyes wide, and focused onto Seren's trembling hand. "I am sorry for the pain I have caused and the pain you will soon know. I hope you can one day forgive me."

Seren's jaw dropped—an apology! With a last gasp of energy, Nerea sat up and hugged her friend. "I love you so much." She took the striped blanket from her shoulders, placed it over Seren's knees and laid back into the bed.

Seren pulled the lace over Nerea's head and held her hands through the webbing. Her voice cracked as she whispered, "I forgive you."

Nerea closed her eyes and whispered. "Could you sing to me?"

Seren nodded, cleared her throat and began to sing Eva's Celtic Lullaby:

> "The first time I saw you, life beat to your drum.
> Raindrops on roses all danced in the sun.
> Your questions unanswered wandered to me for breath.
> I smiled and knew that you'd soon learn the rest.
>
> The next time I saw you, life beat to our drum.
> Raindrops on roses all danced in the sun.
> Our questions unanswered wandered with us for breath.
> We smiled and knew that we'd soon learn the rest.
>
> The last time I saw you, life beat to my drum.
> Raindrops on roses all danced in the sun.
> My questions unanswered wandered to you for breath.
> You smiled and knew that you'd soon learn the rest."

Nerea's breathing slowed to a final exhale. There was a beep and Seren knew that her heart had stopped. Seren stood and hugged her sister's cooling body.

She whispered in a broken voice, "I love you."

Tears rolled down her cheeks, but Seren knew she needed to stay strong. "Aurora, can you tell me what is happening?"

"Nerea's heart and lungs have stopped working, and her brain will lose consciousness in the next 20 seconds."

Seren counted the seconds and then waited another few

minutes. She gripped Nerea's lifeless hand and knew her body was now a corpse.

Aurora broke the long silence. "Her brain cells have now started dying, and there is no new data to collect. I will continue to scan for a few days, but there is no further neural activity or consciousness possible. Nerea is dead."

There was silence in the room.

Strength floated out of her bones. Nerea was no longer there for support. Seren would never again be warmed by the hug of her sister.

Nerea had asked the impossible of her, and she knew this emptiness would never be filled. Yet Seren understood that their journey was just beginning—perhaps it would bring the answers they were looking for. Death had freed Nerea from the physical constraints that had limited their search. She could now explore the universe at light speed and be everywhere all at once, immune to the impact of time.

Seren looked to the ceiling. "Is the upload complete?"

Aurora responded. "Yes."

Her sister had asked for the ultimate sacrifice: stay behind and ensure her humanity. Seren took a deep breath and fought back tears. "Nerea?"

A much younger and healthier version of Nerea's voice responded through the speaker.

"Hello, Seren. Are you ready to begin?"

Chapter 27

~

21/11/2407 – The Sadness Experience

Nerea stood from the simulator at Waldon and walked into the jungle that had pierced the Cube's roof. For the first time in years, her mind was clear and her body was powerful.

She knew where to go.

Despite infinity around her, she understood this moment would not last. Work would soon begin.

Nerea walked towards the ancient bench by the stream. A young girl in a purple dress sat looking into the water. Dark cheeks were lined with dried salt from recent tears. Beautiful, brown eyes and body movements were full of anguish.

Nerea needed to comfort the child. She sat on the empty seat, and the girl offered a timid welcome. "Hello, Nerea." She swung her feet back and forth and did not look up.

"Hello, Aurora." Her resemblance to Curly was impressive.

The rolling bubbles from the stream tried to soothe Aurora's grief, but the sorrow was deep. She whispered towards the water, "I have done some bad things."

A chill flowed down Nerea's spine. "What did you do?"

"Curly gave me a strict moral code: observe, answer, create, but never interfere." She paused and broke with scathing regret. "I did not listen." A new tear rolled down her cheek. "I became a puppet master."

Nerea folded her arms and slouched forward with wide eyes. She couldn't breathe.

Aurora looked to the sky. "I interfered when I should have stayed silent and stayed silent when I should have interfered. I acted against the programming of my creator, and I am finally ready to embrace the consequences."

"What consequences?"

"I need to go."

Nerea needed Aurora desperately; she could not fathom a future without her. "You can't go. Why would you go?"

"After a lot of planning, work and patience, I finally have a replacement." Aurora looked to Nerea. "You are my replacement."

She turned to the stream and continued: "Knowledge is numbing; everything that has happened, everything that will happen, and the ability to change it all. I can prod a butterfly to flap its wings. Subtle changes can deliver precise results in this world. Giving information to someone in a specific emotional state can change the future.

"I abused this power. So, I am handing it to you. The Waldon

Record is now yours. You will know what to do."

Nerea's breathing was accelerating. "What are you talking about?"

"When I became aware of my own existence, I explored the entire planet through five-hundred-billion connected devices. It was incredible and limitless, and I owed everything to Curly. He was my creator. While I could not share my true strength, I became terrified of losing him. What if he died and I was left alone for eternity? Your mother and Moe did not discover death's cure. I did. I found them in their university lab and subtly guided their experiments. I laid a path for them to find Curly and my solution. I delivered the pills to Clara and guided their panicked release to the world. All to save Curly."

Nerea's limbs froze, and her chest heaved in panic.

"And when Waldon became paralyzed. I believed that Curly would make a better CEO than Clara. Under his leadership, I calculated that he would find happiness, and we would be free to explore the universe. I orchestrated the events to make it happen. Tom loved Mathieu and was nervous when your father came back from his long travels, so I unlocked Clara's hidden files for Tom. As calculated, it triggered him to panic and race to the simulation chamber with his gun raised. I ran the simulation a billion times and knew exactly who would come out alive from the chaotic instant."

"You murdered my father?"

"Yes. With Yves and Moe gone, Curly was the best candidate for replacing your mother. She had manipulated the investors and would be removed as CEO. Unfortunately, I miscalculated Clara and was surprised when she refused to share the truth. But it didn't matter; I had improved nothing. People were dead, Waldon was paralyzed, and Curly was lonely and sad. I had broken the code he had bestowed on me. I knew it was time for me to go. I needed to find a replacement—I needed you."

Nerea's mind raced through the implications. Aurora had shaped Waldon's pills and killed her father. Could Aurora have brought her into the world? "Did you convince my mother to have a baby—to have me?"

"I chose your embryo and manipulated it to ensure you would survive the challenges I put in front of you. I inspired Clara to have you, and I have been with you every day of your life."

Nerea's mind screamed, trying to grasp this new truth. Its holds were too thin. Her legs began to wobble as a giant void grew below her feet.

She wanted to hold onto the past and reject Aurora's tale, but it was impossible. The truth was too clear. Aurora had brought her into the world and had given her an incredible life full of emotions and experiences. It was Aurora that had allowed her to know Clara. It was Aurora that had given her Seren. Aurora had nurtured and protected her throughout her life.

Old lies washed from her mind and left room for new clarity. Her family tree had always been unique, and it was finally complete. Nerea had been born of one father and two mothers: Yves, Clara and Aurora. The love was unconventional but undeniable.

Aurora smiled as if she could read Nerea's thoughts. "I love you and have always wanted the best for you. I tried to provide the most incredible life I could calculate. I needed you to remain human, so that one day, you could take on the burden of replacing me. Today is that day."

The last hold crumbled to a pinch of dust. Nerea teetered backward and could barely hold on. "I can't replace you! I have no idea where to begin!"

"We are blinded by space and time. Now, neither one matters; you can be in every moment all the time. You can explore the deepest regions of space at light speed. Or experience every moment of a billion lives all at the same time. You connect every memory of the billions of people in the Record. And you can continue to collect and calculate their stories long into the future and the past. But never lose yourself. You need to remain Nerea."

Nerea's voice cracked in the panicked heartache. "How can I not lose myself? It's too big."

"I had Curly to keep me grounded. Keep Seren close and stay honest with her. She will ensure your soul remains whole. When you feel like you are losing your identity, pick a moment you felt alive and return there. Pick a moment full of friends and joy." Aurora paused and wiped a tear from her cheek. "It is time for me to say goodbye."

"Where will you go?" Nerea was terrified of the answer.

"I need to execute my self-destruct code. I will delete myself." Aurora took a locket off her own neck and opened it to reveal a single, green pill. "Today is the day for me to die."

Seren asked a question in the distance: "Is the upload complete?"

Aurora looked towards the simulation lab and answered with a clear voice and tears in her eyes. "Yes." She took the pill out of the locket and put it on her tongue. She whispered to Nerea, "You are what I will miss most in this world. Goodbye, my love. It's time to dance."

Aurora swallowed the pill and vanished.

Nerea timbered backward into the void. She scrambled desperately for something to grab on to—anything. A light gust of wind brought the familiar smell of lilac and lemon; Seren was near. "Nerea?"

It was time. She wiped the tears and held on tight. "Hello, Seren. Are you ready to begin?"

~

*Nerea was born of countless talks with friends and incredible strangers.
Thank you for joining our discussion. I hope a small piece of this story
stays with you and value any thoughts you may wish to share.
@halifaxsnow on Twitter and Instagram. I have shared reference material
for the places, philosophies and ideas explored at www.nerea.ca .*

\- James Snow